Summer

at

FRASER'S MILL

Summer
at
FRASER'S MILL

URSI ENGEBRETSEN

For Mama and Papa, with love

Table of Contents

New Horizons

Grace Murray burst out into her best impression of Tom Sawyer's Aunt Polly, Southern accent and all—just as the school principal walked in the door.

Of course it would be the day for Grace's teacher evaluation. She had already overslept, spilled coffee on herself in her rush to leave, and left the worksheet she needed for her sixth grade students at home. So she had spent her entire morning planning period recreating the worksheet, just for the printer to refuse to connect to her computer. She'd resorted to writing the worksheet in longhand and photocopied it, hoping her students could read her handwriting since her printing had become awful after years of college note-taking. And through all that chaos, she'd forgotten to change and still had coffee on her blouse—how unprofessional!

Principal Melanie Russo didn't say a word to Grace or the students. She sat on a chair near the door, one leg crossed over the other, a digital notebook resting on her knee, her digital pen poised to write.

Melanie was a tall, thin woman with hair that looked like it never dared to get out of place. She'd been the vice principal of the school until earlier this semester, when the former principal had resigned because of illness. Grace hadn't had a teacher evaluation with Melanie yet, and she wasn't sure Melanie would approve of her methods. Although the new principal was a friendly woman and a good educator, she intimidated Grace, who struggled with organization. School reputation dubbed Melanie an excellent organizer, after all.

The classroom was currently rearranged with the desks in a circle facing the center of the room, with Grace in her chair in the middle. Grace had gotten this idea from another teacher, and although moving all the desks was an annoyance, she agreed the "round table" approach did wonders for classroom discussions. But what would the principal think of it? At least Melanie hadn't come in last week when Grace had tried to do this with her fifth graders. The room had become so chaotic that Grace gave up on the "round table" for fifth grade.

At least the kids were talking now, saving Grace from more character impressions. Olivia Moreno, the biggest talker in this class, held forth on the difference between Anne Shirley's treatment of Marilla and Matthew in *Anne of Green Gables*, the last book they had read, and Tom Sawyer's treatment of his Aunt Polly.

"I think Tom is being bad on purpose," she said. "He's always running away and stealing doughnuts and driving Aunt

Polly crazy. Anne doesn't do any of those things."

"What do you think about that?" Grace asked the students. "Aunt Polly is often upset with Tom, and Marilla Cuthbert is often upset with Anne. Is there a difference between Tom's behavior and Anne's behavior that makes these ladies upset?"

"Anne doesn't do those things on purpose," Nathan Gorecki, a tall brown-haired boy, said. "She wants to be good, but she keeps making mistakes. Like when the mouse falls in the pudding sauce and Anne forgets to tell Marilla about it."

Nathan had been one of the quieter students when Grace started the novel discussions, but he was beginning to hit his stride. Grace smiled and nodded at him.

In the students' last novel study of *Anne of Green Gables*, Grace had resorted to calling on her quieter students with questions. This time she'd come up with a different plan. She created cards with discussion prompts for the kids. They could bring up quotes they liked from the section they were reading. They could try to predict what would happen next in the story. They could talk about characters they liked or disliked. Grace didn't mind if the conversation went off on tangents, as long as the kids were engaged with the story.

"What about when Anne dyed her hair green?" Lucia Sanchez, a small girl with pigtail braids, asked. "Marilla told her never to buy anything from peddlers, and she knew she wasn't supposed to dye her hair."

"But she was sorry about it," Olivia Moreno said. "And she didn't do it to be mean."

Grace jumped in to bring *Tom Sawyer* back into the

conversation. "Do you guys think Tom Sawyer behaves badly in order to be mean?"

"I do," Olivia said.

"Me too," Maria said.

"Can you give me some examples of that?" Grace asked.

Privately, she would characterize Tom's behavior as thoughtlessness. That could be a good direction to turn the conversation—the distinction, if any, between meanness and thoughtlessness.

"Tom makes me think of Calvin and Hobbes," Tim Phillips, a lanky dark-haired boy with a mischievous face, spoke up. "He's always trying to see what he can get away with."

"Yeah," Nathan Gorecki chimed in. "Like how Calvin's always trying to get desserts."

"And run away from school," Tim said. "And even when he's at school, he's pretending to be Spaceman Spiff."

"I don't like Calvin either," Olivia said, shaking her head. "He's such a brat."

"How can you not like Calvin?" Tim demanded.

"Because he's mean," Olivia said.

"You think everybody's mean," Tim said.

Olivia glowered at Tim. This wasn't working well.

"Hey, hey," Grace said. "Let's get along. We can talk about Calvin and Hobbes after class. That was a good comparison though, Tim. Let's go back to Tom Sawyer."

This was no time for the students to go off on tangents and argue with each other. What if Melanie thought discussion-based classes always went like that? Maybe Grace should have stepped in more quickly when the kids began to disagree.

Near the door, Melanie took notes, poker-faced. Grace tried not to think about it. At least Melanie would see the students were participating.

It seemed like an age until the half-hour of discussion finished. Grace gave the kids some questions to answer in their writing notebooks for the last few minutes of class. Melanie closed her digital notebook and walked out, her high heels clicking on the floor.

Grace sank back in her chair. The class had felt chaotic. Would Melanie think the discussion was effective teaching? Would she think Grace had contributed enough as the conversation leader? If Melanie didn't approve, Grace might be back to pre-packaged lesson plans.

❧❧❧❧❧

Grace was in her office, packing up for the afternoon, when Melanie appeared in the doorway. She had a briefcase.

"Grace," she said. "I thought we might have a little talk."

In Grace's experience, when someone suggested a "little talk" it usually meant he or she had a bone to pick with you. She swallowed. Had she done something wrong?

"Of course." Grace whisked a stack of notebooks off a chair to make space for Melanie.

"I'll get right to the point." Melanie sat down. "First of all, you're doing excellently, Grace. That class was great. The kids were really engaged in the discussion."

Thank goodness. The class sure hadn't felt great. "That's

good to hear," Grace said. "They're good kids, and I think they like the discussion classes."

Melanie nodded. "I've got a proposition for you. Have you ever considered pursuing National Board certification? I think it would be a great experience to help you grow as a teacher."

National Board certification? "Oh, wow," Grace said.

Some of the more experienced teachers in the school were certified and had NBCT after their names. Grace had dreamed about having NBCT after her name too, but the certification process sounded like a herculean task that took a lot of experience. Melanie thought Grace was ready to handle that?

"Wow," Grace said again. "I've—well, I've certainly heard about it, but I had no idea I could be ready to do that. I heard one of the teachers say it was the hardest thing she's ever done."

"It's a lengthy process," Melanie said. "But the certification has a lot of benefits. For one thing, you automatically get your clear teaching credential in California. You've been teaching for three years, haven't you?"

"That's right."

"Then you need to get the clear credential soon anyway." Melanie fished in her briefcase. "I'm telling you about this now because it's good timing. If you start preparing for it now and put together your submissions during the fall, you could have your certification by next summer. Do you want to see a brief overview of the process?"

"Sure," Grace said. "Absolutely, I would!"

Close Encounters of the Grocery Store Kind

On the way home after school, Grace remembered she needed groceries. She dodged around the other pre-dinner shoppers at the store, trying to remember which foods she needed. She had planned to make a shopping list, but forgotten to do it.

This grocery store, like most places in Los Angeles, was larger and busier than Grace's family's store in Michigan. The broader selection of items sometimes led to choice paralysis. Yet, shopping for groceries always reminded Grace of her childhood at Murray's Grocery. Before becoming a schoolteacher in California, Grace had worked in the store as a teenager and during her summer vacations from college. She had now left the retail job and the small town behind her, but working there had taught her lessons about diligence and responsibility that she appreciated in her teaching career.

Grace was weighing whether to get naan or challah bread when her phone rang. She ransacked her purse and got the phone out before it stopped ringing. It was her older sister Katie.

"Hi, Katie!" Grace tried to position her cart out of the way of other shoppers without dropping her phone. "Did you get my message?"

"About the National Board certification? Yes! I was going to message you back, but I thought you'd be out of class by now and figured I might as well call. Is this a good time?"

Grace laughed. "If you don't mind me being a little distracted," she said. "I'm at the grocery store, but I can hear all right, and I'm not in anybody's way. Can you hear me okay?"

"Oh, good grief, I don't want to interrupt you when you're at the store!"

"No, it's all right, really. We haven't talked in ages, and later it'll be dinnertime for me and bedtime for you." Grace decided on the naan bread and started toward the produce section.

"All right, but please tell me if you need to get off."

"Absolutely." Grace held the phone with her shoulder so she could open a produce bag. "How are you doing? And how are Arthur and the kids?"

Katie filled Grace in on her family's doings. The kids had all had a stomach bug, which had been miserable to handle with everyone sick at once, but Arthur had been able to get off work to help. Now that things were back to normal, Katie had been working on a plan to homeschool her oldest boy, Gabriel, for kindergarten in the fall.

"So tell me about this National Board certification," Katie told Grace. "Is it a lot of work?"

"Well, I've been reading up on it, and it is quite a bit of

work." Grace checked an avocado for ripeness. "You have to complete four components—one's at a testing center and the other three are all things you send in. The deadline isn't until next spring, but you have to collect student work and make videos and things during the year."

"Wow! I thought you were busy already. How are you gonna have time to do all that during the school year?"

Grace might have known Katie would be worried about her taking too much on. "I'll do it in manageable chunks," she told her. "I'm planning to get started during the summer. I'm going to work for Shipt, delivering groceries—that way I can work whatever hours I want—and the rest of the time I'm going to read all the National Board stuff and figure out what I need to do for the certification."

"Excuse me," a deep voice said. That wasn't Katie. It was a customer trying to get past. Grace apologized and repositioned her cart in the aisle.

"No, sorry, Katie, I was talking to somebody else," Grace said into the phone. "What were you saying?"

"I was just wondering what this would do for you," Katie said. "Is this some extra certification the school wants? It sounds like a lot of work for something that isn't a graduate degree."

"Well, it actually would do a number of things for me," Grace said. "The National Board certification was designed not only to give certification to good teachers, but also to help participants go through the process to become better teachers. I've heard it can be a more enriching process than a master's degree. Also, if you have National Board certification, you automatically get your clear teaching credential in California, which is something I would need to get anyway if I want to keep on teaching."

Why was the store's music so loud? She was having a hard time hearing Katie. Grace pressed the phone to her ear and went around a corner to a quieter spot.

"That makes sense," Katie said. "It just sounds like a lot of extra work the school is suddenly trying to get you to do. You keep talking about all that grading you have to do in the evenings—even on the weekends. You must be working eleven or twelve hours a day. Can't you ever get a break?"

"If I were a lawyer or something, I'd be working much worse hours," Grace said. "Don't worry, Katie. This is something I want to do. I had heard about it before, but I didn't think I was ready for it. Melanie says she thinks otherwise, so I'm gonna go for it. What's the point of becoming a teacher if I don't try to be the best one I can be?"

"I guess you're right. I'm sorry—I'm not meaning to throw cold water on your plans, I just don't want to see you get burned out taking on a huge project if you don't really want to do it."

Did Grace really want to do it? Absolutely. Melanie had opened a door for her, and she couldn't wait to go through it.

"Well, thank you," Grace told Katie. "I appreciate that. I really want to do this, I promise. I think it'll be really interesting. And it'll be a nice change of pace doing Shipt shopping and going through the National Board material after school gets out. It'll be like a vacation."

She heard squawking in the background on Katie's end, followed by a shriek.

"I'd better get off," Katie said. "Gabe and Elijah are fighting over Legos again. I hope everything works out real well with all that certification stuff."

Katie had never fought over toys, being the mildest of the three siblings. But Grace and their brother Thomas used to fight over Legos all the time. Grace wished Katie luck with the boys, smiling as she hung up.

What did Grace still need to buy? She needed milk and eggs, and something for dinner. Grace headed toward the dairy section.

"Well, if it isn't Grace Murray." A cheerful guy's voice made Grace turn. It was Lucas Taylor, a fellow teacher at her school.

Tall and blond, Lucas looked like he spent a lot of time at the gym. Although he was around Grace's age, it was his first year teaching. He had gotten his master's degree in history before coming to the school, where he taught high school history.

"Oh, hi, Lucas," Grace said. She raised a hand in greeting and continued toward the dairy section.

Lucas followed her. "I come to this store all the time after school, and this is the first time I've run into you. Funny how you never run into people you know at the grocery store."

"I guess that comes with living in the city," Grace said. "Back home, I knew pretty much everybody who came through the store."

"You're from Michigan, right?" Lucas parked his cart next to Grace's.

"Yes, I am, from a little town nobody ever seems to have heard of called Fraser's Mill." Grace held out her right hand and pointed to a spot halfway up her little finger. "It's around here, west of Cadillac."

Lucas laughed. "My grandma always does that too—using her hand as a map. She lives in Michigan."

"Really? Where in Michigan?"

"Charlevoix. It looks like that's not too far from you. We've been a short drive from each other dozens of times, and didn't know it."

"It really is a small world."

"So, do you live near here?" Lucas asked. He put a box of butter into his cart. The cart's contents looked like he cooked a lot. Vegetables, fresh herbs, and even a whole raw chicken sat in the basket. Impressive. The guys Grace had known in college seemed to live on Hot Pockets, and Grace's dad and brother were good at grilling and terrible at everything else.

Lucas was looking at Grace expectantly.

"Huh? Oh, yes, my apartment isn't too far away," Grace said.

"Wow. I'm even more surprised we haven't run into each other here before then. Now I know your secret—you come right after class." Lucas smiled broadly. "I'm not stalking you though, don't worry."

Grace laughed. A customer was trying to get to the milk, and Grace moved her cart. "Sorry, I'm in the way," she said. She turned to Lucas. "Guess I'll see you at school tomorrow."

Lucas smiled. "See you tomorrow."

Finally, Grace could finish shopping. With all these interruptions, this was taking forever. She still didn't have anything for dinner. At this point, she might as well get quick frozen food. She didn't feel like multi-step meal prep tonight, since she had a mountain of grading from her fifth grade classes. Besides, she wanted to start looking at the steps to become an NBCT.

In the frozen aisle she ran into Lucas again. "Long time no see," he said. "You know, believe it or not, the frozen food at this place isn't too bad."

He wasn't buying frozen food himself. Was he being helpful or condescending? With Lucas hovering over her shoulder, Grace decided against the frozen pizza and went for a package of beef with broccoli. She liked Chinese anyway, and frying beef with broccoli seemed more like real cooking than making frozen pizza did.

"Well, I'll see you around," Lucas said.

"See ya."

Grace moved on and got a bag of frozen blueberries. If she was going to make beef with broccoli, she needed rice. Rice was in the next aisle.

When she got to the next aisle, there was Lucas again. She wasn't going to say anything to him this time. In her opinion, saying hello to an acquaintance in the grocery store once was fine. Saying hello twice was probably okay. Saying hello a third time was embarrassing.

"Here we meet again."

Lucas must not share Grace's opinion about saying hello in grocery stores. Grace flashed him a smile and continued on. If Lucas would leave the aisle, she'd buy a large container of Nutella.

Internally, she kicked herself. This was ridiculous. She

hardly knew the guy. Why was she embarrassed to buy pre-made food and desserts because he was hanging around?

Grace had often found that embarrassment wouldn't listen to reason. But sometimes one could avoid embarrassment. Grace waited until Lucas had gone around the corner, grabbed the largest jar of Nutella on the shelf, and sped to the checkout, avoiding a near collision with a shopper rounding a corner.

An Evening In

The sun beat down in the parking lot as Grace loaded groceries into her car. That car had seen her through the last three years. It had 150,000 miles on it, but it still ran fine. The car's air conditioning didn't work, but Grace didn't mind. She liked fresh air. Tonight she rolled down all the windows and pulled her curly hair into a bun so it wouldn't blow in her face.

This National Board thing was exciting. Grace had been wondering what next step she should take in her teaching career. The last three years, Grace had had her hands full without adding more schooling into the mix. But now she was ready to go after that additional education. She'd been thinking of a master's degree, but this could be even better.

Grace's apartment was within two miles of the grocery store, but the drive took a while at rush hour. At one traffic light, Grace had to wait through two light cycles before she could turn left. Finally, she arrived at her apartment complex, unpacked her car, and lugged her things up the stairs to the third floor. The air conditioning in the building felt cool against her sweat-damp skin.

Apartment C1. Grace unlocked the door and dumped her grocery bags and backpack inside.

Wow, she'd left a mess. The kitchen and living room looked like a whirlwind had torn through them. She'd better clean up before Jen got back.

Jen was Grace's roommate. Between Jen's commitments and the time she spent with her boyfriend, Grace didn't see her much. She usually had the apartment to herself in the evenings. However, when Jen was at the apartment, she liked to keep things neat—natural for her, and difficult for Grace.

First things first. Grace had food to put away. Then she could deal with the coffee-soaked napkins on the table (left there this morning when she was running late), the dishes in the sink, the recycling on the counter, and the sewing supplies and books all over the living room. She'd better get the rice going, too.

Why hadn't she bought that frozen pizza?

Chores were better with music. Grace chose a music album on her phone—three young Italian singers, doing a tribute to the Three Tenors—and started putting away the groceries.

She still hadn't gotten any exercise today. She'd have to go down to the apartment complex's fitness center to squeeze in her usual run. Going there saved a gym fee, but she preferred to run outside in the fresh air. She often planned to get up early and run before school, when it wasn't hot yet. Most mornings she ended up snoozing her alarm four or five times and getting up just in time to get ready for class. In the evenings, by the time she was free to work out, it was too dark to feel safe. So she usually used the fitness center.

Grace finished putting away the groceries, put on the rice, preheated a pan for the beef with broccoli, and dealt with the mess. She had a lot of grading to do. She might as well do that during dinner. Then she could start looking up the stuff for National Board certification.

Grace was sitting cross-legged on the floor in front of her coffee table, eating beef with broccoli and marking papers, when Jen came in.

"Hey, Jen." Grace put down her grading. "How'd your day go?"

"It was okay." Jen went to wash her hands in the kitchen. "You wouldn't believe how much homework I have," she called. "And Ryan and I are going out for dinner tonight. I'll just have to be up late."

"Couldn't you and Ryan reschedule?"

"No," Jen said. "This is the only day before the weekend that works for both of us. I'll be so glad when finals are over."

She disappeared into her room. Grace resumed her dinner and grading. The sauce on the beef with broccoli was becoming overpoweringly sweet and spicy. Good thing Grace had a glass of milk.

Jen came through wearing a sundress, sandals, and sunglasses, and carrying a woven straw purse. Her smooth chestnut hair was pulled into a perfect ponytail. Grace often wondered what it was like to have hair that behaved normally. Her own hair tended to stick out in all directions.

"Bye, Grace," she said. "Ryan and I are going to the Crab Loft and then to the beach."

"Have fun. Don't forget about all that homework," Grace said.

Jen made a face. "Don't remind me! I'll have to drink so much coffee later."

She went out, leaving Grace alone again with the last bit of her dinner and an everlasting pile of grading. She was getting stiff from sitting in one position.

The air smelled stuffy, too. Grace hauled herself off the floor and opened a window. It let in a blast of warm air, normal for a California May. Grace still wasn't used to the California climate. At this time of year, back in Michigan, opening a window would let in a delightfully cool piney breeze. Her parents would enjoy the spring breeze all evening after the store closed, sitting on their front porch, reading and talking. Here in California, summer weather began in February.

On the beach where Jen and her boyfriend were going, the weather would be nicer. It was a perfect evening for the beach, but Grace needed to choose her priorities carefully. Jen might be okay with spending her evening out and then sitting up half the night doing homework, but if Grace did that, she'd be tired and groggy at work tomorrow. She didn't know how Jen managed to survive on so little sleep. The woman must live on caffeine.

Grace cleared her dishes, settled on the flat-cushioned couch that Jen had bought at a bargain sale two years ago, and started on her pile of grading again.

Her head began to throb. Probably eyestrain. Mom always

told her to take a break from close-up work and look far away every twenty minutes, but Grace always forgot to do it. She put down the papers and looked at the calendar on the far wall.

It was a quote-of-the-day calendar, and the date read March 15th. She had forgotten to change the page over two months ago.

The quote was hard to read from that distance, but Grace could just make it out. "There is nothing like staying at home for real comfort." It was attributed to Jane Austen.

First of all, why did people attribute quotes to Jane Austen when they were really quotes from characters in her books? This one, Grace was almost certain, was said by the obnoxious Mrs. Elton in *Emma*. Furthermore, it was a stupid quote. Staying at home for real comfort? Maybe if one had a lot of leisure time. Grading papers and working out and prepping for National Board certification was good and worthwhile, but Grace wouldn't call it comfort.

It would be nice to be able to manage both work and recreation, like Jen. Grace had resisted when her sister Katie had worried she was working too much, but maybe Katie was on to something there.

What Grace needed was a vacation. The problem was that there was never time for a vacation. She didn't make enough money at her teaching job not to work in the summer, especially since she was paying back student loans.

At least working for Shipt would be a change of pace. Grace had done that the last two summers. She was quick at fulfilling other people's shopping orders—she hadn't spent so much time working in her family's grocery store for nothing — and the flexible schedule was nice.

Her phone buzzed on the coffee table. Grace picked it up. She had a new email. The sender was Lucas Taylor.

Why on earth was Lucas sending her an email? They didn't have any activities together at the school. Only the first few words of the email showed on Grace's lock screen. "Dear Grace, I hope you don't think this is…"

Grace unlocked her phone.

"Dear Grace," the email read, "I hope you don't think this is forward, but I was wondering if you would like to have dinner with me sometime. We seem to have a lot in common, and I'd like to get to know you better."

Grace hadn't expected that. Putting the phone down, she flopped against the back of the couch.

She hadn't thought about Lucas like that. He was just one of her coworkers she'd run into at the school every once in a while.

On the other hand, he was friendly, and he was good-looking, she guessed. From the few conversations she'd had with him, he seemed knowledgeable about a number of topics. And he was Catholic. Grace had been single long enough to know guys like that didn't grow on trees.

What was the worst that could happen if she went out with him? They might not click? Grace had gone out with guys before and found there was no connection. It hadn't been the end of the world. Besides, maybe it would turn out that she was more interested in Lucas than she thought. Maybe, as fellow teachers, they had a lot in common. It was worth getting to know him better. And maybe spending time with somebody outside of work would help Grace balance her work and her recreation more effectively.

She'd think about it and reply later. If she responded too quickly, she might come across as someone who was sitting by her phone, waiting for men to email her. Which she wasn't.

Grace picked up the stack of grading. She was determined to get it done before seven. She still had to go on her run, and she hadn't even gotten to peek at the National Board certification stuff yet.

A Night Out

At nine P.M., Grace emailed Lucas back saying yes, she'd like to have dinner with him sometime.

Less than ten minutes later, Lucas replied, saying that was fantastic. He was looking forward to it. Would this Saturday evening at six work? He knew a good seafood restaurant, unless she was allergic to shellfish.

Grace wasn't allergic to shellfish, and Saturday happened to be her least busy evening. She told Lucas that would be great, and she would meet him at the restaurant at six. It would be nice to get out of the apartment and go on an outing for once.

Lucas thanked her enthusiastically and asked for her phone number in case they needed to communicate on Saturday. Grace sent him the number.

This could be really good. Grace's family and friends were always asking why she hadn't found a young man yet. Back in Fraser's Mill, people had often tried to set her up with this guy or that guy, but it hadn't worked out. Most of the young men in Grace's hometown didn't share the academic interests that were important to her. Since leaving the small town, Grace had been too busy to date much. At last, she was going out with a guy with whom she probably had a lot in common.

❧❧❧❧❧

Saturday afternoon found Grace in her room agonizing over what to wear. Picking a first date outfit was always complicated.

Grace assessed her closet. Her yellow flowered dress, a favorite, hung in front. No good. If this date didn't go well, she would remember it every time she wore the dress. Red dress? Too Valentiney. She didn't want to appear like she was throwing herself at Lucas. She wanted to dress nicely, but not too nicely, and she wanted to wear something she wore frequently, so she wouldn't have a weird memory attached to that outfit afterwards.

She finally picked out an outfit she wore at school: a cream-colored blouse with yellow polka dots, a black pencil skirt, and heels, with a pair of sandals in her bag for backup. Maybe they would go to the beach after the restaurant. She could just smell the tangy ocean air now.

She fussed over her hair. Should she put it up? Her curls weren't behaving well—one section above her left ear stuck out. She ended up pulling her hair into a bun, pinning the offending section back. Good thing they made bobby pins that matched blonde hair.

The restaurant was half an hour away, close to the ocean.

Grace made sure to leave early. At this time of day—especially on a Saturday—the L.A. traffic tended to be at its worst.

She arrived at the restaurant at five minutes to six and sat in the car to wait, reapplying her lip balm. Her stomach felt odd, and her hands were tingling as though she'd had too much caffeine. It was ridiculous to feel this nervous. It wasn't a blind date or anything. She had talked to Lucas before. He was a nice guy. There was nothing to be apprehensive about.

Her phone buzzed with a text from Lucas.

"I've found us a table inside. See you soon!"

Grace put away her phone, made sure her car keys were in her hand so she wouldn't lock them in the car, and checked her hair. She was ready.

Going from the sunny parking lot to the dim restaurant, Grace squinted to see. She never could understand why restaurants kept the lights so low.

She went up to the hostess. "Hi," she said. "I'm here with someone—"

"Are you Grace?" the woman asked. "Your table's over there."

Lucas must have described her to the waitress. What must he have said? Self-conscious, Grace looked in the direction the woman had motioned. Lucas was sitting in a booth. He waved.

Grace slid into her side of the booth. "Hi, Lucas."

"Grace!" Lucas was all smiles. He had a menu and a drink in front of him. He must have been here a while. "How are you?"

Jittery, but she wasn't going to say that. She put her purse down beside her. "I'm doing very well. How are you?"

"Great, now that you're here." Lucas winked broadly. "I've

ordered us an appetizer—Miyagi oysters with champagne mignonette."

"Oh, thanks." When Grace had agreed to go to a seafood restaurant, she'd been thinking of shrimp pasta or lobster ravioli. The thought of oysters didn't sit well with her stomach. Also, that sounded expensive. Was Lucas paying for this, or were they going halves? Either way, she hoped it wasn't too much money.

A waitress appeared. "Can I get you anything to drink?" she asked.

"Water, please," Grace said. "Thank you."

The waitress disappeared, and Grace and Lucas were alone again. Grace's stomach still felt odd and jittery, and all the conversational topics she had thought of beforehand had vanished.

As usual, Lucas wore a suit. Grace couldn't recall ever seeing him without one. His tie had spaceships on it. He must be a fan of sci-fi movies.

"So how's your English teaching going?" Lucas asked.

Thank goodness—that was an easy topic to talk about. Grace launched into an explanation of the novel study she was doing with her sixth graders. Lucas listened and nodded, asking occasional questions.

The waitress returned with Grace's water and a large platter of oysters on ice. A bowl of suspicious-looking pink sauce with small white things in it stood in the middle of the oysters.

The oysters were bigger than Grace had expected. Maybe she had been imagining clams.

"Shall we say grace?" Lucas asked.

He launched into the prayer. Grace joined him slightly late.

It was difficult to be grateful for this particular food, but she would be grateful for whatever entrée she ordered.

Lucas handed her a plate. Grace put an oyster on it. How did one eat these things? She unwrapped the napkin from her silverware and spread it in her lap.

Lucas was already eating his first oyster, which he doused in the pink sauce before loosening it from the shell with his fork. Grace thought she'd leave the sauce for a moment. She wrangled her own oyster out of the shell and put it in her mouth.

"So tell me," Lucas said, wiping his mouth on his napkin, "what's your strategy for not getting bored, teaching children's books all the time?"

The question was inconveniently timed. Grace was trying to convince herself to swallow the oyster. It felt soft and chewy, and she knew now that she didn't like the taste. Besides, Lucas's question was loaded.

"Mm." Grace swallowed hard. "Personally, I don't think things like *Tom Sawyer* and *Anne of Green Gables* are boring. I mean, they're not college-level reading, but that doesn't mean they're just for kids."

"Ah." Lucas's brow furrowed. "I admit I haven't read those in a long time. I suppose you could find themes in those stories that are pertinent for adults as well."

Pertinent for adults? What kinds of books did Lucas read?

"Absolutely," Grace said. "The characters in those stories are incredibly well-written, and the settings are really well done. There's a reason Mark Twain and L.M. Montgomery are such famous authors."

Lucas put sauce on another oyster. "I don't read a lot of American novelists. I'm more of a Tolstoy and Dostoevsky man myself. Those Russian authors had such a depth of understanding of the human condition."

Lucas wasn't even an English major. Was he seriously dismissing all the great American novelists in one breath? Grace fished in her brain for a coherent reply, but the waitress reappeared with a change of subject.

"Ready to order?" She tapped her pen on her notepad.

Grace hadn't even looked at the menu. "I think —"

"Give us a minute, please?" Lucas interrupted.

The waitress returned the notepad to her pocket. "No problem."

"I know what you ought to try," Lucas said, before the waitress had even left. "They have an incredible grilled whole branzino."

"Branzino?" Grace tried to find it on her menu.

Branzino headed the fish section. Grace liked fish, but she had the idea that "whole" meant the fish came with the head and tail attached. She didn't know if she could face that, especially after the oysters.

"It comes with a roasted butternut squash salad," Lucas said. "Otherwise, I'd recommend the sauteéd veal piccata."

No. No fish with head and tail. No veal. Maybe Grace's taste in food wasn't highbrow enough to match Lucas's.

"Thanks," Grace said. "But I guess I'm not the most adventurous eater. I'm going to get pasta." The menu had only two pastas, penne with cream pesto and linguine with clam sauce. No shrimp pasta, no lobster ravioli. Clam sauce might be all right. "I think I'll go with the linguine."

"Oh!" Lucas raised his eyebrows. "That'll probably be good too. This place does a great job with everything."

He sounded like someone who ate there every week. Judging by the prices on the menu, it would be tough to afford that on a teacher's salary.

When the waitress came back, Grace ordered her selection, and Lucas ordered the grilled whole branzino.

That was settled. Grace could relax.

"Want more oysters?" Lucas asked, moving the platter closer to Grace. "There are plenty left."

She took a deep breath and said what she should have said in the first place. "I'm sorry, Lucas, but I'm afraid oysters aren't my thing. I never had them before, and I think they take some getting used to."

"Oh, of course. If I'd known, I would have gotten a different appetizer." Lucas ran a hand through his hair. "Sorry about that. It didn't occur to me you might not have had oysters before."

Grace shook her head, smiling wryly. "I guess I haven't been to a lot of seafood restaurants."

Maybe Lucas was all right, after all, even with his different tastes in books and food. If he asked her, she might be interested in going on a second date. She wasn't sure.

"So tell me," Lucas said, "what kinds of things do you like to do when you're not at school?"

What did she like to do in her free time? Everything that came to mind seemed boring.

"Well, I go running," she said. "I like reading—I guess that's pretty obvious. And I like old movies and TV shows. Especially Westerns. I've seen a lot of *Bonanza* and *The Virginian*."

"I don't think I've seen either of those. I haven't seen a lot of westerns, now that I think about it. What is it you like about them?"

"Well, I grew up watching them, so they feel kind of nostalgic." Why couldn't she think of a better answer? That wasn't the only reason she liked westerns.

Lucas nodded. "I know what you mean. I feel the same way about *Star Wars*."

That was what was on his tie — Han Solo's spaceship. Grace should have recognized it. She'd seen the *Star Wars* movies years ago with her brother, but apparently she didn't remember them well.

Grace rubbed the back of her neck. She and Lucas had to have something in common besides work. She was determined to find it.

"So what do you like to do in your free time?" she asked Lucas.

Lucas confessed he wasn't much of an outdoorsman, but he did like frisbee. A group of his friends often played ultimate frisbee in local parks, and he mentioned Grace should join them sometime. Growing up in San Francisco, he had also done acting, which Grace found interesting, coming from a small town with no theater. Lucas had traveled a lot, too — he'd been to most European countries and even to Japan.

Grace struggled to get a word in. But Lucas did have interesting things to say. Besides, Grace couldn't compete with his travel stories. She'd never been outside the contiguous United States.

The food came. Grace enjoyed her linguine with clam sauce and tried not to look at Lucas's fish, which did come with the head and tail.

Grace was still looking for something she and Lucas had in common. "Have you read *The Lord of the Rings*?" she asked.

"Sure," Lucas said. "Several times, when I was a kid. I liked the movies, too."

"Me too!" Grace smiled. "If I had to pick a favorite story, that would be right near the top of the list. When I was little, I couldn't wait until my parents said I was old enough to read it."

Wonderful — they had a substantial common interest. Grace could talk about *The Lord of the Rings* all day. She'd happily go on a second date with Lucas if *The Lord of the Rings* was their conversational topic.

"Now, as an adult," Lucas said, "I prefer the *Silmarillion*. It's Tolkien's magnum opus. *The Lord of the Rings* only scratched the surface of the worldbuilding he was doing. Once you've read the *Silmarillion,* the Ring Trilogy reads like a kid's story."

Grace's smile faded. Even when it came to her favorite books, Lucas's taste was more highbrow than hers. "I read it once," she said. "I had a hard time keeping all the people and events straight. If I ever went through it again, I think I'd want to take notes."

Lucas nodded. "It takes patience and attention to be able to appreciate it. Re-read it, and you'll see what I mean. I think you'll find it quite rewarding."

The check came, and Lucas said, "I've got it," before the waitress had even set it down.

"I could pay for mine," Grace said.

Lucas shook his head. "No, let me."

"You're sure?" Grace asked. That bill had to be a lot.

"Of course. I insist."

"Well, thank you."

Lucas paid the bill, the waitress brought back his card and receipt, and he didn't make a move to go. He was telling about the high school history he taught, which Grace had no doubt was excellent, but it was getting late.

"Well," she said, when she could get a word in, "I should probably get going. I have a bunch of things I have to do."

"Of course." Lucas got up. "Let me walk you to your car."

Grace felt a pang of embarrassment at the sight of her car's numerous rust spots, which bore testament to Michigan's road salt. But Lucas didn't seem to notice it.

"Whenever I park in a strange parking lot," he said, "I'm always relieved when my catalytic converter hasn't been stolen. There's been a rash of catalytic converter thefts around here lately. I'm glad my apartment complex has gated access."

"Oh, wow," Grace said. "I hadn't heard about that."

Her apartment complex didn't have gated access. That sounded expensive. She always parked her car in an outdoor lot. Hopefully those thieves would be caught soon.

They stood next to the car, Grace holding her keys.

"Well, thank you, Lucas," Grace said. "This was really nice of you."

Lucas smiled broadly. "Thank you," he said. "What a great evening. Let's do it again soon."

Do it again? There had been at least one point during the evening when Grace would have been inclined to say yes. But a nagging feeling inside gave her pause.

"That sounds nice — uh, let me think about it, and I'll let you know. Is that okay?"

Could she have said anything more awkward? She hoped she wasn't wincing outwardly.

Lucas wasn't taken aback. "Sounds great," he said. "You're an incredible girl, Grace. I'm glad we happened to run into each other the other day. You and I have a lot in common."

"Maybe so." Grace smiled.

He was still standing there.

"Well, I'd better get going," Grace said. "See you Monday." She held out her hand as Lucas went in for a hug, and their shoulders collided. "Whoops, sorry."

Lucas laughed. "Awkward. Well, have a good night. See you on Monday."

He was still standing there as she pulled out of the parking lot.

The Perils of Canned Food

Grace hadn't texted Lucas back yet about the second date. She'd started to compose a message a couple of times, but indecision prevented her from sending it. In the meantime, running into him at school felt awkward. On at least one occasion, Grace found herself ducking around a corner when Lucas came into sight.

He was nice enough, and smart enough, but somehow, Grace wasn't enthusiastic about going out with him again. She had to admit he was nicer than most guys she had met. Actually, he checked most of the boxes for what she was looking for in a guy. If she hadn't been stressed about the stupid oysters, and if he hadn't made that off-hand comment about getting bored reading children's books and said *The Lord of the Rings* was a kid's story, things would have gone better. She should probably go on the second date and give him another chance. Grace had read a number of articles that said attraction could grow if you gave it time.

It was the last week of school, and though it was less stressful than Grace's finals weeks in college, it did involve extra work.

She was giving her students final quizzes—not really exams, but things that needed review in order to wrap up the semester. Grace had review classes all day with her three fifth-grade periods and three sixth-grade periods.

On her way to lunch after morning classes, she checked her phone. Three missed calls from her parents? That was unusual. Her parents didn't usually call during the school day. Maybe something bad had happened. Grace stopped in her tracks and called them back.

No answer. Rats! She'd better send a text—not that Mom was likely to answer a text when she hadn't answered a call, but sending it would make Grace feel better.

"Sorry I missed your call," she wrote. "I hope everybody is OK! I just tried to call, but nobody answered."

Grace made sure her phone ringer was on and went to get her lunch from the teachers' break room.

She was grading a stack of papers and eating a naan bread sandwich when Mom called. Grace left her things and went in the hallway to answer the phone.

"Grace." Mom's voice sounded high-pitched and breathless. "I know you were in class all morning, but I wanted to get a hold of you because it's important. Your dad broke his foot, and we're at the hospital."

"What? What happened? Is he going to be all right?" Dad was the last person who seemed likely to break his foot. He was a careful man. She could see him getting injured trying to lift something that was too heavy—he was stubborn that way—but how would he break his foot?

Two other teachers were calling to each other across the hallway. Grace headed for her classroom for the next period, always empty at this time, so she could hear better.

"It was a stupid can of baked beans," Mom explained. "One of those huge ones for potlucks or picnics. It weighed seven pounds and five ounces. Your dad was putting something on a high shelf and lost his balance. He knocked that can of beans off the shelf and it landed on his foot."

"Good grief! That sounds awful." Dropping something on your foot was painful enough without any bones breaking.

Grace went into her classroom and shut the door behind her. Now she could hear better.

"It was miserable," Mom said.

"Poor Dad! What did he do?"

"He yelled for me—I was in the back. I found him sitting on the floor by the canned goods. He couldn't stand to put any weight on the foot, so we figured it might be broken. I ran next door and got the doctor. He said we'd better go to the hospital in Cadillac and get it X-rayed."

"Are you at the hospital now?"

"Yes. We got here around one o'clock, and we had to wait a long time for everything. Your dad's still waiting to have his cast put on. He'll have to wear it for about six weeks, and he won't be able to put any weight on that foot at all."

"He won't like that," Grace said. "How is he? Does it still hurt a lot?"

"Doc gave him some pain medicine before we went out to the hospital, so that helped some, but it's still bad. Not that he would let on. He's just sitting there saying his Rosary and waiting for the doctor to come back. I already told Katie and Thomas. If you all would say some prayers for your dad, we'd be grateful."

"Of course I'll pray! Boy, Mom, that sounds horrible. Poor Dad."

"I know. He's worried about the store, too. We had to leave Natalie to run everything all alone, and there's a bunch of deliveries coming. Today was already a busy day, and now this had to happen."

"Wow. I'm so sorry. I hope Dad won't be too stressed about the store. He just needs to rest and get better."

"I've been trying to tell him that. He says he doesn't know how we're going to manage, with him on crutches for six weeks. For the first few days he isn't supposed to do much at all, and he'll have to keep his foot elevated."

"What are you going to do? Can you get people to cover for Dad?"

"We'll have to try. Oh, the doctor's back. I've got to go. I'll fill you in on more later. Love you."

Grace sat down on the edge of her desk. Six weeks was a long time, and her father was an active man, always busy working in the store and helping around the house and in town. He would hate being on crutches. The store wouldn't do as well without him, either. Mom and the other store employees would have to work extra, making up for him. The whole thing would be hard on everyone.

Lunchtime was nearly over, and Grace still hadn't finished

her lunch. She'd better go finish it, or she'd be hungry and cranky all afternoon. Going without lunch did bad things to her. She never understood those people who could go half the day without eating anything and say they were fine.

The teacher's lounge was empty. Grace's sandwich and other belongings were still at the table as she had left them. Grace bolted the sandwich and hurried to her next class, nearly forgetting to silence her phone. The last time she'd left it on, it had rung in class.

Mom was unlikely to call again during class, but Grace planned to call later to hear about Dad's progress. Maybe she'd be able to talk to him then. She wouldn't feel satisfied that he was okay until she heard it from him in person.

The review classes Grace led for her sixth graders that afternoon weren't the most coherent classes she had ever taught. She was grateful today wasn't her teacher evaluation. Some of the students still seemed confused about the material at the end, and Grace resolved to make things clearer tomorrow. The students didn't deserve to be left confused just because she was distracted today.

She sighed with relief when it was time for dismissal. "Remember, only three more days, and you're done for the summer," she told the students. "It's important to stay focused for those three days so you finish the school year strong."

As the students filtered out, Olivia Moreno came up to Grace's desk. "Miss Murray, what are you going to do during the summer? Do you take a vacation, or do you have to work?"

"Well, some teachers take vacations," Grace said. "But I'm

going to do some extra teacher training and work delivering groceries on the side. I used to work in my parents' grocery store, so I've had a lot of practice."

"My big brother works in a grocery store," Olivia said. "Maybe you'll be at the same one."

"That would be cool." Grace smiled. "What are you going to do this summer?"

"We're going to Yosemite in July. Have you been there?"

"No, I haven't. I heard it's beautiful."

Olivia raced off to find her friends, and Grace gathered her things to go home. Yosemite sounded fun. Maybe she'd go there someday when she had time and wasn't working in a grocery store all summer.

It was funny, when she'd come out to California, she'd thought she was leaving the grocery business behind. But here she was, about to do it again. It was going to be a hot summer delivering groceries with no car AC. Too bad Los Angeles didn't have the cooler northern weather Grace had known growing up.

Grace was at her apartment, baking frozen pizza for dinner, when the phone rang with her parents' number. She picked up. "Hello?"

"Gracie, it's me." A familiar paternal voice with a Southern drawl came over the phone.

"Dad! How are you doing?"

"Just fine, sweetie." Dad's voice sounded tired but cheerful. "The doc got my foot set and we're on our way home. Your mom said I should call. She said you were worried about how I was holding up."

"Thanks, Dad. I'm glad you're doing better. That sounds so painful."

"It's all over now. Doc's got me on crutches for six weeks —"

"And you've got to keep that leg elevated," Mom's voice said in the background.

Dad chuckled. "And I've gotta keep the leg elevated. Only problem is," his voice turned serious, "it's gonna be mighty hard to run the store. I'm gonna be stuck in the house for a while, and even when I can get back in the store I'm not supposed to put weight on the foot. What your mother's going to do without me, I don't know."

Grace could hear her mother's voice in the background again. Dad chuckled. "Your mother's telling me I should stop worrying about that," he said. "I know, the Good Lord will get us through it. But I wish I could find somebody with experience to help out. The only people to hire around here are usually teenagers who haven't worked in a store before."

"Oh boy," Grace said. "Do you think it would do any good to put up a 'hiring' sign in the window or something?"

"It can't hurt to try. We'll put one up tomorrow."

"Is there anything I can do?" Grace said. "I feel so bad for you, worrying about the store when you just need to rest and let your foot heal. Maybe I could do something remotely, over the computer?"

"Now, Gracie, I didn't call to worry you," Dad said. "Your mother and I know how busy you are. You've got a job to do, and that certification to get ready for. Besides, I can do computer stuff for the store when I'm laid up. We'll find help here in Fraser's Mill, and it'll be fine."

"Well, I'll say some extra prayers about the store, as well as your foot," Grace said. "I love you guys."

"Love you, Gracie."

Off the phone, Grace took the pizza out of the oven and poured herself a glass of milk. As she studied National Board materials over dinner, her thoughts kept drifting back to her parents and the store. She wasn't getting much done.

How on earth would her parents manage with Dad unable to work in the store? He was essential to the business. Growing up, Grace had always been impressed with his knowledge of his trade. He excelled at figuring out how much food to order from their wholesale supplier and setting prices in the store. On the floor, he worked the hardest of anyone to ring up purchases, clean up spills, and talk people into buying things. Mom knew the store as well as he did, but she couldn't do the work of two people.

Maybe Grace had better say some prayers for her parents and get to bed early. If she got enough sleep, she could go on a morning run. That might help clear her mind.

An Idea

When Grace's alarm went off at 5:30 in the pitch dark, it took all her willpower to get out of bed. Why did she do things like this? She could go back to bed and work out at the fitness center later.

No, she was tired of being indoors. An early-morning run was just what she needed. The sun would be up in no time. Grace said morning prayers, put on her running clothes, and headed out.

She shivered in her light long-sleeved shirt and running shorts over leggings. Mornings started out cold in this desert climate. But the sun was rising in a blaze of coral and gold, and it would be warm soon enough. Grace did some warm-up stretches and started for the exit of her apartment complex.

Now that she was out, she was glad she had gotten up early. The L.A. air, as usual, smelled like exhaust, but the sunrise—as much as she could see of it around the buildings—was glorious.

She hadn't seen a sunrise in a while, especially since the sun had started rising so early with the approach of summer.

Right now in Michigan, with a three hour time difference, Grace's parents must be up and about. Mom was probably in the store, unless she had another employee open today. How would Dad manage at home by himself with a broken foot? Would Mom be able to check on him regularly?

It was too bad Grace's parents didn't have anybody to take over Dad's place, at least until he could get around again. Grace knew how it was being short-staffed in the store. Poor Mom would get worn out.

If only Grace were there, and able to help. She had plenty of experience, and she would be able to give her parents a break. But as Dad had said, she had a job to do here in California. Her parents would manage somehow — they always did.

Grace came to a stoplight. Jogging in place, she waited for the "walk" signal. It was much nicer running outside than in the stuffy exercise room at the apartment complex, even though she had to be careful about cross streets and driveways and other pedestrians. This was just the thing to clear her head so she could focus on the things she needed to do today.

She had another full day of reviews with her fifth and sixth graders. After that, she really should sit down at home and work through her goals, to-do lists, and schedules. She had to do so many things, transitioning from the school year into the summer, and if she didn't make a good plan and stick to it, something important would surely fall by the wayside.

Afternoon review classes went well for Grace's sixth graders. Grace was proud of how these kids had taken in this semester's material. The discussion classes seemed to have helped, because the kids kept referencing conversations they'd had about different book characters over the last few weeks. Even Nathan Gorecki, who hadn't talked yet this week, contributed to the review.

Still, compared to the more experienced teachers, Grace felt inadequate. When she overheard conversations in the break room or the hallway, she was often amazed by the other teachers' sophisticated lesson plans and the accomplishments of their students. Hopefully the National Board certification process would give Grace some of the knowledge and experience she needed to be a more effective teacher.

In her bedroom after school, Grace pulled a box from under her bed to find a notebook. She needed to brainstorm goals and to-do lists in order to sort out finishing the school year and to start her summer out strong. It was easier doing that on paper than on her computer.

Partially-used notebooks, saved birthday cards, stationery, and printed-out teacher resources filled the box. Grace flipped open one of the gently used notebooks. The first page had a heading, written large in blue marker: "Grace's 5-Year Plan."

This notebook was old. Grace always wrote plans and lists and then forgot about them, but she remembered writing that plan, home from college one summer, sitting on her bunk bed in

Fraser's Mill. That must have been about five years ago, actually. It didn't feel that long ago.

Under the heading sat a numbered list. It began: **1. Graduate from English program.** She'd done that, three years ago now.

2. Find a good school that pays well. She'd done that too. St. Francis de Sales Academy in Los Angeles was just the kind of school she had always wanted to find. As an English teacher, she could introduce the kids to all the great books she'd loved growing up. How much better could it get?

3. Find a guy who's actually compatible. She was still working on that one. Maybe Lucas would turn out to be that guy.

4. Start getting higher education so you can teach more effectively and help other teachers. Younger Grace hadn't known how much time and energy a teaching job would take. Grace hadn't been ready for higher education until now. But now she was ready.

5. Move someplace where you can accomplish bigger things with your career than in Fraser's Mill. That had been a longtime wish before Grace had moved to Los Angeles. Out here in the big city, the opportunities for growth in Grace's career were almost limitless. She still didn't feel used to the city—it seemed overwhelming and impersonal—but maybe that would change with time.

She hadn't done too badly with her old five-year plan. She'd fallen a little behind on some items, but her goals had stayed the same. Now she needed a clear plan to move forward toward those goals, more detailed this time. Five-year plans, she decided, were silly. You didn't know how long these things would take.

The important thing was to know your goals and find concrete ways to achieve them.

Grace found a pen, flipped to a clean notebook page, and wrote a large heading: "Grace's Goals."

Her finished page looked like this:

1. Finish the school year well. Prepare reviews and quizzes carefully for the next two days.

2. Work on National Board prep at least one hour every evening.

3. Be more consistent with daily exercise.

4. Make a Shipt shopping schedule for the summer to make enough money but not get overwhelmed.

The first summer she'd done Shipt, she hadn't figured out her schedule beforehand, and she hadn't made as much money as she'd wanted. The second summer she'd made a rigid schedule and burned herself out by not being flexible enough. There ought to be a happy medium.

Back in Fraser's Mill, it had seemed easier to juggle work and life. She hadn't been so rushed all the time. What was it that was so different now? Was she just busier now she wasn't living with her parents?

Wait a minute. All the goals she had written down, besides finishing the school year, were things she didn't have to be in California to do. She was planning to work in a grocery store. Back home, her parents needed help in the grocery store. Why not forget the Shipt shopping and help her parents in Michigan instead? Was that a crazy idea?

She had sworn to herself when she graduated college that she was done with the grocery store and the small town.

Fraser's Mill was no place for someone with big dreams. The people Grace had known growing up who had stayed in Fraser's Mill were all working on farms or in retail or at the sawmill. There wasn't anything wrong with that, but Grace didn't find it fulfilling. She needed to find something big and important to do, and there wasn't anything big and important for her in Fraser's Mill.

Even if Los Angeles still felt overwhelming and impersonal, getting ready for National Board certification gave her a challenge that interested her. She could make a difference in the world by instilling a love of good books and critical thinking in the next generation of schoolchildren. She wouldn't give that up for anything. But visiting Fraser's Mill for a few weeks this summer wouldn't harm her teaching work. And her parents could use the help.

Grace put away her notebook, preheated the oven to warm leftover pizza, and called her parents.

"Dad, I've got an idea," she exclaimed as soon as Dad answered the phone. "You remember how I said maybe I could do remote work for the store? Well, I've thought about something else. You know how I was going to work for Shipt over the summer? Well, what if—instead of doing that—I came out to Fraser's Mill and worked in the store for six weeks or so, until your cast came off?"

Dad's silence stretched for so long, she wondered if the phone had disconnected. "Gracie," he said at last, his voice serious, "you're a good daughter. But I can't ask you to do that. You've got all kinds of things to do in California. You don't need to spend half your summer helping out here. You work hard the whole school year, and you oughtta get to relax a little."

"I know you wouldn't ask me to come, Dad. But I hate the thought of you and Mom trying to run the store when you have a broken foot."

"I know you care about us," he said. "But I also know my own daughter. I know how you feel about being stuck in a little town in the middle of nowhere. As much as your mother and I would love to see you, I don't think it would be a good idea. You're trying to get ready for that National Board certification. You need to concentrate on that. I know your mother would say the same."

"I was thinking I could do National Board stuff in the evenings," Grace said. "I don't know—I thought it might work! Do you really think it's such a crazy idea, Dad?"

He chuckled. "I won't call it crazy, but I don't advise it either," he said. "I'm not gonna say no, you can't visit us. And I'll mention the idea to your mom. But she'll probably be more against it than I am. She thinks you need to settle in where you are—maybe make some friends. And isn't there some guy out there you were going out with?"

"Lucas," Grace said. "I went out with him on Saturday. I don't know him that well, but I think we could have quite a bit in common."

"See what I mean?" Dad said. "If you come back to Fraser's Mill, how are you gonna get to know this guy better? And how are you gonna get ready for next school year? I think you'd better stay there."

Grace sighed, leaning against the kitchen counter. "I see what you're saying, Dad. I don't know. Maybe it is a wild idea. But I still think I could help you and Mom a lot if I came."

"I'll tell you what, Gracie," Dad said. "Why don't you take some time and think about what I said. Pray about it too. And don't jump into anything you'll regret later. Your mom and I will be all right, no matter what you end up doing."

"All right, Dad," Grace said. "Thanks."

A Thief in the Night

As Grace got ready for work the next morning, she mulled over what Dad had said. Should she stay here? Should she go? Why did decisions have to be complicated? She had prayed last night, but she still didn't know. "Dear Jesus," Grace prayed again, "please show me what I ought to do!"

She went out to the parking lot, chucked her backpack into the passenger seat of her car, and started the engine. An ear-splitting roar met her ears. Whoa, that was loud. What on earth was going on? Had she lost her muffler?

Heedless of her school clothes, Grace jumped out of her car and flattened herself on the pavement to peer underneath. She hadn't spent a lot of time under her car, so she couldn't identify a lot of car parts — she didn't know what the muffler even looked like — but something seemed off. Were there supposed to be two ends of pipe facing each other with nothing in between? Had something fallen off her car?

Grace got back in the car, stopped the engine, and called Dad.

"Dad, I've got a car problem." She explained the noise and what she had seen under the car.

"Two ends of pipe?" Dad asked. "Why don't you send me a picture."

Grace sent the picture and called back. Dad sounded serious on the other end. "You'd better call the police, Gracie," he said. "Your catalytic converter's been stolen."

"Stolen! Oh, no!"

She'd forgotten Lucas's comment the other day about catalytic converter thieves. Now they'd targeted her car.

"The catalytic converter's got precious metals in it," Dad said. "I've read about other people getting them stolen. I bet it happened during the night. You'd better get off and call the police right away."

"Yes—yes, Dad, I will." Grace's voice quavered. How could somebody do this to her? How awful did you have to be to sabotage somebody's car?

"I'll be praying for you. You call me right back if you need anything," Dad said. "I wish I could get a word with those crooks that stole from my little girl's car."

"Me too, Dad," Grace said. "I'm so mad, I could cry."

Her hands were shaking. It was a struggle to keep her voice calm on her call with the police.

The middle-aged, dark-haired policeman who showed up a few minutes later was friendly and sympathetic, but said he couldn't do much. These thefts were happening all over the place. He advised Grace to see if her insurance covered a replacement for the catalytic converter.

Grace called the school and let them know she wasn't coming in. She needed to figure things out.

An internet search told her she would need comprehensive insurance to cover the part replacement. Grace rifled through her box of important papers, only to find comprehensive insurance marked as "not included" on her paperwork.

Grace flopped on her bed with a groan. Why hadn't she gotten comprehensive insurance? Because her car was inexpensive, comprehensive insurance cost extra, and she had been a poor college graduate when she took out the insurance policy. She'd have to pay out of pocket for the part, if she could find a garage to replace it.

It took all morning—and some phone calls with her dad and brother—to research a garage in Los Angeles that would replace the catalytic converter. In the early afternoon, Grace got her car towed there. At least her insurance covered the tow.

In the late afternoon the garage called with awful news. The catalytic converter would cost somewhere around three thousand dollars. And it wasn't in stock. According to California regulations, they could only use factory parts for the replacement, and so many people had had their catalytic converters stolen that there was a shortage. Grace was looking at a couple months' wait to get her car back.

Oh, no. A hard knot formed in Grace's chest. What in the world should she do? Three thousand dollars? That was probably more than half the value of Grace's Honda CR-V. And two months? Practically the whole summer!

Well, this answered part of the question she had been praying about, although not in the way she had expected. If she didn't have a car for two months, she couldn't work for Shipt, which required its shoppers to have their own cars. The only thing that made sense was to go to Fraser's Mill after all.

She called her parents and tried to explain the situation, her words tumbling over each other.

"Grace, Grace, it's okay," Mom said. "You can slow down and breathe. We've got time."

Grace took a deep breath. "All right. I'll try."

The first issue was whether she should even get the car fixed for that amount of money. Dad told her the vehicle market was so bad right now, it would probably be best for Grace to get hers fixed, as long as there wasn't anything else significantly wrong with it. "You can't even get an old sedan for a decent amount around here," he said. "And in California it's probably worse, with those smog regulations."

Grace sighed. "You're probably right. And I don't want to get rid of my car. I like my car."

"There's your answer then," Dad said. "So what are you going to do in the meantime?"

"I'll just have to come to Fraser's Mill," she said. "I won't have any way to get around here until my car's fixed, so I can't shop for Shipt. And I don't have any other way to make money here. You've got to agree with me this time!"

Dad laughed. "All right, all right!"

"Are you sure?" Mom asked. "Will you be able to get ready for teaching in the fall? I want to make sure this won't jeopardize your job or your preparation for the National Board certification."

"I'm absolutely sure my job will be fine," Grace said. "I already signed my contract for next year. I'm gonna teach the same classes again, fifth and sixth grade English language arts. It won't be hard to get ready for that. And I can do all my National Board prep in the evenings after the store closes."

"Well, then, if you really want to, we'd love to have you."

"Thanks, Mom. I really want to."

Jen got to the apartment late that evening after studying at a coffee shop. She was horrified about the catalytic converter theft and surprised at Grace's plan.

"That's nice of you to help out your parents," she said. "It's going to be lonely here without you. I'll be glad when you get back."

Grace did feel bad about leaving Jen without a roommate for six weeks. At the same time, she and Jen didn't hang out that much anyway, and Jen had her boyfriend. She would still have someone to spend time with when Grace had left.

Grace bought her plane tickets that evening. Ticket prices were high so close to the day of the flight, but at least she got a discount for a round trip. She'd fly to Michigan on Monday. That would give her Saturday to pack and Sunday to rest before flying out Monday morning. Her return flight would be July 16th, giving her enough time to help her parents until Dad's cast came off. Then she would have a few weeks in California to get ready for the school year, which started in August. The timing would be tight. Looking at the dates on her calendar made her nervous. But it was exciting, too, a completely different summer than she'd originally planned.

The Last Day

Up early the next morning, Grace looked forward to the day with optimism. It was the last day of school. She had an Uber scheduled to take her there. After today, she just had to clean up her classroom and pack for Michigan.

On her way into school, Grace ran into Melanie Russo.

The principal smiled cheerily. "Have you thought any more about the National Board certification?"

That was almost the only thing that hadn't changed for Grace over the past few days. "Yes," Grace said. "I'm planning to prepare for it this summer. Then I'll get my things together over the school year to submit in the spring."

"Excellent. I'm looking forward to giving you a nameplate with NBCT on it." Melanie nodded at Grace and walked toward the principal's office, her high heels clicking on the floor.

Maybe that could be Grace someday—a school principal, walking around confidently, advising other teachers, making a big difference in the world. She could see it now. Only, she probably wouldn't be wearing high heels. How did Melanie make it through eight hours with those shoes? Grace whisked herself and her flat sandals into her classroom.

◌°◌∾◌∾◌∾°◌

Grace was eating a tuna sandwich, an applesauce cup, and a granola bar for lunch when Lucas walked into the break room. Oh, no. She still hadn't gotten back to him about that second date. Now she'd have to tell him about going to Michigan. This was awkward.

Lucas plunked himself down next to her. "I haven't seen you all week! I started worrying you were avoiding me." He winked. "How are you?"

Grace mustered up a smile. "I'm hanging in there. Only a few more hours, and we're done."

"Right? I'm ready for vacation," Lucas said. "You're going to work for Shipt and get ready for your National Board certification, aren't you? Are you doing anything else?"

Grace fiddled with her sandwich. Time to try to explain. "Actually, I'm not working for Shipt anymore," she said. "I had a change of plans."

"Ah. So what are you doing now?" Lucas leaned forward.

"Well, it's a long story," Grace said. She filled him in on Dad's broken foot and her stolen catalytic converter.

"Wow." Lucas ran a hand through his hair. "That's tough, not having a car for two months. But isn't there something else you could do, besides flying all the way out to Michigan? I mean, it's generous of you to help your parents. I respect that. But isn't there somebody that lives closer who could help? Maybe one of your siblings?"

Did he think nobody in her family would have thought of that already? Grace shook her head. "My sister's married with three kids—she's swamped. And my brother has an internship in Florida."

"Oh." Lucas's brow furrowed. "How long will you be gone?"

"Until the middle of July. My dad should have his cast off by then, and I can fly back and get ready for school. Maybe my car will be fixed by then, too."

"The middle of July." Lucas shook his head, sitting back against his chair. "You're a very devoted daughter. I admire that kind of self-sacrifice in a woman."

"Well, my parents are pretty great. And they didn't ask me to come. I wanted to come and help." It must be time for class. Grace took a large bite of sandwich and started gathering up her things.

"I can take that." Lucas picked up her napkin. "Got any more trash?" He reached for Grace's granola bar wrapper.

Grace let him take it. "Thanks."

It was unusual, having lunch with a coworker. She usually spent her lunch break grading papers.

Lucas wadded up the trash and threw it halfway across the room, into the trash can. "I call that a perfect half-court shot." He leaned toward Grace, his face serious. "Well, since you're going to be gone for most of the summer, you and I should do something fun before you leave. How about Saturday night? We could do dinner and a movie."

She had told herself she would probably say yes to that second date, but there was no way Saturday would work. Grace swallowed her last bite of sandwich, hard.

"I'm sorry," she said. "I've got a million things to do before I go. There's no way I could do dinner and a movie, or even just dinner."

"What if we changed it to tonight or Sunday?"

Grace shook her head. "It wouldn't work. I'm sorry."

Lucas sighed. "In that case, I guess we'll have to see each other when you get back."

"I guess we will," Grace said. "Well, have a great summer, Lucas." She smiled at him, turning to go.

"What, no hug?" Lucas asked.

Awkward. "Oh—yeah, sure." Grace gave him a one-armed hug. "Have a good summer, Lucas."

"Good luck in Michigan," he said. "Don't wear yourself out."

Grace laughed. "Thanks. I'll be fine. It'll be good."

She went off to her classroom, conflicting emotions swirling in her brain. It was unfortunate that she had to leave, just as she had begun to get to know Lucas. He was clearly disappointed about it. He must really be interested in her. Now anything that might be going on between them would be left in limbo until Grace came back. At the same time, maybe a few weeks away would give Grace more clarity about her feelings.

❧⟡❧

In the hallway after lunch, some of the teachers stood talking about upcoming summer activities. It sounded like they were planning to hang out together. Nobody seemed to notice Grace as she went by. Well, she didn't have time to talk in the hall anyway. After all, she wanted her last day's classes to be good.

It took longer than Grace had expected to get out of school after the last class, because a number of her students hung around to say goodbye. Several, including Nathan Gorecki, proclaimed her their favorite teacher.

"Miss Murray, I loved being in your class," Olivia Moreno, who had waited until last to leave, told Grace. She handed her a wrapped package. "I'm gonna miss you next year."

"I'll miss you too, Olivia. Thank you."

These kids had been Grace's students for two years now, and it was strange to think that in the fall they would all be in someone else's class. But that was the life of a teacher. You had just a little time to help these kids, to share your love of learning with them, and then they would move on and you'd have new students to help. A good teacher could have an impact on so many people.

Grace was still holding the wrapped package. "Should I open it now?"

Olivia smiled, showing braces on her teeth. "Sure."

Grace unwrapped the tissue paper from what turned out to be a coffee mug. All over the mug, in sixth grade handwriting, were book titles, diagrammed sentences, and parts of speech.

"Oh, I love it! Thank you so much."

"The ink won't wash off," Olivia said. "I baked it in the oven after I wrote on it. I know you like coffee, so I thought you might like it. The books are all ones we did in class."

"It's perfect." Grace came around her desk and gave the girl a hug. "Have a wonderful time with your family at Yosemite."

It was rewarding, teaching students like Olivia. Grace couldn't think of anything she'd rather do for a living.

59

Back to Fraser's Mill

After a busy Saturday and a Sunday mostly spent going to Mass and napping (Grace had been short on sleep the last few days), Monday arrived quickly. And with Monday came her plane flight. Jen drove her to the airport.

As usual, LAX was a madhouse. Grace wrestled her three suitcases out of Jen's little car, hugged her roommate goodbye, and headed into the airport. She checked her bags, made her way through TSA security, and found her gate. So far, so good. She was on time, and her belongings were in order. A lot of experience in airports had taught Grace that a plane trip was one situation where it paid to be organized.

Restaurants were everywhere, but greasy airport breakfasts tended to make Grace feel sick on the plane. She had eaten cereal and an egg at her apartment, and she brought a bag of snacks to eat later. She wasn't about to pay nine dollars for a tiny tray of cheese, crackers, and grapes on the plane when she could bring all those things with her for a much cheaper price.

She craned her neck to see the screen by the boarding door. It said, "Flight 475, Chicago: now departing at 9:15 A.M."

Wait a minute. Grace had been supposed to take off at 9 A.M. The flight was delayed.

That wasn't so bad, as long as it didn't keep getting delayed. As it was, Grace would have an hour and fifteen minutes in the Chicago airport. That was still a comfortable buffer.

After working so hard to be organized for her trip, of course Grace had forgotten something: she hadn't brought anything to do while she waited. She'd packed books, but they were all in her checked luggage. It wouldn't be practical to use her laptop, especially since it had to be plugged in to work. Grace already heard several people complaining that the electrical outlets in the gate area didn't work. She'd better conserve her phone battery. This was a great time to say her Rosary.

Midway through the second decade, Grace checked the gate screen again. Uh-oh. It said "Now departing at 9:30 A.M." That left one hour in the Chicago airport. Grace added another intention to her Rosary: "Please, God, don't let me miss my next flight!"

Grace was beginning to think maybe she'd better rebook her second flight when the woman at the counter announced the plane was boarding.

It was a full flight. Grace squeezed into her assigned seat between a sleeping man with wireless earbuds and a lady with a baby, who had to get up to let her in.

But the plane sat on the tarmac. They were delayed again.

"Do you know what the delay is about?" a woman's voice asked somewhere behind Grace.

"I heard it was mechanical problems," a man's voice replied. "They're probably still working on it."

The delay went on. Now Grace couldn't rebook her second flight even if she wanted to. Great, now she would have four hours of anxiety about missing her second flight. What was wrong with this plane, anyway? Hopefully the mechanics would be able to fix it, and it wouldn't break again in midair.

The shadows outside the plane window had grown shorter. They were finally in the air. Barring any more problems, Grace would be in Chicago in a matter of hours. She put her head back against her seat, trying to relax.

The baby next to Grace had large brown eyes and a worried expression. She kept dropping her toys on the floor under Grace's feet, and Grace kept reaching down to get them.

"I'm sorry," the baby's mother told Grace. "You don't have to keep picking up those toys. I should've brought one of those ones that attaches to the kid's outfit so they can't throw it."

Grace laughed. "It's all right. She's super cute. I don't mind."

The mom's thanks were drowned out by the baby's sudden shrieks. Maybe her ears hurt from the altitude.

"Ssh, ssh," the baby's mom said. "It's all right, sweetie." She got up and stood in the aisle, bouncing the baby. The baby's wailing quieted to a whimper.

The flight went on. Grace shifted in her seat, trying to find a better place for her feet. She couldn't wait to stretch her legs. She tried to sleep, but she wasn't used to sleeping at this time of day, and the plane seat was uncomfortable for a nap.

Finally the plane landed. It took forever to taxi to the gate. As soon as the great number of people in front of her had slowly gotten their things together and moved forward, Grace grabbed her carry-on suitcase and followed at their heels. Inside the airport, she looked for signs to direct her to her gate. Rats. It was at the other end, and her flight had been boarding for ten minutes. She had ten minutes to get there. Grace took firm hold of her suitcase handle and ran, weaving her way between groups of people, taking speed-walking conveyor belts as often as possible. Too bad this airport didn't have a shuttle.

It wasn't easy running with a rolling suitcase. The thing kept wanting to tip over or twist around, and it slowed Grace down. She nearly collided with several people. A stitch started in her side, but she couldn't stop now.

She arrived in the right concourse. There, at the end of a long stretch, was her gate. Grace pushed herself to run faster.

The plane was there — she could see it out the window — but the boarding had finished. The gate was closed. Nobody was behind the counter to take tickets. All that running had been for nothing.

Grace sank down on a chair to catch her breath. Clearly, she hadn't been meant to catch that last flight. She would just have to rebook it. But first she needed a drink of water. And she had to call her parents.

She waited in line to rebook her flight. "You're in luck," the man at the counter said. "There's one more flight to Manistee tonight."

Thank goodness. Those small airports didn't have a lot of flights. If you missed the last one of the evening, you had to wait until morning for the next one.

It was late in Chicago. It would be even later in Michigan's time zone. Grace felt bad for Mom, who would be driving out to the airport to pick her up.

The second flight was uneventful. Almost before she knew it, Grace had landed in Manistee. She found her suitcases and hustled outside into the cool Michigan night.

A familiar car was at the curb—Mom's Dodge Durango. And there was Mom, waving from the front seat.

Grace's mother, Liz Murray, had her blonde hair pulled back into a low ponytail, and her usual cheery smile lit up her face— although it wasn't unheard of that she could lose her temper. Grace had always been told she got a lot of her personality from her mother.

Mom gave her daughter a big hug. "Hooray! You're finally here. You must be so tired after all that running around and all those delays." She opened the back hatch of the car. "Can you fit your suitcases in here?"

Soon they were on their way to Fraser's Mill, the road winding through pine forests and birch groves and little towns. Everything was dark except for the Durango's headlights. Grace was driving because Mom couldn't see the road as well as she used to in the dark.

Fresh air blew through the rolled down windows. California's air always smelled vaguely sweet, especially after a rain. Probably because of all the flowers that grew there even in winter. Lots of people liked the smell, but Grace found it cloying, like too much perfume. The Michigan air was piney and bracing and not sweet at all. It smelled wonderful.

On the way home, Mom regaled Grace with the full story of Dad's broken foot and told her about the last few days.

"The problem with that man is, he won't let anybody do anything for him," she said. "He goes stumping all over the house with those crutches, trying to do all kinds of things he shouldn't be doing until his foot gets better. Doc's going to have his hide if he catches him at it."

That seemed unlikely. Grace remembered the doctor—who lived next door and had his office in part of his house—as a mild man who would usually just shake his head at patients who weren't following his orders. Maybe he'd gotten crankier with age.

They rolled into Fraser's Mill, the gas station and garage greeting them, the first buildings at the edge of town.

A new building loomed right past the gas station—a large, dark-colored structure still under construction. According to a sign out front, the building would be a new dollar store.

Other than that, Main Street looked the same as Grace remembered it. She passed the Free Methodist church, the diner, and the hardware store. Almost home.

There was the red pole barn that was Murray's Grocery, closed for the night. And there, just past it, was the white two-story farmhouse where Grace and her siblings had grown up. A light shone behind the blinds in the living room.

And there was Dad, standing tall in the doorway with his cast and crutches clear in the porchlight.

"That man!" Mom exclaimed. "He's going to drive me crazy. I told him not to go walking all around while I was gone. He's probably been doing projects and chores this whole time. That foot will never heal." She helped Grace get her suitcases out of the back of the car.

Grace left the suitcases on the driveway and ran up the porch steps. "Hi, Dad! I'm home!"

He hugged her as well as he could with crutches under his arms. "Welcome home, Gracie."

Grace's dad, Ben Murray, had graying hair and a friendly face. He was known as a mild man, not easily ruffled, and a hard worker. Ben had grown up on a farm in Georgia, in the middle of the Bible Belt, although he and his family were Catholics. After meeting Liz in college, he moved north to Michigan, where she had grown up. They'd married, settled down, and bought the grocery store in Fraser's Mill thirty years ago now.

"We've got dinner saved for you," Dad told her. "You must be hungry and tired after missing your flight and everything."

"I've just gotta get my suitcases," Grace said.

Long past midnight, Grace sat at her parents' kitchen table, eating leftover meatloaf. Dad had gone to get ready for bed, at Mom's insistence, and Mom was still going through the fridge suggesting anything Grace might possibly like to eat.

"I'm fine, Mom, really—this is great," Grace told her. "You ought to go to bed. We've got to work in the morning."

Mom closed the fridge and faced her, hands on hips. "I've got to work in the morning," she said. "You're three hours behind us, and you've just traveled all day. You aren't doing a lick of work in that store until one P.M. tomorrow, and that's final."

"Yes, Mom."

"Now, you'd better finish eating and get up to bed. I put fresh sheets on the top bunk. I'd have put them on the bottom bunk, but I know you never sleep there. There are clean towels in the closet if you want a shower, but you'll have to use an old towel for a bath mat because the bath mat's out hanging over the back fence to dry. I'll go see what your father is up to now."

Mom bustled away. Grace washed her dishes and lugged her suitcases upstairs to the room she and her sister Katie used to share. The old bunk bed took up most of the small room. Katie had had the bottom bunk, and Grace had had the top. Even when Katie had gone away to college, Grace kept the top bunk and used Katie's bunk as a place to set things down.

Katie and Grace had decorated the room with all kinds of things that had caught their fancy growing up. Assorted pictures covered the walls—movie stars from Westerns, places the girls had wanted to go someday, quotes they liked. The dressers showcased porcelain figurines, music boxes, old dolls, and little baskets of hair ties. The top of one dresser was a little shrine, with a statue of the Blessed Virgin, a crucifix, blessed candles, a bottle of holy water, and a third-class St. Anthony relic.

It was all as Grace remembered it—cluttered, but full of good memories. She ought to work on her apartment bedroom back in California to make it feel homey like this.

The trip and the late hour had left her exhausted. She left unpacking for tomorrow and went off to get ready for bed.

Doc

According to her mother's order, Grace had set her alarm for sleeping in. When the alarm's bird-chirping sounds jolted her into wakefulness, her body protested that it was too early to get up. Yet, mid-morning light streamed through the chinks in the blinds. Grace rolled over and turned off the alarm. Nine A.M. — only six A.M. her usual time.

When she came downstairs, having washed and dressed, she found the kitchen empty except for a few dishes in the sink.

"Dad?" Grace called.

"In here," Dad's voice said from the living room.

He was sitting in front of a card table with his laptop, his injured foot elevated on another chair. "Morning, Gracie! Your mother made me promise to keep my foot up. How'd you sleep?"

"Just fine. Did you eat?"

"Yup, eggs and oatmeal with raisins. Coffee's in the coffeemaker if you want any."

"Thanks."

Right, coffee. Grace headed back upstairs to look in her suitcase for the French press she had brought. The coffee Grace's parents drank was on par with the kind at the gas station. She couldn't convince them French press coffee was better than theirs, but she had convinced them to get a few more kinds of coffee for the store.

She was filling the tea kettle at the kitchen sink when she noticed movement outside the window, which looked out over the gravel driveway. Someone was out there. Standing on tiptoe in front of the sink, Grace saw a dark-haired man hunched down next to Mom's car.

What the heck? What was he doing? Trying to steal the car? Or cut out the catalytic converter? Didn't that kind of thing only happen in L.A.?

After struggling with the deadbolt, which Dad had replaced a few years ago and reinstalled backwards by mistake, Grace flew out the kitchen door, the screen banging behind her. It was chilly outside, and the gravel driveway stung her bare feet.

"Hey! What are you doing?" she demanded.

Still crouched next to the car, the man looked up. Grace had thought she knew pretty much everyone in town, but this man was a stranger. He looked to be in his late twenties or early thirties, with a narrow face and wavy dark hair.

"Who are you?" the man asked.

"I live here." She planted herself facing him, hands on hips. "What are you doing with my mom's car?"

"Ah! You must be Grace." He straightened up—and up.

At five foot seven, Grace didn't consider herself short, but this guy towered over her. He held out his hand. "Doc Johnson. Professional car thief. Glad to meet you."

Grace opened her mouth, found she had nothing to say, and closed it again. The car thief was waiting, hand outstretched, an amused gleam in his eyes.

Grace ignored the hand. "You're not really a car thief."

"If I was, I wouldn't steal this car."

"What's wrong with it?"

He motioned with his head. "Flat tire."

Grace looked. "Oh." Between last night and this morning, the front tire on the driver's side of Mom's car had gone completely flat.

"There's a nail right through it," the thief told her. "Just got in from the city?"

She turned back to him. "What makes you think that?"

"We don't get a lot of car thieves out here." His face crinkled in a grin. "And your dad told me you were flying in from L.A."

Why did this stranger know so much about her?

"Who are you really?" Grace demanded.

"My name's Jim. Dr. James Johnson. I live next door. Most folks around here call me Doc."

"In the doctor's office? What happened to Doc Williams?" Doc Williams had been the town doctor for as long as Grace could remember. She had just seen him when she visited her parents at Christmas.

"He retired in January, and I took over his practice. He's my uncle." The car-thief-turned-doctor still looked amused.

Didn't Doc Williams know nepotism was a bad idea? And how was this guy old enough to be a doctor?

"Is your dad up?" Doc asked. "I'm gonna check on his foot."

He wasn't just a doctor—he was Dad's doctor. She had accused Dad's doctor of being a car thief. She would never hear the end of it.

"He's up," Grace said.

"Thanks. I can help change that tire after work, unless you still think I'm trying to steal the car."

The expression on Doc's face could only be described as a teasing grin, and it sealed Grace's decision.

"No need," she said. "I've got it."

Doc went into the house, and Grace was left with the car, the flat tire, and the gravel driveway, which hurt her feet.

First things first. She had to get her shoes.

Inside the house, Grace sneaked past the living room doorway to go upstairs. Doc was looking at Dad's foot and didn't notice her. So far so good. She would confer with Mom about the flat tire. She could even look up how to change a tire online if it came to that. No need to ask Dad and get laughed at by the new know-it-all doctor. Grace put on her shoes and hurried over to find Mom in the grocery store.

☙❧

Mom was manning the cash register. "What are you doing here?" she exclaimed. "I hope you got enough sleep. It's only six-thirty in California, and you don't work till one."

"Oh, I got plenty of sleep," Grace said. "Mom, we've got a

problem. There's a flat tire on your car. We must have run over a nail on the way back from the airport last night. Do you know how to unhook the spare tire from under the car?"

Mom shook her head. "Don't even think about it," she said. "You're not gonna try to change a tire. You can get killed doing that. If the jack slips and you're underneath the car, you're dead. I never liked it when your father did it. You're not doing it."

There was no arguing with Mom when she used that tone. Grace sighed. "Then what are we supposed to do?"

"Maybe we could pump up the tire enough to get it down to Ed's," Mom said. "You can try the bike pump in the garage, if you want. But you're not changing any tires. There's no need to be a hero. Or you could always call AAA, and they'll come and do it."

"No, I don't feel like bothering them. I'll try pumping it up."

❧❧❧❧

Good thing there was no need to be a hero, because Grace felt decidedly unheroic after spending ten minutes trying to figure out how to attach the bike pump to the car. She felt even less heroic after she had started pumping air into the tire. She was just an ordinary woman who didn't work out her arms enough. They were beginning to feel like noodles, and the rim of the wheel, almost touching the ground, didn't seem to budge at all.

This would probably take a while. Grace continued pumping. And pumping. She wasn't cold anymore.

Why hadn't she accepted Doc's help when he offered it? She wasn't in the habit of refusing people's help. What had come over her to insist on doing it herself? Maybe it had been the expression on his face. He had been so obviously amused at the city girl who took a helpful neighbor for a car thief. It was Grace's first day back, and already she had been reminded she was out of place in this small town.

The screen door opened and shut. Footsteps crunched across the gravel.

Grace looked over.

Doc stood watching her, his arms crossed over his chest. "How's it going?"

"Just fine." Grace pushed a strand of hair out of her face.

"Sure you don't want any help?" Doc asked.

"Absolutely sure." Grace put all her weight behind pumping up the tire. She might be tired, but she wasn't going to be a damsel in distress and accept his help. Even a city girl could pump up a tire.

She wasn't looking at Doc, but she could hear amusement in his voice. "Have a good workout, then."

More footsteps across gravel, then the door of the doctor's office opened and shut. Grace continued working on the tire.

Was the pump doing anything? Grace still couldn't tell if the tire had budged. At this rate, she'd be here till doomsday. At least it wasn't too hot. Grace hated exercising in the heat.

After what felt like an hour, the tire was filling. The rim of the wheel lifted farther from the ground. Thank goodness — Grace's arms couldn't hold out much longer. She straightened up and stretched, breathing in the cool spring air.

The tire looked like it could be driven a short way. Grace

put back the bike pump and ran into the house for the car keys, which were kept in a bowl on the kitchen counter.

She stopped to tell Dad what was going on.

His forehead furrowed. "Gracie, you didn't have to do all that," he said. "I could have found somebody to change the tire."

"That new doctor from next door already offered to do that," Grace told him. "I wanted to do it myself."

Dad shook his head, but he smiled. "I'm proud of you."

"Thanks, Dad."

❧❧❧❧❧

Ed's gas station and car garage sat at the edge of town, half a mile away. Since it was the only garage in town, the small car repair lot was always jammed with cars. Grace maneuvered Mom's car into the only available space.

Grace went into the tiny office, catching a whiff of cigarette smoke. Ed, a thin, unshaven man, was on the phone filling out paperwork with his free hand. Paper covered his whole desk — forms, receipts, phone numbers, and a huge calendar with scribbled notes covering every inch of what used to be white space. Photos of classic cars covered the wall behind the desk.

Grace waited in the doorway until Ed hung up the phone.

"Hi there." Ed put down his pen and looked up at Grace. "How can I help you?"

"My mom's car has a flat tire," Grace said. "There's a nail in it."

"Flat tire, eh? What kind of car?"

"It's a 2003 Dodge Durango." Grace pointed it out through the office window.

"The silver one? I know that car. You're Ben Murray's kid, aren't you?"

"Yes, I'm Grace."

"You've been away a few years. You done with school yet?"

A lot of people still asked that question, years after Grace had graduated from college. Either she looked younger than she was, or people in general were bad at guessing ages.

"Yes, I actually teach school now in L.A.," Grace said. "I came back to help out in the store because my dad broke his foot." She started working the car key off the key ring so she could leave it with Ed.

"I heard about that." Ed's face was all sympathy. "You tell your dad to get better soon, you hear? I'll take a look at that tire and see if I can fix it. Got a few other vehicles to do first, but I should get to it before the end of the day. What's a good phone number for you?"

That was one problem solved since Grace had come home, anyway. Leaving her number and the car key with Ed, she headed back to her house.

Thick dew still covered the grass, so Grace walked in the road, her tennis shoes almost noiseless against the asphalt. A tiny red squirrel scampered across the road and up a tree. Birds warbled and trilled all around. Fraser's Mill had more birds than Los Angeles. Despite the car problems, it was a beautiful morning.

It was almost time for Grace's first shift at Murray's Grocery. Hopefully she'd still remember the things she'd learned about running the store. Otherwise, what was the point of her coming all the way out here to help?

The First Day

After lunch that day, which seemed too early because Grace's brain was stuck on California time, Grace went down to the store and clocked in. Mom and Dad had never taken her off the list of timeclock employees. She found a big apron in the back room (she didn't plan to spill on herself, but anything could happen), tied it on, and went to relieve Mom from the cash register.

"I'll go see how Natalie's doing with the unpacking in the back room," Mom said. "Holler if you need me or if you forget how to do anything."

"Mom, I worked here every summer when I was in college." Grace adjusted the screen above the cash register. "I'll be fine."

"Well, it's been a while," Mom said. "Just call me if you need me."

She disappeared, leaving Grace in charge of the store. Grace could see only one customer at the moment—a woman named Dorothy, who was an old friend of Grace's parents. Dorothy's hair was going from red to gray, but as she put baking supplies in her basket she appeared as energetic as ever. She was known for being involved in every town project and church event, including running the ladies' guild. Besides that, she regularly volunteered to read children's stories at the library and was a champion grandmother. The woman must have some extra source of energy other people didn't have.

Grace had often benefited from Dorothy's advice growing up. Maybe she should ask her for advice on getting more done throughout the day. Life was slower-paced here than in Los Angeles, but working in the grocery store in the day and doing National Board prep in the evening was probably going to be a full schedule.

The grocery store's door opened, and Grace looked over to see Dad maneuvering his crutches through the doorway.

"Dad! What are you doing here?"

Her father looked sheepish. "Don't tell your mother I was here. She hasn't let me in the store since I broke my foot."

"So you picked the first time I was running the store to sneak in without her knowing? Dad, she'll kill you."

"Don't worry, I won't take long. Did your mom show you all the new stuff yet?"

"Most of it, I think."

"You saw the fresh produce?" Dad crutched his way over to a display near the front of the store. "See this? It's from the Martins. It's all grown using organic processes, although they can't get their farm certified organic yet."

"Oh wow, I saw the local produce sign, but I didn't know it was from the Martins. That's so cool."

The display was impressive for so early in the year. It contained asparagus, several different kinds of greens (some Grace hadn't heard of), small new potatoes, and rhubarb. A big sign on the display read: "Local Produce! Grown with Organic Processes!" Some jars of honey stood at the front of the display. The Martins must keep bees now.

"We've also got local eggs," Dad said. "The Hoffmans started raising chickens. They've got all kinds of eggs, even blue ones."

Dorothy was coming toward the cash register, and Grace hurried behind the counter to check out her groceries.

"It's great to have you back, Grace." Dorothy smiled. "Your parents could certainly use the help. I remember when Walt was on crutches. He kept trying to do landscaping projects, getting down on his knees in the dirt. He said he wasn't putting any weight on his foot. But his cast would be covered in mud all the way up to the knee!"

"Now, that's just Walt for you," Dad called. "You can't keep the man away from his projects."

Dorothy shook her head. "Men! They never listen. I tried to convince him to ask for help on the town social media page. I know somebody would have been happy to help him."

"The town has a social media page?" Grace could hardly believe Fraser's Mill was that modern now. Her family had had dial-up internet until she was halfway through college.

"Yes, for the last couple years. I run the page, but anybody in town can post on it. Anytime there's a local event, or if somebody needs help with a project, or if bad weather's coming, people can share on the page. It's a great way to stay in touch with the community. There's another page for the Ladies' Guild at St. Anthony's, too."

"Wow, I'll have to check those out. It sounds like you've been busy."

"Oh, I just keep going along," Dorothy said. "There's so much to do, and only so much time to do it in."

Grace handed her her receipt. "I think you're the busiest person I know."

Dorothy smiled. "I couldn't do any of it without God's help." She gathered up her bags of groceries and went out.

So that was Dorothy's advice for getting things done: not planners, not calendar apps, but a firm trust in the Lord. Maybe Grace should pray more about her day-to-day busyness, too.

Dad came up to the counter. "I've got a project idea for you. I wanna hear what you think about it."

"Sure, Dad! What is it?"

"Ever since I broke my foot, I've wanted to rearrange the dry goods so there aren't so many heavy cans on the higher shelves. We can put cereal and pasta and rice up top—things that won't hurt anybody if they fall—and put all the cans lower down."

He led Grace to the side wall of the store, where there was one large display of canned food and another of non-perishable boxed food.

"Sure, I think that would work," Grace said. "I'll wait for a slow time and then start on it."

"Your mother thinks it's a waste of time," Dad said. "She

says I only knocked that can down because I'm naturally clumsy. But I say it's best to avoid accidents in the first place."

"Avoid accidents? Are you dropping things on your feet again?" a male voice asked from behind them.

Grace turned around. The new doctor from next door surveyed them with his arms folded.

"Ben, how many times do I have to tell you not to put weight on that foot?" he asked. "You're supposed to be completely non-weight-bearing until you get the cast off."

"Oops, sorry, Doc. I keep forgetting." Dad lifted the foot with the cast off the floor. "That better?" His smile was disarming.

Doc lifted one eyebrow. "As long as you don't put it down again as soon as I go out the door. You're supposed to get rest. What are you doing in the store?"

"What are you doing in the store?" Grace cut in. "Don't you have patients to see?" Sure, it probably wasn't a good idea for Dad to be standing around in the store, and Mom was going to be mad at him, but he didn't need a doctor hovering over him all the time.

Doc grinned, his face crinkling. "I need apple juice. The clinic's out of it, and we need it for patients with low blood sugar."

"Gracie, you know where the apple juice is?" Dad asked.

"Sure I do." Grace headed for the right aisle.

"No, I'll get it—I know where it is." Doc overtook Grace and headed for the apple juice. Grace gave up and went back to the register.

Doc came back with three packages of juice boxes. He must

be stocking up, or the clinic had a lot more patients with low blood sugar than Grace would have thought.

"That'll be $9.27," Grace told him.

Dad crutched his way up to the counter. "Doc, you got any tips on getting around better with crutches? Or carrying things when you've got a crutch in each hand?"

Doc shook his head. "I think you're already doing about the maximum activity possible for somebody who's on crutches."

One would think that in the twenty-first century they would have better equipment for people with foot or ankle injuries. They were always making advances in modern medicine, weren't they?

"Isn't there anything Dad could use that works better than crutches?" Grace asked. "They make all kinds of walking aids for people who have trouble walking. Isn't there anything else for people with injured feet?"

"That's all right, Gracie," Dad said. "Doc, don't worry about it."

Doc pursed his lips. "Well, you could get a knee scooter. That way you won't forget and put weight on the cast. But they're expensive as heck."

"Would insurance cover something like that?" Grace asked.

"In some cases. Want me to look into it, Ben?"

"Knee scooter?" Dad asked. "What's it like?"

Doc pulled out his phone. "I'll show you a picture."

He showed Grace and her dad the knee scooter. It looked like the kind of scooter Grace had as a kid, except that the rider put a knee on the elevated seat of the scooter instead of standing on it.

"That's pretty ingenious," Dad said. "I'd get around better with that, for sure."

"Then I'll look into it. Take care of yourself. Don't drop any more cans on your feet." Doc picked up his purchases and went out, whistling.

Grace shook her head. "I can't believe it."

"What?" Dad asked.

"He knew about knee scooters this whole time, and he even knew they might be covered by insurance, and he didn't tell you about them. You've been struggling with going around on crutches for how long? Isn't this the sixth day? What a jerk!"

"Now, Gracie," Dad said, "it's not Doc's fault. Like he said, those things are expensive as heck. Could be we can't even afford it. Besides, I hadn't complained to him before about the crutches. He probably thought I was doing fine. And I am doing fine. Lots of people have to be on crutches. Won't hurt me to deal with it for a few weeks."

Grace shook her head. "I still think he should have offered you that option from the start."

"Oh, Doc's all right." Dad waved a hand. "Well, I'd best be going. I'm pushing my luck in here—your mom could come in any minute. I'll be back at the house if you need me."

"Thanks, Dad. You really ought to go sit down for a while. You must be putting a lot of strain on that other foot."

"Don't you start bossing me too!" Dad chuckled. "Between your mother and Doc, I feel like I'm taking orders in the army."

The afternoon went on. Traffic in and out of the store stayed fairly slow, but Grace kept busy by restocking depleted shelves with products from the back. They were out of juice boxes to replace the ones Doc had bought, however. Those shelves would have to stay empty for the moment.

Grace was in the back doing inventory while Natalie Vanderberg, another employee, manned the cash register. Someone knocked on the back door. Grace opened it to find Alex Martin standing there with a crate of vegetables.

Alex—short for Alexandra—had grown up with Grace and still lived on a farm nearby. Alex wore her long brunette hair twisted up in a hair clip. A plaid shirt tucked into blue jeans emphasized her wiry frame. A grin stretched across her face.

"I heard you were back in town." Alex put down the crate and pulled Grace into a hug. "How long are you here? Is this your vacation? Do schoolteachers get all summer off?"

"We get June and July off," Grace said. "I was going to work for Shipt, but then my dad broke his foot, so I thought I'd come help out here for a few weeks. I'm here until July 16th."

"Yay!" Alex's brown eyes danced. "There are all kinds of things going on this summer—it's going to be great. Are you gonna have any time to hang out?"

"I'd love to, when I can," Grace said. "There is one project I've got in the evenings—I'm getting ready to apply for National Board certification."

"What's that?" Alex asked. "Sorry, I know you're working. I don't want to hold you up."

"Oh, that's okay, I'm just restocking." Grace put packages of flour and sugar onto a rolling cart. "You can follow me around, unless you have to get back to the farm."

Alex smiled mischievously. "I told Mom you were back, and she told Dad and Sam I'd be late getting back from town."

Grace laughed. "Have I told you I love your mom?"

As Grace worked, she told Alex about the National Board certification process. "I figure I'll work my way through the instructions in the evenings," she said. "Then I'll know just what to do in the fall when I start putting together the things I'll need to submit."

Alex shook her head. "I think you need an intervention. You're planning to spend your days in the store and your nights squinting over a computer? I thought I had a lot of work, but that's even worse."

"It's no worse than teaching classes all day and grading in the evening." Grace shrugged. "Don't worry, I'll still get outside. I'm planning to go for a run every day before work."

Alex raised an expressive eyebrow. "You must be used to getting up early now. I remember in high school you would always roll out of bed just in time to get down to the store. Then you'd agonize all day about how you hadn't worked out yet."

Grace laughed. "Well, actually, I did that most of the time this last semester. But I don't have to drive to work every morning here, so I'm gonna try to use the extra time and get my run in."

Despite her mom's prediction that she would be late coming back, Alex only stayed a few more minutes. She had a lot of work waiting back home.

Grace relieved Natalie at the cash register. It was interesting saying hello to the townspeople who came through, some of whom she hadn't seen in five years. She'd only been home for brief visits since she'd moved to California.

A young woman, about Grace's age, with designer sunglasses

on top of her smooth brown hair, approached the counter. Grace couldn't place her. She wore a striped tank top and white shorts — early in the year to do so. Wouldn't she get cold?

"Excuse me," the newcomer said. "Do you have coconut water?"

"Let me check," Grace said. She hurried away to the drink area. Lemon juice, apple juice, bottles of pop, boxes of tea, bags of coffee — no coconut water. Maybe it was in a different section. Grace checked the baking aisle. Nothing. She checked the drink cooler, in case it was mixed in with the iced coffee and pop. No success.

The young woman was leaning back against the counter, checking her pristine nails, when Grace got back.

"I'm sorry," Grace said, "we don't seem to carry it. I could talk to my mom and see about adding it to our inventory."

"Oh, don't worry about it. I'll just go to Cadillac. They've got it at Walmart."

She was going to drive forty-five minutes each way to get coconut water? Who did that?

"I'm sorry I wasn't able to help," Grace said. "Are you new in town? I'm Grace Murray."

"I'm Hannah. Hannah Fraser." The young woman turned to go.

"Hannah Fraser, like Fraser's Mill?" Fraser's Water-Powered Sawmill stood at the north edge of town. It was the oldest business in town and was still in operation.

Hannah flipped her hair back. "That's right. My grandfather founded the town."

"It's funny — I grew up here, but I don't think I ever met you." Grace tapped her cheek. Why didn't she recognize Hannah?

"I didn't grow up here," Hannah said. "I'm from Chicago. When my grandparents moved to Florida a few years ago, they sold my parents their house for a summer cottage. I'm staying there this summer."

"That explains it! Well, nice to meet you, Hannah."

"Uh-huh." Hannah continued out the door.

"Is she gone?" Natalie popped out from one of the aisles, string mop in hand.

"Is who gone?" Grace asked.

"Hannah Fraser." Natalie wrinkled her freckled nose. "Just because she's rich, she thinks she owns the town." She put muscle behind the string mop, her long blonde braid swinging back and forth. "She doesn't even live here. But she goes all over town taking photos and videos and posting on social media about what life in a small town is like."

"How do you know so much about her?" Grace asked. "I thought she just moved into town."

"Yeah, she did," Natalie said. "But she posted on the town social media the first day she came here, telling people to follow her video channel and her social media page. She's an influencer."

Grace knew little about influencers. She had the general idea that they did advertising for assorted products.

Natalie leaned on her mop. "She's always going around with Doc. My sister said she snapped him up the minute she came to town. And he's the only new guy we've seen in town in forever." Her voice was peeved.

"The new doctor?"

"Yeah. He just got here this winter. Have you seen him? Isn't he good-looking?"

"Good-looking? Yeah, I guess."

Natalie was a little young to be interested in guys Doc's age. Maybe Natalie's sister, a few years older, was interested in him. Sure, he was handsome, and his arrival must have made a stir in this small town. The girls in town must think of him as an eligible bachelor. But Grace didn't see the appeal. She encountered too many handsome guys on a regular basis in L.A. to have her head turned by this one, whose personality grated on her.

Grace worked until seven P.M., when the store closed. She could imagine the outrage if a grocery store in the city closed as early as seven, but the people here were used to it. With the small number of employees the store had, it made sense to close early and let the workers go home. Grace swept the floor and wiped down the counter by the cash register. She smelled something funny, but she couldn't identify the smell or where it came from. It didn't seem like a big issue, so she added up the day's totals and locked up for the night. She headed over to the house, where Mom had kept dinner warm for her.

Her parents had already eaten and were sitting on the front porch. They often did that in the evening. Grace got a plate of food and came out to join them. Dad was reading something aloud and stopped to make comments to Mom, who was taking notes.

"Come join us, Grace," Mom said. "We're going through the

first few chapters of that novel I'm trying to write. We could use somebody with an English degree."

"I'm afraid my degree isn't in creative writing," Grace said. "But I do get a lot of practice going over people's grammar."

Mom tucked her pen behind her ear. "That's just what I need. Every other sentence I write is a run-on sentence with commas in all the wrong places." She glanced at Grace's plate. "Did you find the carrots? They were on the back of the stove."

"Yes, here they are," Grace said, pointing out the carrots on her plate. "Thanks, Mom. Roast pork is one of my favorites."

"I bet you don't have a lot of time to cook, teaching school," Dad said, looking up from Mom's novel. "What do you eat? Rotisserie chickens and pre-bagged salad?"

Grace laughed. "Pretty much. When I get home from school the last thing I want to do is spend the whole evening cooking."

"Not much fun doing fancy cooking for just one person, anyway," Dad said. "Well, Liz, I've got a couple more comments for you."

Grace's parents returned to their analysis of Mom's manuscript, and Grace ate her roast pork, potatoes, and carrots. The evening was fair with a light breeze. If she stayed out there much longer she would want a hoodie.

A crash from the driveway next door made her look over. Doc was halfway underneath a long blue car, doing something to it. At least, Grace assumed it was Doc. She couldn't see much of him. Well, it was a nice night to work on your car.

But as nice as it was outside, Grace couldn't stay. After she finished eating, she excused herself and went inside. She was going to figure out more of this National Board stuff.

She found general overviews, starting guides, and guides that focused on different subject areas in which a teacher might get certified. It was all pretty complicated, and Grace found herself going down an Internet rabbit hole into more and more specific stuff before she even understood the general overview. There ought to be a starting guide to the starting guide. Maybe the whole thing was a test of the teachers' reading comprehension: if you couldn't figure out the information, you weren't smart enough to be a certified teacher.

Grace realized she had been twirling her hair for who knows how long. She twisted the curly mess into some kind of bun and stuck three hairpins into it. That should keep her from touching it anymore.

Her parents were still on the front porch, their voices floating up through Grace's open window. Maybe she should go join them. She had looked at this stuff long enough for one evening. She'd get a headache or eyestrain if she wasn't careful.

Grace closed her laptop, grabbed a hoodie, and went down to the porch.

Trials

For the first two days after Grace's arrival, Mom insisted on Grace not working until the afternoon. She would open the store herself, and Grace would close. That way Grace could catch up on the sleep she had lost from having jet lag.

On Wednesday night, after her second shift at the store, Grace confronted Mom during her evening front porch writing session. "You oughtta let me open the store tomorrow," she said. "You've been running yourself ragged, staying up late and getting up early and helping Dad with his foot. This time you can sleep in, and I can open the store."

"But that's at eight A.M.," Mom exclaimed. "That'll feel like five A.M. in California."

"I'll go to bed in plenty of time to get enough sleep," Grace said. "I want to do this, Mom."

"Let her, Liz," Dad said from his rocking chair. "She's young. She can handle it. You need a rest."

"Thanks, Dad," Grace said. "What about it, Mom?"

Mom sighed. "I guess that would be all right. I'll come in in the afternoon. But you'd better not kill yourself doing all the work."

"I promise I won't."

It was hard getting up at seven A.M., but not as bad as Grace had thought it might be. Her crash came at lunchtime. When Mom came to relieve her at one P.M. so she could go home for a sandwich or something, Grace decided on a nap instead. She set an alarm on her phone and flopped down on the bottom bunk in her work clothes.

She awoke, startled by a loud noise. What was that? Eyes half-shut, she listened. It was knocking. Somebody was at the front door.

Dad probably couldn't answer it. Grace shot out of bed and hurried out of her room, running to the stairs.

Her foot caught the first step wrong. All at once she was sliding, skidding down the stairs like she was snowboarding, everything whooshing past. With a sickening drop in her stomach, she braced herself for the crash at the landing.

Hitting her back on several stairs along the way, she landed hard, half-sitting on the second-to-last stair.

Ouch. Grace caught her breath and took stock of herself. Her back hurt. But it felt like it was more from rug burn than from anything being injured. She had done something to her ankle, but it didn't hurt sharply when she moved it. So that must be all right too. She hauled herself to her feet, one hand on the banister and the other hand on her back. How could she have been so clumsy? She must have been groggy after waking up. Well, she wasn't groggy now.

Someone was still at the door. Through the window, Grace could see it was Doc. What was he doing here?

Grace yanked the door open. "Hello."

Doc stood on the porch, his expression perturbed. "What on earth was that noise?" he asked. He looked at Grace, who was still holding her back. "Did you just fall down those stairs? Are you all right?"

"I'm fine," Grace said. "I didn't exactly fall. I kind of skidded."

She was still breathing hard. She used to think the swinging pirate ship ride at the county fair was scary. It had been nothing compared to the sickening drop in her stomach as she hurtled down the stairs.

Doc crossed his arms. "You skidded?"

Of all the obvious questions! What was this guy doing here, anyway, knocking and waking her up and causing all this?

"Yes, I skidded, all the way down!" Grace motioned to the long staircase behind her. "I heard you knocking and I tripped at the top."

Doc shook his head at her. "You might wanna be more careful on those stairs. Only one person with a broken bone per family, please." The corner of his mouth quirked.

He thought it was funny! And he probably thought Grace was the world's biggest klutz, too.

"I'm not in the habit of sliding down the stairs." Grace held her chin high. "I was taking a nap, because I'm still on California time, and I heard somebody pounding on the front door. I figured my dad couldn't get the door, so I ran to answer it. I think I was still half-asleep, and I caught my foot."

"Wow." Doc shook his head again. He peered around Grace at the stairs. "I wouldn't want to slide down those. At least you've got carpet. Are you sure you're not hurt?"

"Absolutely sure," Grace said.

"You don't have a concussion? Do you know what day and date it is?"

"I didn't hit my head. I don't need to do a concussion checklist, thanks." She began to turn away from the door, but stopped. "Why did you knock, anyway?"

He held out a white business envelope. "Your parents' mail got put in my mailbox by mistake," he said. "I guess I should have stuck it in their mailbox. Could have saved you the trouble of falling downstairs."

He was grinning, and Grace fought a strong wish to tell him off. He hadn't done anything. But he had a point. Why did he have to come over with that stupid piece of mail?

Grace opened her mouth, decided against saying the thing that came to her mind, and took the envelope from Doc.

"I'll see you around." Doc turned to go. He stopped. "Are you sure you know what day and date it is?"

Grace grimaced at him, shut the door, and locked it.

Inside, she put the piece of mail—the utility bill, as it happened—into the mail basket near the entryway. Where on earth was Dad? Maybe he was outside somewhere. She hoped he was being careful with his crutches. The last thing she needed was for Dad to get in another accident and require Doc's services. She had seen enough of Doc for one day.

Grace had the early shift again on Thursday morning, but this time she had gotten enough sleep before waking up at seven. She washed her hair, leaving it to air dry, drank an extra-strong cup of French press coffee for energy, bolted a bowl of cereal and a banana, and hurried over to open the store.

That lingering funny smell was stronger today. Grace followed her nose. Now the smell obviously came from the produce section—not the vegetables from the Martin farm, but the ones from the store's main supplier.

Grace traced the stench to the potato bin. Ugh. She held her nose, her stomach lurching. She would have to deal with that. But first she had to prepare for customers. She got the door unlocked, the lights on, and the cash register ready for the first transaction. No one else was there—Natalie started at eleven. Grace had the first three hours in the store by herself.

She turned her attention to the potato bin. The potatoes on top of the bin looked fine. But it was hard to tell through the plastic of the five-pound bags. Why didn't her parents sell potatoes individually? Probably more of a hassle. Maybe more expensive, too. Grace sighed and began lifting bags of potatoes out of the box, examining each one. There had to be something rotten somewhere. Small flies hovered around—some kind of fruit fly, Grace figured. But they weren't hanging around the fruit. Maybe these flies liked potatoes. In any case, it wouldn't do to have a bad smell and flies in the store.

At the bottom of the bin, one of the bags Grace picked up

dripped foul brown juice. A putrid smell arose. Yup, that was the culprit. Rotten potatoes. Ugh. The smell was so bad, she had to breathe through her mouth. And customers could come in any minute.

Grace ran for a big trash bag. She'd better get the rotten potatoes out of there first. Then she would need to check for any other bad ones. And she'd have to clean up all that awful brown liquid in the bottom of the bin. At eight A.M., it was already one of those days.

A customer's shuffling footsteps came in while Grace was still dealing with the situation. She had found all the rotten potatoes—there had been two more bags—and taken them out to the trash. The good bags of potatoes were all stacked next to the bin, and she was about to clean out the bottom of the bin.

"Phew!" the customer exclaimed. "What's that smell?"

Grace looked up to see Walt, Dorothy's husband, a burly, bearded man.

"It was potatoes that went bad," Grace said. "I threw them out, but I've still got to clean out this bin."

Walt shook his head. "That's a rough start to your morning."

Grace groaned. "Tell me about it. It's probably my fault it got this bad, too. I started smelling something funny in here a couple days ago. I should have realized something was wrong before now."

By the time Walt had finished his shopping, Grace had finished cleaning out the potato bin and put the rest of the potatoes back. There. She could have a normal rest of the day.

Twenty minutes later, while Grace checked out a customer's

groceries, a thud came from the other side of the store. A loud "Oh, no!" followed the thud. That didn't sound good.

Elaine Keller, a woman in her seventies who had been the town librarian for as long as Grace could remember, came around a corner, her face distressed.

"Grace, I'm terribly sorry," she said. "I dropped a gallon of milk, and it broke and went all over the floor. I can help you clean it up."

Milk—oh no. Even a trace of spilled milk would reek later.

"No, no, that's all right," Grace said. "I'll get it. I can get you a new jug of milk, and then I'll deal with the spilled one."

Elaine put her hands on her hips. "You shouldn't have to clean up after my clumsy mistake."

Grace put her own hands on her hips. "This is standard procedure. If you went to a big grocery store in the city and dropped a jug of milk, they'd do just the same thing."

Elaine shook her head. "I shouldn't let you do it," she said. "But since I don't know where you keep the cleaning supplies, I'd have to go all the way home to get mine. And then I wouldn't have the energy to walk back here again. So I'm afraid you're stuck doing it."

Grace couldn't help smiling. "I'll go get your replacement milk, and you can finish the rest of your shopping."

Her smile faded at the sight of the spilled milk. How could one gallon of milk go so far? She'd need the mop and a lot of towels. She couldn't get a replacement gallon from the refrigerator without tracking spilled milk all over the store, so she'd have to start the cleanup first and get the milk to Elaine in a minute.

Elaine didn't mind. "I was the one who caused all that trouble, so I shouldn't complain if I need to wait while it gets cleaned up. I'll just sit here by the counter and read. There's an article on my phone I've been meaning to finish."

Grace used old towels to absorb as much of the milk as possible, then mopped the floor, wringing the mop into the bucket at frequent intervals. Somebody ought to make gigantic sponges for things like this. Grace didn't think even a car-washing sponge would be big enough to do anything.

She finished mopping up the spill, got Elaine her jug of milk, and checked out several customers who had come in during the ordeal. Now she had to mop again with a cleaner so the floor wouldn't stink.

The floor finished, Grace collapsed on a chair by the cash register to rest. Two big messes so far, and it was only ten A.M. She hoped her parents' days in the store weren't usually like this. This was more work than teaching classes.

What should she do now? There was that project Dad had mentioned, switching the canned and jarred food to lower shelves and putting the boxed food on higher shelves. She could do that.

She got the rolling cart from the back room and started putting the high-up cans and jars on it. She could see how Dad had knocked that can onto his foot. They should have a step stool for the things on the top shelf. Grace could reach them, but they were far above her head and she had to stand on tiptoe to get them down. It must be hard for short people.

She brought down several glass jars of pickles and started on the pasta sauce, stretching to grab a jar of marinara.

"Good morning," a male voice said behind her.

Grace jumped, losing her grip on the pasta sauce. The jar shattered at her feet, sending red sauce in every direction.

Grace whirled around and found herself face to face with Doc.

Doc opened his mouth to speak. Grace cut him off.

"You — you — why did you have to sneak up on me like that? You scared me!"

Every towel in the back room had been used, and sticky, tomato-covered broken glass was everywhere. What an awful morning!

Doc was saying something, but Grace wasn't taking in what he said.

"Just look at this!" Grace threw her hands up. "All I've done this morning is clean up rotten potatoes and spilled milk. Now this!"

Tears welled in her eyes, and she turned her back on Doc, resting her forehead against the second-to-top shelf. She was standing on the broken glass. It didn't matter. Tomato sauce and glass covered her shoes anyway.

It wasn't Doc's fault. He hadn't meant to scare her, she was sure. But it was the last straw after Grace's long morning.

A gentle hand touched her shoulder. Doc's words came through this time, although his voice still sounded as though it were coming from a long way off.

"I said I'm sorry — I didn't mean to scare you. I'll help you clean this up. Do you have any towels?"

"No, I used them all up earlier." Grace wiped her eyes on her sleeve.

"Then I'll get some towels from my office." Doc's footsteps retreated.

She shouldn't let him help her. It wasn't his job. Grace looked down at her feet. She didn't want to track the sauce all over. She wiggled off one of her shoes and stepped outside the area with the tomato sauce, avoiding the broken glass. She stood on one foot to take off the other shoe. The store had a policy against people coming in barefoot, but this was an emergency. Grace went for the broom. Better deal with the large pieces of broken glass first.

Doc came back as she was sweeping up the glass. He set a stack of towels on the cart Grace had been using.

He reached for the broom. "Allow me."

Grace held on to it. "It's my job to clean it up," she said. "But thanks for the towels."

Doc raised an eyebrow. "It seems like you could use some help."

"No." Grace bent down to sweep the glass and some of the tomato sauce into a dustpan. "Thanks anyway. You can go get whatever you were trying to get."

Him scaring her had been the last straw this morning, and she'd lost her temper and blown up at him. It was so embarrassing and unprofessional. She couldn't bear to let him help now.

"Suit yourself." He dusted off his hands and went into one of the aisles, whistling, while Grace worked on the floor. She would have to rinse the broom before sweeping up the shards of glass that had gone farther away. What a mess. She would have to wash her shoes too.

Doc wandered over to the cash register. Maybe he intended to wait there until Grace finished cleaning up the floor, but Grace didn't want to let him be heroically patient. She leaned the broom against the shelves, made a wide berth around the broken glass, and went to check out his groceries.

"What are you doing here so early, anyway?" Grace asked, as she scanned a package of ham, a bag of lettuce, and a bag of potato chips. "Don't you have appointments?"

"My ten-thirty appointment canceled."

"Well, I hope the next time you come in, you don't sneak up on people who are lifting jars," Grace said. "I could have dropped something heavy on my foot and broken it, the way my dad did."

Doc nodded solemnly. "I'll make sure to whistle on the way in."

"Just make a regular amount of noise walking in, like a normal human being." Grace grabbed a bag for Doc's groceries.

He took the bag from her hand. "Allow me."

She let him pack up his own groceries.

"You know," he said, the hint of a smile on his face as he turned to go, "you could put a bell over the door."

Grace made a face at him, but it was hard to keep from laughing. He wasn't all bad.

Grace, Baker Extraordinaire

By Saturday things had fallen into a rhythm. Grace and Mom were taking turns on the early shift and the late shift (Grace had offered to take the early shift every day, but Mom wouldn't let her). Grace had only managed to get her run in on days she started later, but some exercise was better than none.

Grace had also bought a bell at the hardware store and put it over the grocery store door. She'd expected Doc to grin and comment on it, but he'd just looked at it with raised eyebrows when he came in. Mom said it drove her crazy to hear the jingle every two minutes, but Dad said he'd often thought they ought to have a bell over the door.

After several days working in the store, Grace came up with another idea for improvement. She broached the idea to her parents one night as they were sitting on the porch.

"The one thing I miss from the grocery store I go to in California," Grace said, "is the fresh-baked goods section."

"What do you mean?" Mom asked. "All our baked goods are fresh."

Grace shook her head. "I don't mean from the suppliers. I meant things made there, at the store. Breads and rolls and coffee cakes and cookies and stuff like that. They're especially nice for a quick breakfast. I was thinking this morning, when I was eating cold cereal, that it would be nice to have a muffin or something. I bet a lot of other people in Fraser's Mill would feel the same way."

Ever since Hannah Fraser had been disappointed in her search for coconut water, Grace had been thinking about ways to stock more interesting items. Business had seemed slower lately than she remembered from years past. Maybe a fresh baked goods section would draw more people to the store.

"You mean we would bake things ourselves to sell at the store?" Mom asked. "Don't we have enough to do as it is?"

"I could do it," Grace said. "Especially in the mornings when I don't work early. I wouldn't go crazy — I would just make a few things. I looked up the food laws around here, and Michigan has a Cottage Food Law that says you can sell baked goods and a few other kinds of things in a grocery store without getting special permission or having a separate kitchen, as long as you label them properly."

"I don't know," Mom said. "If it takes off and does well, people will still want the baked goods after you leave in six weeks. I don't have time to do all that. And your father doesn't know the first thing about baking."

"We can call it a summer special," Grace said. "Only

available for a limited time. We could put a sign out front to advertise them."

"I think you oughtta let her, Liz," Dad said. "It can't hurt to have some special items in the store on occasion. Besides, I wouldn't mind some fresh-baked goods myself."

"The things we get from the supplier are perfectly fine," Mom said. "And I baked you a pie last week."

He chuckled. "Don't I know it. That pie was the best thing I've ever tasted."

"It was a peach pie," Mom told Grace.

"How do we have peaches at this time of year?"

"They come from California, but it's better than nothing," Mom said. "That was the day before your dad broke his foot. Since then I haven't had time to even think about baking."

"Well, is it okay if I do it for the store?" Grace said. "I won't leave a big mess in the kitchen. It won't be a problem for anybody, I promise."

Mom rocked slowly in her chair. "It's all right with me. Just don't run yourself ragged. How are things going getting ready for the National Board certification?"

"Oh, it's going all right," Grace said. "I've been working on it just about every evening. Don't worry, Mom, I'll be fine."

❧❦❧

The first chance Grace got, which happened to be Monday morning, she set out to bake some delicious items to draw the townspeople to the store.

She probably shouldn't make things too complicated. Lots

of places sold pies, but rolling out pie crust took a lot of work and always got flour everywhere. Gingersnaps were simpler, and she had a favorite recipe she had discovered years ago in an old cookbook, that used a secret ingredient: vinegar. Something about the vinegar gave the gingersnaps a special flavor.

She had all morning to bake. The gingersnaps would probably take about an hour and a half, including all the baking time for multiple batches. She wanted to make at least two different things. Apple crisp was a popular treat, and it wasn't as fiddly to make as pie crust. Besides, it took only a few ingredients. Grace put on an upbeat oldies playlist and went to work.

Dad popped his head in the door. "Good luck with your baking," he said. "I'm working on an order to our supplier. I've got to figure out what we're getting from the farm before I order any vegetables."

"I'll bring you some cookies when they're done," Grace told him. "I'm glad you're figuring out the inventory stuff, because I'm terrible at that sort of thing."

"Then I'll just have to show you," Dad said. "I know you're only here for the summer, but it's a good thing to learn. Not that you don't have enough to learn already, with that certification and everything."

He went back to his work, and Grace went back to her baking.

People kept bringing up the National Board certification, as though Grace might have forgotten it. It was true, she'd been spending more time thinking about the grocery store than the National Board lately, but she didn't need anybody to remind her how important it was. She'd buckle down to work on that soon, maybe tonight, maybe tomorrow. But she also wanted to improve the grocery store.

The gingersnap recipe made a massive amount of dough. She hoped lots of people would want to buy cookies, or her family would have to eat the ones that went stale. It was a pity — whenever the store had leftovers, they were usually at the point of being old and unappealing. But eating them kept them from being wasted.

The last batch of gingersnaps was in the oven. Grace pushed back her hair with a sticky hand, surveying the pile of used bowls and measuring cups and spoons. She'd better deal with those and then get to the apple crisp.

She found a large, flat pan with raised edges that would be perfect to make a large crisp. It would probably fit a quadrupled recipe. She'd better check pan size conversions online.

Grace almost forgot about the last batch of gingersnaps while she looked up pan sizes on her phone. The timer had gone off without her noticing. Some good timers were! Grace raced for the potholders and took the cookies out. They were a little dark. Those ones would have to be for the family — she didn't think she ought to sell them.

Time to start the apple crisp. What a lot of apples the recipe called for! Grace didn't have enough, so she went to the store to get more. She'd need to tally up the prices of all the ingredients she used so she could make sure she wasn't losing money selling the baked goods.

Back in the kitchen, Grace found herself grateful for her music playlist and for the sunny, pleasant kitchen. Mom always said wallpaper was a pain and no one wanted old-fashioned, brightly-colored Pennsylvania Dutch pictures anymore, but Grace thought it gave the kitchen a homey look.

At long last she had peeled all the apples, mixed them with sugar, spices, and cornstarch, put together her oat crumble for the top, and got the whole thing in the oven. Now she could work on the labels for the cookies and apple crisp.

In the middle of typing out a list of ingredients on her laptop, Grace noticed a ringing noise. Wait a minute. That was the kitchen timer. Why did she keep tuning it out? The apple crisp must be done.

She'd better not have burned this too. Grace snatched up the potholders from the kitchen table and flung open the oven door. Thank goodness. The huge pan of apple crisp was the perfect shade of golden brown. Grace whisked it out of the oven, and a searing pain shot across the back of her right hand.

"Aah!" Grace nearly dropped the pan, but set it on top of the stove just in time. In her hurry to take the pan out of the oven, she must have tipped the pan sideways. Boiling, sticky juice had poured all over her hand.

It hurt so badly, Grace couldn't think straight. Cold water. She ran to the sink and turned on the faucet, running the water as cold as it would go.

"Gracie?" Dad called from the next room. "What's going on?"

"I burned my hand!"

The cold water numbed her hand a little, which took away some of the pain, but she knew once she took it out again it would be bad. Two different blistered areas had already formed across her knuckles.

She heard the sound of crutches come into the kitchen.

"What happened?" Dad asked.

"The pan tipped when I was taking the apple crisp out of the oven." Grace tried not to cry, but her eyes were streaming.

"I'm so sorry, sweetheart." Dad surveyed the hand under the running water. "That looks bad. You oughtta get Doc to take a look at it."

Oh no, not Doc. She didn't want to have to talk to him.

"I'll be all right," Grace said through clenched teeth. "We have those burn dressing things in the store, don't we? In the first aid section? I can get one and bandage it up."

"No, I wouldn't do that," Dad said. "That's a pretty big area. I wouldn't risk it getting infected. You'd better show the doctor."

"Maybe it's not that bad," Grace said. "It probably says online what kinds of burns you need to see a doctor for." She pulled her hand out of the cold water. Searing pain again. "Ow. I'd better keep it under the water. Would you look up burns for me, Dad?"

"Sure." Dad crutched his way to the laptop at the kitchen table. Grace held her hand under the tap and tried not to think about how much it hurt.

Why hadn't she been more careful getting that pan out of the oven? She had baked fruit-filled things before. She knew better than to tip the pan.

"Gracie," Dad said, "it says here that you should see a doctor for burns on the hand, because they can be more serious. You'd better go to the clinic. You can get an ice pack from the freezer and ice it on your way over."

Grace wasn't about to argue with internet wisdom. She wiped her eyes with her non-burned hand and went to get the ice pack and a paper towel to wrap around it. Even with the ice, her hand hurt like fire. She put on her shoes and headed next door to the doctor's office.

⁂

Grace found herself in the small waiting room she remembered from growing up. The chairs were different, though. They must have been replaced. Four other people were waiting: a mom with a runny-nosed toddler, an elderly lady on oxygen, and a young guy with his arm in a sling. The toddler was playing with one of those big bead-sliding toys they always seemed to have in medical offices. Grace picked a chair far from everyone else and sat down.

A door opened, and Dorothy walked out. "Grace," she exclaimed. "I didn't expect to see you here."

"I burned my hand." Grace held it up.

"Ouch, that looks bad. What happened? Were you working in the store?"

"No, I was making apple crisp." Dang it, Grace's eyes were watering again. She didn't want to cry in public.

Dorothy shook her head. "I'm sorry. That looks miserable."

"I think the ice pack is helping a little."

"That's good. Doc probably has some fancy burn dressings that will help too. Back in the day we used to put butter on burns.

I guess you're not supposed to do that anymore." Dorothy shook her head. "Thank goodness for modern medicine. Well, I hope it feels better soon."

"Thanks," Grace said.

Doc's head appeared in the doorway of the next room. "Ethan," he called.

The woman with the toddler began to extricate the toddler from the bead toy. Doc waited for them in the doorway, looking tall and professional with a white lab coat and a stethoscope around his neck.

Grace sank lower in her chair. It would be great to be invisible. She needed medical attention, but did Doc have to be the one to give it? He'd better not tease her about needing his help.

Doc's gaze fell upon Grace, and his eyebrows shot up. "Abby, you can sit Ethan on the exam table," he told the mom with the toddler. "I'll be right in."

He approached Grace. "You're about the last person I expected to see in here."

Grace made a face at him. "You know any other doctors closer than Cadillac?"

Doc motioned toward Grace's hand. "What happened to you?"

Grace took off the ice pack so he could see the blistered expanse of the burn.

Doc pursed his lips. "That looks painful. But you shouldn't ice a burn. Have you run it under cool water?"

"Yes, I did. I used the coldest water from the faucet."

Doc shook his head. "I see why you might think that was a

good idea, but you should only use cool water on a burn, not cold water or ice. It can damage the tissue."

"Oh." Of course she was doing something wrong. Every time she saw Doc, she was in the middle of some embarrassing, messy, or uncomfortable situation. Grace put the ice pack on the chair next to her.

"Are you okay to wait for a few minutes?" Doc asked. "I've got a couple other people to see. If the burn hurts too much you can run water over it in the bathroom, but not too cold."

"Sure."

Doc disappeared into the exam room. Grace leaned back in her chair, wishing she'd brought a watch, or her phone, or anything to check the time. If Doc had to get through three appointments before her, it could be a long time. Without the ice pack, her hand felt much worse. Maybe she should run water over it like Doc had suggested. No, somebody was in the clinic bathroom.

Looking down, Grace realized her clothes were splotched with flour. She must look like a mess — her hair was coming out of its ponytail and falling in her face, and her eyes felt swollen. What a way to be out in public.

The wait took forever. Grace must've been missing her work shift by now. Dad probably told Mom what had happened — hopefully Mom wouldn't be expecting her down at the store.

Two more people came in, a woman with a walker and a middle-aged woman helping her. The woman with the walker — a smiley, chatty woman — told Grace she was having trouble getting diabetic shoes. Doc would help her out.

"He's just the nicest, friendliest young fellow," she told

Grace. "Always listens. Like I was his own grandmother he was trying to help. And so smart. Knows everything there is about doctoring."

That was an impressive testimonial to Doc's skills and bedside manner. It was hard for Grace to envision him with all those qualities. But clearly this woman appreciated him.

Finally it was Grace's turn. She went into Doc's exam room, which was pristine. Everything looked like it had just been scrubbed and polished. He must spend a lot of time cleaning it, unless he hired a cleaner.

Doc was all business. "Why don't you sit on the exam table," he told her. "Let me wash my hands."

Grace sat on the paper-covered table, swinging her feet. The burned hand felt as bad as ever.

Doc washed his hands and pulled on a pair of blue gloves. He rummaged through a drawer. "How did you get burned?"

"I was taking an apple crisp out of the oven, and the pan tipped and spilled juice all over my hand," Grace said. "The juice was sticky — I think that made it worse."

"Do you have any other burns?"

"Just my hand."

Doc pulled a tube of something out of the drawer. "This is an antibiotic cream," he said. "Let me see that hand again."

Grace held out her hand, and Doc took it in one gloved hand to scrutinize it. "You've got a second-degree burn," he said. "That must be painful. The blisters haven't broken open, so that's good — there's not as much chance of infection. But when you've got a burn like this that goes deeper than the surface, you can't tell how deep it really is. I'm gonna put antibiotic cream on this and bandage it. You'll have to keep the bandage dry and change it once a day. Then you'll need to come back in a few days so I can evaluate it."

Grace sighed. "All right." Would he get to the antibiotic cream already? Maybe that would make it feel better.

Unfortunately, the antibiotic cream didn't do a thing for the pain. But Doc applied it surprisingly gently. He taped a bandage over Grace's hand, not sticking anything to the burned area. His face was serious, and Grace realized why the townspeople liked having him for their doctor. He showed not just competence but also sympathy. Although the hand hurt just as badly, Grace found herself relaxing.

"You might want to take an over-the-counter pain reliever," he said. "That's going to hurt for a while."

"Okay," Grace said.

He put more bandage materials in a small paper bag. "Are you right-handed?"

"Yeah."

"That's rough. You'll probably need someone to help change the bandage. If that's too much for you and your parents, feel free to come back over here, and I'll help with it." Doc took off his gloves in the methodical way doctors always did, balling the first one up in one gloved hand and taking the second one off inside-out. He had nice hands, agile-looking, with long fingers. "Well, feel better soon."

"Wait a minute," Grace said, getting down from the exam

table. "I haven't shown you my insurance card, and I haven't paid a copay or anything."

"Oh, I'll bill you, don't worry." Doc grinned. "I know where you live."

He might be good at bandaging things, but he was still insufferable.

Back at home, when Grace went to put the bandage materials in the medicine cabinet, she hardly recognized the wild-haired, streaky-faced, flour-daubed creature staring back at her from the mirror. She had gone over to the doctor's like that? Well, it's not as though it mattered. She wasn't trying to impress anyone.

She wasn't keeping score or anything, but if she had been, it was currently Doc — 4, Grace — 0.

Out of the House

Grace learned quickly that a burned hand was an ordeal. She'd never realized how many times she washed her hands every day until now. Handwashing was a chore when you were trying to keep a bandage dry.

Mom suggested she take a couple days off working in the store until the burn had had some time to heal, but Grace was firm. She had come all the way out here to work in the store. She wouldn't let a little thing like a blistered hand stop her. So, that evening, she printed up the labels for the gingersnaps and apple crisp according to the Cottage Food Law regulations. Mom bagged the baked goods, and Grace carried them down to the store and arranged them on a little display near the front. Tomorrow's customers had better appreciate them after all the work and pain that had gone into the cooking.

On Tuesday morning, as Grace was working (with a large plastic glove over the bandaged hand, so she could keep it clean), Alex came in to deliver some produce. She stopped at the front and leaned her elbows on the counter.

"Hey, Grace," she said. "What's your schedule like tomorrow night?"

Grace raised an eyebrow. "You're trying to talk me into something."

"This doesn't take a lot of time. And you're good at it. You'll like it," Alex said.

"I can't think of anything that falls under all those categories."

Alex waved that away. "You'll love it. Listen. Two of the altos in the Latin Mass choir are out of town this week and I'm the only one left. You sing alto. You oughtta come to choir practice tomorrow night at seven-thirty and sing with us on Sunday."

"Um, Alex, I haven't sung in the choir in years. Besides, it would take a long time to learn all that music. I don't have a lot of time right now."

"You'll be there on Sunday anyway," Alex said. "And practice tomorrow is just an hour."

"I'd crash and burn. You guys sing so much stuff where the parts are all staggered. When I was in the choir we sang for the English Mass and just did hymns and a few chants."

"It's not that bad," Alex said. "The motets aren't too hard, and I'll be singing with you. You don't have to sing loud if you don't want. It'll be fun!"

Well, if she didn't have to sing loud, her mistakes wouldn't be too obvious. And it would be fun to hang out with Alex.

"You're incorrigible." Grace shook her head at Alex. "All right, I'll do it."

"Yay!"

"But I'm not signing up to sing for the whole summer. I'll see how it goes this week."

Alex headed for the door. "I fully intend to get you roped in for the whole summer," she called back.

◦⌒⌒⌒◦

Just before seven-thirty on Wednesday evening, Grace made her way up the street toward St. Anthony's Church. The church stood near the north end of town, across from the library and town hall. Looming in the distance behind the church was Fraser's Water-Powered Sawmill, the mill that had given the town its name.

St. Anthony's Church had been built in the 1950s. It had managed to escape most of the "wreckovation" renovation efforts of the decades following. The stained glass windows, with pictures of the Sacraments, looked like the illustrations in the Baltimore Catechism, but Grace had always liked the 50s and the Baltimore Catechism, so she didn't mind.

Alex was waiting in the church vestibule. "Good, you're here," Alex said. "You can meet our new choir director."

Grace followed her up the stairs and into the loft. A brown-haired woman in her forties was sitting at the organ bench. "Oh, hello," she said.

"We've got another alto, for this week at least," Alex said. "Mary Jane, this is Grace."

"Wonderful." Mary Jane smiled and slid off the organ bench. "Let me get you some music. Alex, would you please find Grace a hymnal and a chant book?"

As Mary Jane and Alex got Grace's music together, other choir members began to filter in. Dorothy and Elaine arrived, followed by Hannah Fraser, then two young ladies Grace recognized from a family that owned a cherry orchard near Alex's farm. Those women must all be sopranos, since Alex had said she would be the only alto unless Grace came. As for the men, there was Alex's brother Sam, Charlie Keller—Elaine's grandson who managed the diner down the street—and Doc Johnson. Of course Doc would be there. Just Grace's luck, now she would probably sing terribly.

Mary Jane called the practice to order, and the choir sang warm-ups. Mary Jane kept stopping them to talk about good singing technique and to remind everyone to listen to one another. "The most important thing about singing as a choir is singing together," she said. "You can't sing together if you don't listen to the people around you."

They practiced motets, in which each voice part had its own different timing, and here Grace had her opportunity to crash and burn. She didn't know the motets, and the sopranos (especially Hannah) were loud. It was hard to listen to Alex's medium-volume alto, read the music to follow along, and watch the conductor.

Mary Jane stopped the choir in the middle of the first motet. "Just a moment," she said. "We seem to be coming apart. Altos, how are you doing?"

"The counting is a little confusing," Alex said. "I think I'm holding something too long, but I don't know what."

"I got lost about one line in," Grace said.

"All right. Altos, let's run your counting in the first two systems—you've got a lot of eighth notes. Everybody else, you may sit down for a minute."

Everyone else sat down, and Mary Jane went to the organ. Hannah whispered something to Doc, who was sitting next to her. Doc's handsome face took on an amused grin.

If they were laughing at the altos, they wouldn't laugh long. Grace set her chin high. She listened intently to Mary Jane playing through the alto part.

"Now you try it with me," Mary Jane said, and Grace and Alex sang along with the organ.

The next full run of the piece went better than the first time. Mary Jane beamed. "Let's talk about dynamics now," she said, and handed out pencils.

Choir practice wasn't so bad, once you got the counting down. If Grace could remember how to sight-read sheet music, it would help.

After the second motet, which was easier than the first one, and two hymns, Mary Jane said it was time for the choir to split into two groups. The men would practice some chants with her, while the women would take a short break before practicing their chants.

As Mary Jane played the starting notes for the men, Doc slapped his pocket and pulled out his phone.

"Sorry, Mary Jane," he said, "I have to go. I'll practice the propers at home."

"Not again." Hannah groaned. "You always get called away."

Doc headed toward the stairs. "See you, everybody," he said. "Nice to have you join us, Grace."

That was odd, Doc singling Grace out to say goodbye. He was probably relieved she hadn't fallen down any stairs or broken any jars or burned herself today.

While the men practiced their chants, Grace realized she was thirsty. She'd better go down to the drinking fountain in the church vestibule.

As Grace came back from getting her drink, she ran into Hannah coming down the stairs. Hannah held a sleek pink water bottle.

"Hi," Grace said.

"Hi." Hannah stopped on the stairs. "I didn't know you knew Doc."

"He lives next door to my parents," Grace said. "And I had to go to his office a couple days ago when I burnt my hand making apple crisp." She held out the bandaged hand.

"Wow, that's a big bandage," Hannah said. "Does it hurt?"

"Not anymore, unless I press on it."

"So are you thinking of joining the choir?" Hannah asked.

"Maybe. I'm not sure yet. I thought I'd try it for a week."

Hannah took a sip from her water bottle. "I get that. I wasn't sure about joining myself, but Doc talked me into it. He said they needed sopranos. It's too bad he got called away in the middle of practice. That happens to him all the time."

"I guess rural doctors must always be on call," Grace said.

"Seriously. He and I were playing tennis the other evening when he got called away. It's always a bummer." Hannah smiled. "But we're going to play again tomorrow night to make up for it."

Hannah brushed past down the stairs, and Grace went up to the loft. It was pretty clear how Hannah felt about Doc. But why did she come down here just to tell Grace about how close she and Doc were? Was she warning Grace off? Grace laughed to herself. Hannah needn't worry. Nothing was further from Grace's mind than going after Doc.

⬿⬿⬿⬿⬿

"Well, how did you like practice?" Alex asked afterwards, as they walked down Main Street together.

"It wasn't easy," Grace said. "But I think it was good. I had some problems reading the square notation for the chants, but Mary Jane said she'd email me some recordings."

"The practice recordings she sends are really helpful." Alex tossed her choir water bottle and caught it again. "I'm not great at reading sheet music, but when I listen to my part and practice it along with the other parts, it really helps."

They were almost at the grocery store, and Grace had an idea. "Hey, want to come down to the diner and get a milkshake or something?"

"Hmm, I don't know," Alex said. "I've got a bunch of chores I have to do at home."

"We won't be long. And we haven't gotten much of a chance to catch up since I got back."

"Well, I guess it would keep you from being cooped up in the house," Alex said. "Sure, I'll go. But I can't stay long."

"We can get milkshakes to go, and I'll walk down to the farm with you."

It was a warm evening, and the sun hadn't set yet. Chuck's Diner was down by the gas station at the south end of town. It had been there since before either of the girls was born. Chuck Keller, Elaine's husband, started it. Their grandson Charlie ran it now.

The diner served standard American diner food, plus a few German and Italian house specialties, and its milkshakes were famous. It was the only restaurant in town, if you didn't count the tavern or the ice cream stand.

Grace and Alex went through swinging glass doors and into the diner. It was a long, narrow building, with booths on one side and a serving counter lined with bar stools on the other. Charlie looked up from wiping down the counter. He brightened when he saw them.

"Alex!" He whisked his counter-wiping cloth out of sight. "And Grace! Long time no see."

Alex laughed. "How did you get here so fast? Did you run all the way from the church?"

"No, I changed into my Superman suit and flew here," Charlie said with a wink. "What can I get you? We've got gluten-free peanut butter cookies."

That was meant for Alex — she couldn't eat gluten. Grace slid onto a bar stool beside Alex and peered at the menu on the wall behind Charlie's head. Although it had been a while since she'd been there, the menu hadn't changed much.

"I'd like a chocolate milkshake, please," Alex told Charlie.

"Right away. And you?" Charlie looked at Grace.

"A peanut butter milkshake, please."

Charlie whisked around making the shakes.

"Hey, Alex," he called. "How's that prize pumpkin coming?"

Alex laughed. "You know I just planted the pumpkins yesterday. Don't you know how long it takes a pumpkin plant to sprout?"

"I have no idea," Charlie called. He applied whipped cream to the milkshakes with a liberal hand. "I bet you'll get the blue ribbon at the contest."

"Thanks. I don't know if I will, but I'm sure gonna try," Alex said.

Charlie put the two shakes on the counter and pulled out two napkins with a flourish. "Here you are — on the house."

"On the house?" Grace stared.

Charlie smiled. "You get one because you just came back to town. Alex gets one for being Alex."

Alex blushed under her tan. "Thanks, Charlie."

"You're sure?" Grace asked.

"Sure I'm sure." Charlie pushed Grace's shake towards her.

"Well, thank you," Grace said.

Although Alex had said she needed to get back to the farm, she seemed in no hurry to leave. Charlie leaned on the counter, chatting with the girls and teasing Alex. He and Alex seemed to know each other pretty well. Maybe something was going on there.

Once a group of customers came in and Charlie went to take their orders, Alex slid down from her bar stool, her gaze lingering on Charlie. "I guess we oughtta get going."

She and Grace started up the street together.

"You probably shouldn't walk all the way with me," Alex

said. "You'd have to walk back by yourself in the dark. I'm sorry—I didn't realize how late it was getting."

"Well, I don't want you to walk all that way by yourself in the dark either," Grace said. "I've got an idea. I'll borrow my mom's car and drop you off at the farm."

"Oh, you don't need to do that," Alex said. "I walk this way all the time. I'm not gonna get mugged in Fraser's Mill. And I've got a flashlight."

"No way. It's a two-minute drive. I'm taking you."

"Okay, fine." Alex smiled. "Thanks."

They walked up the road, waving to townspeople they passed along the way.

"I've got a nosy question," Grace said, "so you don't have to answer it unless you want to. Is there something going on between you and Charlie?"

Alex raised her eyebrows. "What do you mean?"

"Well, the two of you seem to know each other pretty well."

Alex sipped her milkshake. "We've known each other a long time," she said. "We both grew up in Fraser's Mill, and we both sing in the choir. We do get along pretty well. I mean, Charlie's a nice guy. But we're just friends."

"Really?"

The corner of Alex's mouth quirked. "Yeah. Why? Did it look like something else?"

"If you're just friends, what was with the free milkshake?"

"What do you mean? He gave you one too."

Grace shook her head. "I've gone to the diner all my life before I moved, and Charlie's never given me anything for free before. I bet he just did that because he wanted to give you a free shake. He obviously likes you."

"No way." Alex shook her head. "He's just a friendly guy. There's nothing else going on."

"Nothing? That's it?"

"Yes, that's it." Alex sipped her milkshake.

Grace shook her head. "I don't believe you. You're smiling."

"I'm not. You're just trying to matchmake. I oughtta pay you back by picking somebody for you." Alex's eyes gleamed with mischief.

"In Fraser's Mill? Ha! You just try."

Who was there in Fraser's Mill, anyway? No one compatible with her, she was sure. The only eligible guy that came to mind — if he was single, which Grace didn't know — was Doc. Perish the thought! Of all the guys who would be completely wrong for Grace, Doc headed the list.

It was silly to even think about guys in Fraser's Mill. Finding a compatible guy in L.A. was difficult enough. And the situation with Lucas was still confusing since Grace had left him hanging after that one date. Grace didn't have time for Alex's mischievous setups right now. She had goals for this summer, and she needed to focus on them.

The Chicken Situation

Grace got back to the house to find her parents in a state of excitement.

"Your father's got a knee scooter!" Mom announced the moment Grace came in the door. "He won't stay still for a minute. He's been scooting all around the house. I'm trying to convince him to put the thing away and get ready for bed. He can't take it up the stairs, which is a mercy."

"Gracie, come look at this," Dad called from the living room.

Grace came in to find her father with a contraption that looked like a cross between a scooter and a tricycle. The seat of the scooter supported his injured leg, and he pushed himself around the room with his other foot.

"This is great," he said. "It's a hundred times better than crutches. I can get around the house, and I can put things in this basket on the front."

"That's great, Dad," Grace said. "Where did it come from? Did Doc buy it? Did you?"

"It's rented," Dad said. "It's expensive to buy one if you're just using it for a few weeks. Doc found a place to rent one pretty cheaply. The insurance covers part of it."

"I hope the insurance covers the rest of the medical bills you'll have if you get injured using that thing," Mom said. "Aren't you going to put that away for the night? You're acting like Thomas, the time we got him the bike for Christmas."

Dad chuckled. "As I recall, Thomas fell asleep that night hugging the bike wheel."

"Well, you're not doing any such thing. Leave the scooter with Grace—it's not going anywhere—and come upstairs. Here are your crutches."

"All right, all right," Dad said, hauling himself off the scooter and struggling to get balanced with the crutches. "That thing's gonna make a world of difference."

Grace had the early shift, so it was time for her to get ready for bed. Showering with her bandaged hand was tough. So far she had used a large rubber glove with rubber bands around the wrist to keep the water out of the bandage, but some water had found its way inside. She couldn't wait until she got the bandage off.

Grace had said her night prayers and was ready for bed when an email from Lucas popped up on her phone. Why was Lucas emailing her at this hour? Well, California was three hours behind.

Lucas wondered how things were going for her at the grocery store. So much had happened since Grace got to Michigan that she wasn't sure how to begin. She told Lucas about how she had hit a small snag burning her hand while cooking, but that her dad's injury was healing all right and the store work was going okay. She asked how things were going for him.

Lucas emailing her must be a sign that he was still interested. She'd wondered if her trip to Michigan would make him forget about a second date. But he must at least be interested in corresponding and getting to know each other better.

And his email writing was excellent. Grace's English teacher self appreciated that. It was one sign of compatibility between her and Lucas. She dozed off, thinking of how she just needed to get to know him better to figure out whether they would really work together.

In the morning she read Lucas's reply. He was sorry to hear about her burned hand. His own summer was going well—he was taking the summer off and using the time to travel around. Most recently he had been to Santa Barbara and played ultimate frisbee with some friends from college. He was going to San Diego next week. He was also re-reading *War and Peace* and had a lot of insights on Napoleon.

Grace replied that that sounded like a good summer. Privately, she was glad she wasn't stuck in L.A. this summer shopping for Shipt and poring over National Board materials. In that case she might have envied Lucas's travels.

But she wasn't envious of him now. For such a small town, Fraser's Mill had more going on than Grace had remembered.

During Grace's shift that morning, the bell over the door jingled, and there was Dad in the doorway with his knee scooter.

"Dad, what are you doing here?" Grace kept her voice low. Mom was around somewhere. She wouldn't be happy if she came along and found Dad there with his injured foot.

"Move over, young lady." Dad rolled toward the cash register on his scooter. "I'm gonna work the register. You can tell your mother to take a break and work on her book."

"She won't want to do that." Grace moved over to let Dad through. "She'll just be mad you're in here. She would never agree to take a break in the middle of the morning just to work on her book."

"You just do as I say, and we'll see how your mom takes it."

Grace sighed. Well, this wasn't her idea. Mom could decide how to react to it.

Mom was in the back, unpacking boxes.

"Mom," Grace said, "Dad just came in on his scooter, and he's taking over the cash register. He says to tell you you should take a break and work on your novel."

"What?" Mom shook her head as though she'd heard wrong. "Take a break? And let him run the register? He would just wear himself out and probably reinjure his foot. Take a break, indeed! I just got on a roll with this unpacking. That man's gonna drive me crazy. I'll talk to him."

She hurried into the store. Grace followed behind.

"Benjamin Murray," Mom exclaimed, "if you think I'm gonna write my book and let you slave away in the store with a broken foot, you've got another thing coming. If you really want to work, can't you do paperwork in the house?"

"I finished all the paperwork already," Dad said, his

demeanor unruffled. "Besides, if you don't work on that novel, you'll never get it written. You haven't touched it all week. I hate to see your story-writing get sidelined. There ought to be a way for you to spend more time on it."

"Since when does my story-writing come before your welfare? I won't allow it, Ben."

"It won't hurt me to mind the cash register while Grace takes over for you in the back. You go work on that story, and when you've written five hundred words you can come back and I'll let you take over."

Mom put her hands on her hips. "Five hundred words?"

"Five hundred, and not one word less. I'm gonna ask to see it later, so don't you cheat."

"Fine." Mom shook hands with her husband over the counter. "It's a deal. I bet I can get that done in half an hour and get you back in the house where you belong."

Shaking her head, she went out the door, still wearing her grocery apron.

Dad chuckled. "Did you see that? I reckon she'll get more done on that story today than she has in weeks."

Grace shook her head. "Well, I'm impressed. But are you sure you're not going to hurt your foot or over-exert yourself?"

"Positive. Go on, young lady, you've got a job to do. I can't let my employees stand around talking when they oughtta be working."

Grace gave up.

After lunch that day, Natalie discovered a problem.

"I was just checking dates on food," Natalie told Grace, "and all that chicken in the fridge is gonna be past-date tomorrow!"

"Oof." The last Grace had seen, the fridge was full of chicken. She hurried over to the meat section.

There lay packages upon packages of chicken, all marked with the same date. They must have gotten in a large shipment the last time. Why hadn't more customers bought it? If somebody didn't buy it by tomorrow, they'd have to see how much they could freeze for their own use. But their family could never use so much chicken. Maybe they could sell it quickly to avoid wasting too much.

What was the best way to get people to buy things? Have a sale? There had to be some way to get the customers' attention.

"I've got an idea," Grace said. "Somebody can stand out at the edge of the road with a sign that says there's a big sale on chicken."

"That's a great idea," Natalie said. "We oughtta get a lot of customers that way."

"Yeah, maybe we'll even attract some people who are just passing through," Grace said. "I'm gonna go ask my mom about it."

"Who's gonna stand out there with the sign?" Natalie asked.

"That's a good question." Grace and Natalie were the only employees up front in the store.

"Don't look at me." Natalie shook her head so hard her braid swung back and forth. "I'm not gonna do it. I would die of embarrassment."

That left one person.

"Fine, I'll do it," Grace said. "I better ask my mom about marking down the chicken."

Mom sighed when Grace told her about the situation. "Yes, we've got to sell the chicken if we possibly can," she said. "You should mark it down. And maybe advertising by the road will bring in more sales." She mopped her brow. "If it's not one thing, it's another. I'm at my wits' end trying to manage things in this store today."

If she was going to be a sign twirler for a day, Grace needed a sign. She found a broken-down white cardboard box in the back room. One side of the box would work for a sign. Grace found some markers and wrote in eye-catching letters, "Huge Sale on Chicken! Today Only!"

Now she had to stand by the road and let the sign work its magic. She'd better get a baseball cap, or she'd get a sunburn.

As she went to find the baseball cap, a thought struck her. Hadn't Dorothy mentioned a town social media page? Grace pulled out her phone. She could advertise on the page about the sale.

It took some time to find the town's page, because she didn't know the page's name, but she eventually found it. The top post was by Dorothy, telling people about an upcoming fireman's supper and dance at the fire hall, and the second was by Hank Liddell, the town sheriff, warning people to be careful while driving through town because there were chickens kept in some of the front yards.

Grace smiled. A town had to have a low crime rate if the only message from the sheriff was about chickens.

The town social media page was public, so Grace composed a message about the chicken sale. She grabbed her hat and went out by the road with the sign.

A job as a sign twirler might not be so bad, if the pay was reasonable. At least today was nice weather, and to be fair,

Grace wasn't twirling the sign. She'd probably drop it if she tried anything too fancy.

The chicken-selling business wasn't brisk, even with the sign. Grace saw a couple customers look at the sign on their way in, but when she came in for a drink an hour later (it felt like several hours later) the supply of chicken hadn't diminished much.

Well, the store always got busier right before dinnertime. Grace hoped some people coming to shop for dinner would decide to buy chicken. She splashed cold water on her face, readjusted her baseball cap, and returned to the side of the road.

Did this kind of thing happen a lot? Did her parents often end up with large quantities of food they couldn't sell? Grace didn't remember it from when she was growing up. Maybe this was random. Maybe they hadn't had as many customers this week. Or maybe the townspeople had all bought beef and pork instead.

Five o'clock came around. With it came Doc, heading toward the grocery store from next door. He stopped to look at Grace's sign, his mouth pursed in an expression Grace couldn't read.

"Did your parents hire you as a sign twirler?" he said. "You oughtta get one of those Chick-fil-A signs with the cows on it that say 'Eat Mor Chikin.'"

"We don't have any Chick-fil-As out here," Grace said. "And we could probably get sued for copyright infringement."

Doc grinned. "You see any Chick-fil-A lawyers out here?"

Maybe he thought this whole thing was funny, but he hadn't spent half the afternoon standing in the sun holding a sign.

"Nope." Grace waved the sign back and forth. "But I do see

someone that ought to take advantage of this marvelous sale on chicken. Unless the townspeople pay you for your doctor visits with chickens and bags of apples."

Doc laughed. "Not quite. But sometimes people do try to pay with gift cards they don't want."

He disappeared into the store. A few cars rumbled down the road. Grace held her sign at the best angle for the people in the cars to read.

When Doc emerged from the store five minutes later, he carried a full shopping bag. Grace hoped there was chicken somewhere in that bag. She wasn't going to ask.

Not long after, Charlie drove up and parked in the store's small gravel parking lot. "I heard you were having a sale on chicken," he called to Grace. "We could use some at the diner."

The diner! That was wonderful. Whenever the diner needed food, they bought a lot of it. Grace followed Charlie into the store in case he wanted help carrying the chicken out to his car. She wasn't disappointed. Charlie bought nearly all the remaining stock.

Three packages remained. If they didn't sell by closing time, the Murrays could eat them. Grace hoped Dad had ordered more chicken with a newer expiration date, because there wasn't any fresh chicken left for tomorrow. It was already an embarrassment that the store didn't always have what the townspeople wanted, like Hannah's coconut water. It was worse to be out of common items like chicken. There ought to be some way to organize these things better so the store's supply matched up with the customer's demand.

Running a grocery store was a lot more complicated than Grace had realized when she was younger. How did Grace's parents do it all, even when Dad wasn't injured?

The Storm

At dinner that night (chicken, of course), Dad said he didn't trust the weather. The air had been still all day, and the weather report predicted a possible thunderstorm.

"I think we're in for a doozy," he said. "Those weathermen are wrong more than half the time, but I don't like the look of the sky out there, and I haven't heard a bird all evening."

"Do you think we'll have a power outage?" Mom asked.

"Could be. We'd better get the generator ready, just in case."

Power outages occurred frequently in these parts, mostly from fallen trees bringing down power lines. Grace's parents had a system worked out for such times. They kept flashlights stowed in different areas of the house and lots of bottled water because their electric well stopped working without power. They also had a generator for the store.

"Does the generator need gas in it?" Mom asked.

"Yeah. We haven't used it since last year, so I siphoned the gas and used it in the car."

"I can refill it," Grace said. "Where's the gas can?"

"Thank you kindly, sweetheart," Dad said. "Would you mind setting it up in case we need it? It's gotta be at least twenty feet from the buildings, and it has a rain tent that goes over the top. Those things and the gas can are in the garage."

So after dinner Grace wheeled the generator out of the garage, filled it with gas, and set it up with the generator tent over it. She hoped they wouldn't have to use it. She didn't know how to hook it up.

As it neared bedtime the wind picked up and rain began splashing against the windows. Dad, who loved to watch storms despite his gloomy predictions, sat on the front porch in his rocking chair and watched the rain and the lightning.

"Ben, you'll catch your death," Mom said. "The wind's blowing right this way. You'll get soaked sitting there."

"Don't worry, I won't get my cast wet," Dad said. "The rain's not coming this direction. I'm keeping an eye on it."

"You would keep an eye on a tornado." Mom patted him on the shoulder in a way that belied her stern tone. "I'll get you a cup of tea."

Grace smiled. Her parents' relationship was cute. She headed up to her room to work on National Board prep and listen to the rain on the roof. The sound was soothing. Rain had been a rarity in California, especially during the summer, and Grace missed it. She liked rainstorms, even ones with a lot of thunder and lightning. Maybe she felt that way because Dad had always been so interested in them.

She tried to read through the National Board materials, but as often happened, she found herself distracted. On this occasion, an email dinged on her phone. She had a message from Lucas, telling about more of his travels. He wondered exactly when she would be getting back to California.

July 16th, Grace told him. That would give her enough time to settle back in and get ready for the school year before it started in August.

August had seemed far off before Grace left for Fraser's Mill. It seemed a lot closer now. She'd better start working more seriously on the National Board stuff. She kept forgetting about it and doing other things instead, and she shouldn't. It was the one thing she was doing this summer that would affect her future in a big way. She had to get organized and figure out how to work through the material. Maybe she could join some kind of support group. There were lots of support groups online.

Grace logged into her social media. Before trying to find a support group for the NBCT stuff, she'd better comment on that post she had made about the sale on chicken. Engaging with customers on social media would probably make the store look good in the community. Grace wrote a comment saying the chicken was sold out and thanking those who had bought it.

As Grace added her comment to the post, she had an idea. Why not make a social media page for the store? Of course, one of her parents or another store employee would have to run the page after she went back to California, but that shouldn't be too much trouble. It was something to suggest to her parents.

The rain grew louder, coming down in sheets. Good thing Grace wasn't out in it. This kind of weather turned umbrellas inside out.

Footsteps approached, and Mom appeared in the doorway. "It's getting pretty windy," she said. "Your dad thinks we ought to go down to the basement. There's a tornado warning, and if that tree by the driveway comes down it could hit the house."

If Dad said they should go to the basement, it must be serious. Grace closed her laptop and gathered it up with its power cord. She snagged a red-and-white blanket from her bed—the basement was chilly.

Downstairs, Mom was supervising Dad as he went down to the basement on his crutches. The basement stairs were steep, narrow, and uncarpeted. "Take it slower, Ben," Mom warned him. "There's no rush."

The Murrays' basement was half laundry room and workshop, half storage and board game area. It was furnished with a plastic lawn chair and a nubbly loveseat exiled from the living room. An old-fashioned ring-shaped fluorescent bulb provided light. Grace settled into the plastic lawn chair with her blanket, and her parents took the loveseat.

"Grace, why don't you take a look at the weather?" Dad asked. "See how that tornado warning is doing."

According to the internet, their area was in the center of where Doppler radar had indicated rotation in the clouds, warranting the tornado warning. The crashing thunder and pouring rain sounded loud even from here in the basement.

"Thomas will be sad he isn't here," Dad said. "He likes storms. Although I reckon he gets plenty of them in Florida, with those hurricanes."

"I'll text him and tell him what he's missing here," Grace

said, grinning. "I'll make him as jealous as possible. He owes us a visit, anyway."

"It's that internship," Mom said. "He's supposed to get some time off in August, and he says he'll come visit then."

"Aw, shucks," Grace said. "I'll be back in California by then. I wish we could all coordinate our schedules to spend a vacation together, or fly to see each other more often. Why do plane flights have to be so expensive?"

At that moment, the lights flickered out.

"Power's out," Dad said unnecessarily. "Good thing we got the generator all ready. As soon as this tornado warning's over, I'm gonna go out and set it up."

"Benjamin Murray, you are not going out of this house until it's done raining. Grace and I can get the generator going."

"You've never hooked it up before," Dad said. "It's not as simple as you might think."

"We can figure it out, Dad," Grace said. "You can't get your cast wet."

Dad sighed. "All right, fine. But nobody's stirring out of this basement until the tornado warning is over. The big maple next to the driveway could fall on the house."

At last, the better part of an hour later, the tornado warning ended. Grace dashed upstairs to see how things looked outside. She hit the kitchen light switch. Nothing happened. Right, the power was out. Outside the window was dark, but the storm had quieted.

Her parents followed her upstairs, Dad struggling to climb with his crutches.

"Wait for me, Grace," Mom called from behind her husband. "I'm coming out with you to start up the generator."

"I can go," Dad said again.

"No, you won't," Mom said. "You can stand at the kitchen window and watch us do it. We'll be fine."

Grace grabbed a jacket from the coat closet—it was Dad's, and the sleeves were way too long for her—and opened the kitchen door. The rain had all but stopped. The air felt cool and misty. Everything was dark; the whole town must have lost power. The maple tree Dad had been worried about still stood between the Murrays' driveway and Doc's.

Grace stepped onto the driveway and splashed into an ankle-deep puddle, cold water rushing into her shoes. "Yikes!" she exclaimed.

"Look out for the puddles, Mom," she called into the kitchen. "The driveway's full of them. I just got soaked."

"Thanks," Mom called. "I'll get my rain boots."

Grace had left her rain boots in California. She should have thought to bring them with her to Michigan, but California was so sunny she tended to forget rain existed.

Together Grace and Mom started the generator to power the store, being careful with the power cords and the wet ground. Dad called instructions from the kitchen window.

The generator finally powered on. The food in the store was safe. Grace's shoes were dripping—those were going to take a while to dry.

Cozy and warm again in the living room, with the light from flashlights and a couple of non-toxic scented candles, Grace brought up the subject of a social media page for the store.

"I don't know," Dad said. "Seems to me we've got a lot to do around here. Running a social media page must take a lot of time."

"It wouldn't take too long to post something every couple days," Grace said. "It wouldn't have to be anything complicated. If we'd had our own page today, we could have posted about the chicken. Lots of small businesses are on social media, and I think it's really helpful for the store owners and the customers."

"Well, I suppose we could try it out," Mom said. "Maybe some of the employees would help with it. They're more tech-savvy than I am."

"It won't take too much time to keep it up," Grace said. "Somebody would just have to check it a couple times a day and make posts when there's something to share about."

"If it'll bring in more business, it'll be worth a little time," Dad said. "Go ahead, Gracie. Maybe it'll be a good thing."

Since Grace's computer didn't work unless it was plugged in, she couldn't start a page for the store tonight. Instead, she and her parents played a game of Clue by flashlight.

If the power was back on by tomorrow, she absolutely needed to figure out a system for National Board preparation. Despite her plans earlier this evening, this became yet another day when she'd done nothing about it at all. But she couldn't help it now. She ought to order a new laptop battery. What kind of professional teacher used a laptop that only worked when it was plugged in?

The power was still out the next morning. Dad said he hoped it wouldn't stay off much longer. The generator would only run for sixteen hours, and then it would have to cool down before being refueled.

Grace went over to the store early to grab a quart of milk for cereal for herself and her parents. Mom had put dry ice in their home refrigerator and taped it shut so people wouldn't open it by mistake.

The first store customer that morning was Ed Hoffman from the garage, shaking his head about the damage the storm had done to his wife's garden and chicken coop. "But it's not as bad as what happened to Walt and Dorothy's house," he said. "That big tree behind their house came down and hit the roof over their extra bedroom. Wrecked the whole room. It's gonna be hard to get that fixed. We're trying to convince Walt to let us help rebuild it instead of calling in a contractor from who knows where."

That must have been awfully scary for Dorothy and Walt. It was a blessing the tree had fallen on a spare room with nobody in it.

During her break that morning, Grace told Mom about the situation. Mom was horrified.

"That's terrible! We've got to do something. I'm gonna make a few calls and hook up the stove to the generator."

Grace didn't learn who Mom called, but it must have been effective. When Grace got off work at three that afternoon, Mom asked her if she would take a huge pot of chili and two pans of cornbread over to Dorothy's house. Volunteers were there sawing the tree into firewood and beginning to rebuild the spare room.

Grace didn't want the enormous chili pot to tip over while she was driving. She taped down the lid and wedged it in a box on the floor of Mom's car. She put the pans of cornbread on the middle seat. If she drove slowly, they shouldn't slide off. She also brought a box with paper bowls, plastic spoons, and napkins.

The whole town showed storm damage. Large branches littered the yards, and detached roof shingles lay everywhere. Garbage cans were overturned with garbage spilling out. The only buildings with power were the ones with generators. Several power lines were down, and it would take time for the power company to fix them.

Grace pulled up in front of Dorothy's house, near the church, to find the driveway jammed with cars and several guys climbing on the roof. A large section of the roof was smashed in. Grace couldn't imagine how to fix something like that, but the guys looked competent.

She lugged the pot of chili up to the front door, but nobody came to the doorbell. Everybody must be in the backyard. Grace took the chili around to the back.

Things were even busier out back. A crew of guys with chainsaws were sawing the tree into chunks. There was Doc, loading wood onto somebody's pickup truck. Charlie stood inside the broken spare room, yelling to the guys on the roof. Dorothy stood watching, hands on hips.

"Dorothy, I brought food," Grace called. "Chili and cornbread for the helpers. My mom made it."

"Your mother is so kind!" Dorothy took the chili pot from Grace, ignoring Grace's protests that she could carry it. "I'll set everything up here. You can bring the cornbread. This smells delicious."

As Grace came back to her car, Elaine walked up the driveway with a large bag in hand.

"Have you seen Dorothy?" Elaine asked. "I've brought some cookies for those guys working on the house. I thought they might like a snack."

Grace laughed. "My mom thought the same thing. Dorothy's out back setting up food for the helpers."

It was amazing how the town came together to help out. Dorothy and her husband had lived in the town for forty years, so they'd come to know just about everybody. But Grace got the feeling these people would have helped a neighbor in need even if they hadn't known him.

She hung around to help serve food and watch the progress on the house. Dorothy's husband, Walt, who knew something about building, shouted orders from the ground.

"He wanted to help on the roof," Dorothy said. "The idea! He'd fall off and break something. And of course he said, 'It's only one story high.' I told him, 'You're going up there over my dead body.'"

Grace laughed. "That's the kind of thing my dad would try to do, and my mom wouldn't let him either."

Dorothy ladled chili into a bowl. "But we have such kind neighbors. Ed, Charlie, Doc, Jack, Elaine, you…I can't tell you how much we appreciate all of you. Our kids would have helped, of course, if they'd been here, but they're all too far away and have their own families to raise. The good Lord knew what He was doing finding Walt a job in Fraser's Mill, fifty years ago—this town is like family to us."

Grace smiled. "That's wonderful."

"I couldn't imagine living anywhere else," Dorothy said. "Not that people shouldn't live other places, of course. I know you're going back to do your teaching in L.A. And I hope that works well for you. It's important to be in the place where you know you belong."

Grace nodded. "Thanks, Dorothy. I love my work teaching."

Dorothy smiled. "I know you're making a big difference to those kids."

She went off to investigate the progress on the roof and left Grace with the food table.

Doc stopped by for a bowl of chili. He had been working hard—his T-shirt was soaked with sweat, and his face glistened. In casual clothes, he seemed bigger than usual. He must work out a lot. Did Fraser's Mill even have a gym? Maybe they'd gotten one since Grace visited last.

"How's the hand?" Doc asked.

"Well, it doesn't hurt much anymore," Grace said. "I got the bandage wet last night though—my mom and I went out to set up the generator after the storm, and I forgot about my hand."

"Did you get a dry bandage afterwards?"

"Yeah."

"Then it shouldn't be too bad. Good thing your dad didn't try to do it with that cast on."

Good thing Doc didn't know that was exactly what Dad had tried to do before they stopped him.

"You want cornbread with your chili?" Grace hovered a piece of cornbread over Doc's chili bowl.

"Sure, thanks. Who made all this food?"

"My mom. She wanted to help out."

"Tell her thanks from me." Doc nodded at Grace and went over to talk with the guys running the chainsaws.

He must have been in a hurry — he hadn't teased Grace about anything. Oddly, she almost missed it.

⌘

The power came on that evening, which was a relief, because the store was out of dry ice. All the people who had lost power had been buying it for their refrigerators. Now the Murrays could stock up before the next big storm.

As she worked on National Board prep before bed, looking for a support group of teachers preparing for the same certification, Grace got another lengthy email from Lucas. He had gone to Monterey and had a great time. Now he was making plans for a family reunion at his grandmother's in a few weeks. He wanted to know how things were going in Grace's neck of the woods.

"Hi Lucas," Grace wrote. "My neck of the woods is very muddy at the moment, and has a lot of broken branches and some damaged houses. But it does have a lot of friendly people."

She filled him in on the windstorm and the people helping Dorothy and Walt.

Lucas replied almost immediately. "Wow, that sounds like quite a storm. I hope it doesn't do that while I'm visiting my grandmother. How's your National Board preparation going? Are you excited for the new school year?"

"I'm trying to work on some National Board stuff tonight," Grace replied. "It's going okay, I think."

Hopefully she'd be able to work out a good system for the National Board prep soon, because the work she'd done so far seemed haphazard and disorganized. She'd better finish this email and find that teacher support group.

"I hadn't thought much about school starting again," she wrote. "Wow, that's coming sooner than I'd realized. I usually get excited when I start lesson planning. How about you?"

Signing off, she went back to searching support groups. Lucas's email had strengthened her in her resolve to focus on her goals.

Yet, as Grace fell asleep that night, the image that played in her head wasn't National Board certification or the start of the school year. It was her friends and neighbors from Fraser's Mill, coming together to help Dorothy and Walt repair their home.

That Michigan Game

Grace was working on Saturday morning when Alex rushed in with a box of asparagus. "Did you see the post on the town's page?" She bounced with excitement. "They're gonna be playing euchre at the church hall this afternoon! Do you wanna be my partner?"

"Euchre?" Grace asked. "I forgot that existed. In college the only card game anybody played was poker. Nobody seems to play euchre outside of Michigan."

"Well, we still play it a lot here," Alex said. "Dorothy set it up, so the Ladies' Guild is hosting it. She wanted to do something nice for the town after they helped with her house."

"I hope I still remember how to play." Grace took the box of asparagus from Alex and started putting it in the display. "I'll probably be terrible."

"Playing euchre is like riding a bike. You never forget. Come on, it'll be fun. I'll see you there." Alex whisked out of the store before Grace had a chance to protest.

She might as well go. After all, it was Saturday. She could take a break from doing National Board prep tonight.

❧❧❧❧❧

In the afternoon, Grace walked to the church hall. She was running slightly late.

As she entered the parking lot, Alex drove up in a battered white pickup.

"Howdy, pardner," Alex called to her. "Ready to win?" She jumped down from the driver's seat and smoothed her bandana print skirt.

"As ready as I'll ever be," Grace said. "I can't promise to be good."

"Nonsense, you were great in high school. Just use that schoolteacher brain of yours and you'll be fine." Alex started toward the church hall, Grace hurrying after her.

The church hall was a modest-sized building. Today it was crowded with round tables. Near the door, Dorothy and Elaine were setting out cookies and lemonade.

Dorothy hurried over to Grace and Alex. "Just in time," she said. "We need two more people. You two can play against Doc and Hannah."

Oof. Doc and Hannah?

Across the room, Doc and Hannah sat opposite each other. Doc was saying something, and Hannah was laughing.

Grace scanned the rest of the room. Weren't there any other

tables that needed people? Apparently not. Maybe she could get somebody to switch with her and Alex.

Alex elbowed her. "Come on, let's go."

"Doc and I don't get along," Grace hissed at her.

Alex's eyebrows drew together. "Huh? You get along with everybody. Besides, it's the only table left."

Grace sighed. Alex was right.

But she would probably make a fool of herself and do terribly at this game, if the recent pattern still held. She seemed fated to embarrass herself in front of Doc all summer.

Doc and Hannah looked up as Grace and Alex approached.

"Hey," Doc said. "Look who showed up. It looks like we'll be playing euchre after all." He pulled a deck of cards out of his pocket. "Dorothy said they were running short, so I brought my own."

"How do we know it's not a marked deck?" Grace asked.

Doc raised an eyebrow. "You can take my word for it, or you can scrutinize every card. Your choice."

"I'll take your word for it." Grace sat at the near side of the table. Alex went around.

Hannah nodded toward the two newcomers. Was it Grace's imagination, or did she look less than thrilled to have them there? Hannah was dressed up for a Saturday afternoon—she wore a white dress that showed off her tan, long earrings, and sunglasses on top of her head. She always had sunglasses. Maybe her eyes were sensitive to the sun. Doc wore a polo shirt and khakis.

"Good thing you came," Doc said. "We were about to go play tennis instead."

Hannah raised an eyebrow at him. "You still owe me a match to make up for that one you missed."

Somebody tapped a microphone, and all heads swiveled toward the sound. It was Dorothy.

"It's time to start," Dorothy said. "If anybody has questions or disagreements about the rules of euchre, Elaine and I both have rulebooks, so just come find us. There's also a suggested donation for the cookies and lemonade. The pro-life group at St. Anthony's will use the donations to buy baby clothes and diapers for local moms who need assistance. You can start playing whenever you want."

"Ready, Hannah?" Doc asked.

Hannah flipped her hair over her shoulder. "I'm ready."

Grace gave Alex a double thumbs-up. "Good luck, pardner!"

"Yippee!" Alex said. "Come on, Doc, separate the deck."

Doc separated the cards and dealt the first hand. Either he was purposely giving Grace bad cards, or she had rotten luck. No matter which suit ended up chosen as trump — the highest-ranking suit for the round — she couldn't win anything when her hand was mostly nines and tens.

"You start, Grace," Doc said.

The players first had to decide which suit would be trump. The face-up card on the table was the queen of diamonds. Grace didn't have a lot of diamonds. "Pass," she said.

Hannah took a long time to look at her cards. Maybe she hadn't played this game much. Or maybe it was part of her strategy. "Pass," she said.

"Pass," Alex said, poker-faced.

Doc discarded a card and picked up the queen of diamonds. "Diamonds are trump."

Unless Alex had great cards, she and Grace were losing this hand. Grace's only diamond was a nine. Since she sat to the left of the dealer, she had to go first. She put down the nine of clubs.

Hannah put down the jack of diamonds. What in the world? Why waste the jack of diamonds—the highest card—on a nine?

Doc's eyebrows went up at his partner's action, but he didn't say anything. Hannah took that trick.

Doc took the next trick—which started out with spades, a non-trump suit—with the ten of diamonds. Even a low trump card would beat a card of a different suit. But Doc couldn't have played that unless he didn't have any spades.

"You don't have any spades?" Alex asked. "I'll remember that."

Doc grinned. "I believe you."

It was his turn to start. He placed down the jack of hearts. The jack of the same color as the trump suit counted as a trump card too. No wonder Doc had picked up that diamond—he seemed to have no end of trump cards. Grace played the nine of diamonds. Hannah played the queen of clubs.

"Wait a minute," Alex said. "Hannah, you reneged. Grace played a club in the first trick, and you played the jack of diamonds."

"Yeah, that's right," Grace said.

Doc whistled and sat back against his chair.

Hannah looked annoyed. "What did I do?"

"You were supposed to follow suit when I played the club in

the first round," Grace said. "You can only play a different suit if you don't have the suit that's being played."

"Oh. Whoopsie. Can I just take the card back?" Hannah flipped her hair back.

Alex shook her head. "Catching the other team reneging is two points for us."

Doc slid his remaining cards to the center of the table. "She's right, Hannah," he said. "It's okay. People make mistakes. Let's go on. Grace, it's your deal."

Imagine getting two points out of such a lousy hand. Grace marked the two points. She shuffled the cards and dealt.

It became clear as the game went on that Hannah had no idea how to play. She wasted her highest cards on tricks that didn't need them; she played cards that trumped Doc's cards when he was already winning a trick; she reneged yet again. Doc's self-restraint surprised Grace. If she were Hannah's partner, she would be dancing up and down at this point. Doc must like Hannah — that was the only possible explanation. He could put up with her poor euchre playing as long as he got to spend time hanging out with her.

Well, who cared? It wasn't as though Grace was interested in Doc or anything.

"I've got an idea," Alex said after Hannah's second renege. "Hannah, why don't you go to Dorothy or Elaine and get a quick refresher on the rules, and we can take a break for cookies and lemonade?"

Hannah looked indignant, but Doc nodded. "It shouldn't take too long to skim the rules," he told her. "We'll still be here when you get back."

Hannah made her way to the rules table, and Grace, Alex, and Doc went for the refreshments.

"Gluten-free peanut butter cookies." Alex took two. "I'll bet the diner donated them. Charlie always makes them. He says they're the easiest kind to make because they only have three ingredients."

"It's probably hard to burn yourself making them, too," Doc said. "How's your hand, Grace? Made any more apple crisp lately?"

"With this enormous bandage on my hand?" Grace asked. "I'm taking a break from baking. But I'm going to start up again as soon as my hand's better. The things I made before sold out really quickly."

They returned to their table supplied with cookies and lemonade. From the well-filled donation basket, it looked like the pro-life group would be able to help a lot of mothers.

Hannah was still at Dorothy and Elaine's table, listening to Elaine explain euchre rules. Grace stifled a smile. Elaine liked to explain things. By the time she finished, Hannah would know the rules, all right. But it might be a while.

Doc leaned back in his chair and stretched his long legs out under the table in a way that left no room for anybody else's feet. "So how long have you two been playing euchre?"

"My uncle Angelo taught me and my brother one Christmas at our lola's—our grandmother's," Alex said. "My cousins and I used to play it a lot."

Doc looked at Grace.

"My dad taught me," Grace said. "My brother Thomas and I used to play against him and my sister Katie. Dad and Katie always won."

"You oughtta challenge them to a rematch," Doc said. "I bet you'd give them a run for their money now."

Was that a compliment? "Thanks," Grace said. "But we don't all get together very much. Katie lives downstate and Thomas is in Florida."

Doc sat forward, resting his arms on the table. "Now how did you all get scattered so far from each other? Michigan, Florida, California. That's a long way!"

How had they gotten scattered to the far-flung reaches of the United States? It would take some explaining. It wasn't that Grace's family members disliked each other—their careers, as adults, had ended up putting them far apart physically.

"I'm back," a voice said.

Hannah appeared next to Doc, resting her hand on his shoulder. "Can we start playing again? Elaine told me the rules about ten times."

"Suits me," Grace said. "Whose deal is it?"

"Mine," Alex said. "Hand me those cards, Doc, will you?"

They were in the middle of the next hand—Doc and Hannah had taken two tricks—when Doc's phone buzzed in his pocket.

"Whoops," he said, looking at the screen. "Gotta go. Medical emergency."

Hannah groaned. "Just when things were getting good. Text you later, Doc."

"Sure," Doc said absently, pocketing his phone. "Keep the cards—Grace can give them back to me anytime. See you around."

He strode away, leaving the three girls with an incomplete euchre table.

"That poor guy never gets any fun." Hannah shook her head. "I'm going home. We can't play without four people."

"We could see if Dorothy or Elaine will play with us," Alex suggested. "One person ought to be enough to man the rulebook table."

"That's all right," Hannah said. "I've got things to do anyway. I've got to edit a video for my channel."

She got her straw purse from the back of the chair and left Grace and Alex sitting at the table.

"Maybe Dorothy and Elaine can both play with us," Grace said. "If somebody comes along and asks about the rules we can just pause the game."

"Let's try it."

"It'll be more fun playing with them, anyway."

Alex laughed. "More fun than watching Hannah pretend she knew what she was doing, when it was obvious she had no clue? I thought it was hilarious."

Grace laughed too. "I don't think I've ever seen someone so confident and so terrible at the same time."

Clearly, Hannah had only been there to spend time with Doc. If those two weren't dating, Grace figured it was only a matter of time before they were. They were both attractive and athletic, probably wealthy — of course they'd be interested in each other. But what was the point of Hannah blundering through a game she didn't know how to play and didn't even seem to like? Grace just couldn't understand Hannah. Maybe she'd understand her better if she checked out her video channel sometime.

A Few Interviews

Grace came home to a quiet house. Her parents were working on Mom's story in progress.

She flipped through the mail that had come that day. Bills, more bills, and a card from a realtor selling houses in the town Katie and Arthur lived in. Why were realtors in Katie and Arthur's town sending advertisements to Fraser's Mill?

Grace had to get work done, but euchre night had left her oddly tense. She would do something fun for a while, then work on National Board stuff. She grabbed two oatmeal cookies from the kitchen and went upstairs.

Mom made the cookies. The gingersnaps and apple crisp Grace had made before burning her hand had sold so well that Mom had set aside some of her limited free time for baking things for the store. She'd made extra for the family, too.

On the computer, Grace scrolled down the town social media page looking for the posts Natalie said Hannah had put up. A long way down the page, she found Hannah's post advertising her video channel and social media account. She clicked on the link to the video channel.

The newest videos were shot in Fraser's Mill and had titles like "Going Fishing for the First Time Ever!" and "Tour of Historic Fraser's Water-Powered Sawmill." Some were fashion-focused like "What I Wore for a Week in a Small Town" and "Roundup of This Summer's Best Sunglasses." Hannah had a lot of subscribers. At least, it looked like a lot of subscribers to Grace. She didn't know what success looked like for an influencer.

The thumbnail of one of the more recent videos featured Hannah with Doc. Its title read, "Meet Doc: An Interview with Fraser's Mill's Young Resident Doctor."

Clicking into the video felt like snooping, as though she were spying on Hannah and Doc. But this was a public channel, and Hannah had advertised it to the whole town. Grace had the right to watch the videos on it. Besides, maybe understanding Doc and Hannah better would help her feel more charitable toward them.

The video was shot in Doc's exam room. Doc and Hannah sat in chairs turned half toward each other. Doc wore his white lab coat with a stethoscope around his neck. He looked at ease, sitting back in his chair with one leg crossed in guy-fashion. Hannah wore a white tank top, white jeans, gold jewelry, and sunglasses on top of her head. She seemed extra smiley.

"Hello, Internet," Hannah addressed the viewers. "Today, in my ongoing series 'Summer in Small-Town Michigan,' I'm going to interview one of the important citizens of Fraser's Mill: Dr. James Johnson, known to the people around here as 'Doc.'"

Doc chuckled. "That, or 'the young doc,'" he said. "My uncle just retired in January after running this practice for forty years. He's the only doctor most of the townspeople remember seeing."

Hannah asked Doc about his day-to-day life as a doctor. He said it was quite different from practicing medicine in the city.

"For one thing, you have to learn to be a jack of all trades," he said. "During my residency, when a patient came in with a problem, I'd often refer him to a specialist. Around here, it's a long drive for most people to see a specialist or even to get to the hospital. I've got to fix whatever problems they have the best I can."

"So what kinds of things do you do?"

"It depends on the day. There are usually a few routine checkups—a lot of older folks, especially. And people come in with accidents—broken bones, cuts, burns. I'm kind of a one-man emergency room."

"Wow! So if somebody has a heart attack, they call you instead of an ambulance?"

"Yup. The closest hospital is in Manistee or Cadillac. If they call an ambulance, it'll take a while. If they call me, I can usually get there in five minutes or less."

"That must put a lot of pressure on you," Hannah said. "Having so many people's lives depend on you like that. Is it stressful?"

"Well, you know, it depends how you look at it. When there's an emergency, you need a doctor in the right place at the right time. I'm glad I'm close and able to help. But in the moment, it's terrifying." He chuckled. "You get a call that somebody's cut his hand open with a chainsaw, or a woman's having a baby and can't get to the hospital, and you're the only one around. And you just have to say, 'Okay, I'll be there in five.'"

"Wow!" Hannah's eyes grew wide. "So you've delivered babies?"

"A few." Doc grinned. "I got asked to be the godfather of one of them."

Hannah laughed. "That's fantastic. So when you're not delivering babies and acting as an ER doctor, what other kinds of things do you do?"

"Well, I see a lot of people with colds, flu, stomach bugs—especially kids. Some of that's slowed down now because it's summer. But in summer people get heat stroke and work injuries. There's always something." Doc chuckled. "Once, somebody brought in a sick dog. He didn't want to drive all the way into Cadillac to find a vet."

"What did you do?"

"I looked up the dog's symptoms, but I couldn't figure out what the heck was wrong. So I told the guy he'd better just take it to the vet. He said he'd lost faith in me as a doctor—I couldn't even cure a dog!"

Hannah laughed. "What a bad review for your practice! But I'm sure you get plenty of good reviews as well."

Doc chuckled. "It all depends what the town gossip says about you. If it's good, you're in good shape. If it's bad, you'd better find another town."

"So what does the town gossip say about you?"

"You'd better interview the town for that one."

"Fair enough." Hannah flipped her hair back. "Now, here's

something the viewers are probably curious about: what kinds of things do you do on your time off?"

"I play golf now and again," Doc said. "I like tinkering with cars, and you may be surprised to hear this, but I sing in the church choir."

Hannah giggled. "Would you believe that? He literally sits next to me at choir practice," she said to the camera. "Do you travel much?" she asked Doc.

Doc shook his head. "Not much since I got here. There's always a lot going on around town, and I've got to keep my phone on in case somebody needs emergency help. I did visit my parents in April—I got a friend from Cadillac to take over the clinic for a few days."

Hannah shook her head. "You're one of the hardest-working people I've ever met. So I've got to ask: why did you come to a small town to practice medicine? I hear you had big prospects in New York City."

"Well, I could ask you the same thing," Doc said. "What's an Internet sensation from Chicago doing in a small town all summer?"

Hannah laughed. "How many twenty-somethings do you know that have access to a vacation cottage in a place as pretty as this? I thought it would provide a unique setting for a new video series." She turned to the camera. "Well, that's all the time we have—Doc has somebody coming in for an appointment." She turned back to Doc. "Thank you so much for the interview."

Doc held out his hand for a handshake. "Thanks for having me."

"I'll see you later for our tennis match."

Doc grinned. "Sure. You don't stand a chance."

Hannah turned to the camera. "You hear what he thinks about my tennis playing? I might have to video the match so you can see how I do for yourselves."

Hannah ended with an advertising pitch for a brand of vitamins. Grace turned the video off.

Well, that was interesting. The video made Grace wonder, as Hannah had asked (and Doc hadn't answered), why would a young doctor with good prospects want to bury himself in the hard work and obscurity of a small town? If she were in his place, she wouldn't dream of doing it.

Hard work reminded Grace of National Board prep. She ought to stop watching videos and do something important.

A car crunched on gravel outside Grace's window, and she peered out. A big white pickup truck was pulling in. Was that Alex? What was she doing over here at this time of night? Grace hurried downstairs.

It was Alex, holding a large empty pan. "My mom borrowed this from your mom. She sent me to bring it back."

"Oh, thanks." Grace took the pan. "Wanna come in? I could make tea or cocoa or something."

She wouldn't get any National Board prep done, but spending time with Alex was important too.

"Sure, thanks," Alex said. She came in, wiping her boots on the mat.

"Do you want tea or cocoa?" Grace asked.

"Do you have oolong tea?"

"I'll check."

They did have oolong tea, in a tin with such a tight-fitting lid that Grace couldn't get it off. After a lot of prying, and help from Alex, Grace managed to open the tin. She heated water in the kettle.

The teacups were in the back of the cupboard, and Grace had to stand on tiptoe and rearrange things to get to them.

"Hey Grace," Alex said. "Can I ask you for some advice? It's about Charlie."

"Aha!" Grace emerged from the cupboard. "You told me you two were just friends. Is there something more going on?"

"Well—maybe, but maybe not." Alex opened a drawer. "Where do you keep the silverware?"

Grace showed her the right drawer. "So what's going on?"

Alex sighed. "I can't tell. That's the problem. We've known each other for years, and he's always been a friendly guy. But a while ago I started thinking he might like me. For one thing, he started making gluten-free cookies for the diner all the time. He never did that before, even though there are plenty of diner customers who can't eat gluten."

"Uh-huh," Grace said. "That sounds like it could be a sign that he likes you." The tea kettle whistled. She took it off the heat.

"And it's not just that. He's started hanging around after choir practice and talking to me. He didn't used to do that. And you know the other day, when he gave us both milkshakes on the house? That wasn't the first time he did that for me. It was the fifth or sixth time."

Grace poured hot water into the teacups. "That sounds pretty obvious," she said. "I can see somebody giving a milkshake on the house once or twice. But any more than that, and he definitely likes you."

"Yeah, that's what I thought too."

"And you like him, right?" Grace sat down with her tea and pushed the other teacup toward Alex.

"Yeah, I do," Alex said. She sank down in a chair. "To tell you the truth, I've liked him for a while. But the problem is, he never says anything. That's why I told you the other day that we're just friends. It's true. He's never asked me out. I'm starting to think he's never gonna do anything, and he's just going to be weirdly extra-friendly forever."

Grace was familiar with that situation. Sometimes you couldn't tell if the guy needed an extra push or if he wasn't interested enough to ask the girl out.

"I've watched a bunch of videos online on how to tell if a guy likes you," Alex said, "but none of them say what to do if he acts like he likes you, but never asks you out. It's so frustrating." She gestured with tightly-curled hands.

"Hmm." Grace tapped a finger on her teacup. "Well, in my opinion, he's absolutely acting like he likes you. Maybe he can't tell if you like him."

"Well, I'm not gonna go up to him and tell him," Alex said. "I mean, I hang out with him and we talk all the time, and I don't refuse all those free milkshakes. What more can I do?"

"Alex, I'm probably the worst person to ask about how to catch a man," Grace said. "I've been single for ages."

"Just because somebody's single doesn't mean they don't know anything about relationships," Alex said. "Besides, I know you won't tell people, and I don't want this told all over town in case it gets back to Charlie."

Alex was right—you had to pick your confidantes carefully. It was nice to be trusted, even if Grace wasn't sure she'd be much help.

"Maybe you could bake him cookies or something," Grace suggested. "Not for the diner or the choir, just for him. That should give him the idea that you're interested, but I don't think it seems too pushy."

Alex brightened. "That sounds like a good idea. What kind of cookies?"

"Oh, I don't know—any kind you want, I guess."

Alex raised her teacup. "I'll do it. I'll bake cookies tonight and give them to him tomorrow after Mass."

"Tonight? Alex, it's nine P.M.! Isn't that late for you already?"

"It doesn't take too long to make one pan of cookies," Alex said. "And tomorrow's Sunday so Mass isn't until noon, and Sam's going to feed the stock. I can sleep in."

Alex must really like Charlie to disrupt her early-bird schedule for him like this. Grace laughed. "Well, good luck," she said. "Don't burn yourself or anything. You don't want to get your hand all bandaged up like mine."

"I'll be careful," Alex promised. "You know how I said I was gonna find somebody to set you up with? Wanna hear who would be a good match for you?" Her eyes gleamed.

"In this town? You're not trying to set me up with Sam, are you?"

Alex shook her head. "Sam's got a girlfriend. Besides, I know better than to try to match you up with him. I was thinking of Doc."

Grace's pulse thumped oddly, and she stared at Alex.

"*Doc?* Alex, you've gotta be out of your mind. Why in the world would you think that?"

If she had a list of people who drove her crazy, Doc would be at the top of the list. They wouldn't get along in a million years.

"I saw you talking at euchre this afternoon," Alex said.

"For like three seconds," Grace exclaimed. "It was a fluke. We don't get along at all. The first time I saw him, I thought he was stealing my mom's car. It all went downhill from there. I run into him all the time, because he lives next door, and we always get into arguments. We would be terrible together. We would fight all the time."

"Oh, I don't know," Alex said. "You both have strong personalities, that's all. I think people with strong personalities work well with other strong personalities. You don't want to find a guy who's a total doormat. Besides, I think you and Doc are cute together."

"Cute together? More like a train wreck," Grace said. "Besides, I'm positive he and Hannah are an item. They play tennis together and text each other, and Hannah did a special interview with him for her video channel. Not to mention she basically warned me away from him during choir practice on Wednesday."

Alex still wasn't crushed. "She may like him, but if they were together, I think Hannah would have broadcasted it all over town. I don't think they're dating."

"Well, I do," Grace said. "And even if they weren't, Doc doesn't like me, and I don't like him. So it doesn't matter."

Alex sipped her tea.

"Besides," Grace said, "there's this guy from California—

Lucas — that I went out with once before I got here. We've been emailing back and forth, and we seem to have a lot in common. I want to get to know him better and see if we'd be a good fit."

"Ooh!" Alex sat up straighter. "So that's what you've been hiding. Do you like him?"

"Well," Grace said, "he's friendly, and smart, and good-looking — "

Alex shook her head. "I asked if you *like* him."

"Don't you have cookies to bake?" Grace asked. "If you don't hurry up and get started, you're gonna still be baking at three A.M."

"I'm going, I'm going." Alex drained her teacup and started for the door. "I still stand by what I said about you and Doc."

"Alex Santiago Martin, you're gonna go down in history as the world's worst matchmaker."

"I haven't been proven wrong yet," Alex said as she slipped out the door.

An Old-Fashioned Evening

The town was getting excited about the fireman's supper and dance coming up the next Saturday. After Mass on Sunday (at which the choir music went decently well and Mary Jane said Grace's singing was lovely) it was the main topic of discussion in the church vestibule.

Grace planned to go since the store would be closed during the event. Her parents were going, even though Dad couldn't dance with his injured foot, and she thought an old-fashioned evening sounded like fun. It did seem a bit over-hyped, but then again, dinner and dancing at the fire hall was about as exciting as Fraser's Mill ever got, apart from the Fourth of July parade every year. The grocery store was providing most of the food that would be cooked for the dinner, so a couple freezers in the back room were packed with frozen meat from the store's supplier until the people in charge of the dinner picked it up.

Grace's hand was finally healing, and she ditched the

bandages. The skin on the back of her hand still looked funny, but she hoped it would get back to normal with some air. Working in the store without the bandages was a lot easier, and she could take over the baking from Mom.

Dad was getting around better than ever on his scooter, and he made a bargain with his wife: he would work in the store two hours every day while she worked on her novel. He said he needed the exercise, and this was a great opportunity for Liz to get novel writing done while they had Grace around to help. Mom reluctantly agreed to the plan, since her story was finally progressing.

On Friday evening, Alex came into the store, her face wreathed in gloom. She propped her elbows on the checkout counter, her chin resting in her hands. "I don't think I'm going to the dinner and dance tomorrow."

"Why? What happened?" Grace lost track of the money she was counting. She pushed the cash register drawer back in.

"I gave Charlie those cookies on Sunday, and he seemed happy about them, but he hasn't done a single thing since then. He's never going to ask me out."

The cookies had been five whole days ago. Why hadn't Charlie said anything?

"Wow," Grace said. "Gee, Alex, I'm sorry. I thought for sure the cookies would help."

"I guess not," Alex said. "Here's what happened. I took the cookies to St. Anthony's with me in my choir bag. I didn't want to give them to Charlie in front of the whole choir, so I waited until after Mass. Charlie and I talked to Mary Jane about the music for a while, but then she left and it was just us. So I said,

'By the way, Charlie, I have something for you,' and I pulled out the bag of cookies and gave them to him. He said, 'Wow, thanks, Alex! These look great!" He had this huge grin on his face, and I thought he was about to say something else. But then Sam and Doc came up and started asking him about playing pickup basketball that evening. Then my family was leaving, so I had to go."

"Maybe he would have said something, if Sam and Doc hadn't come barging in," Grace said.

"Well, they didn't know anything was going on," Alex said. "I didn't tell Sam about the cookies. I didn't feel like telling anybody about it, in case it didn't work out. Anyway, after that I hoped Charlie would text me later. But he didn't. He talked to me on Wednesday after choir practice, but it was just about random topics. And now that dance is tonight, and everybody in town is gonna be there, and I don't wanna stand around waiting for him to ask me to dance. I'm sick of the whole thing. Clearly, he just isn't interested in me."

"But he seemed so interested," Grace said. "It's been less than a week. I wouldn't give up on him quite yet. Why don't you come to the dance, and we'll have a good time even if Charlie doesn't say anything. And if he wants to say something, you'll be there, so he'll be able to say it."

"I don't know," Alex said. "I hate the thought of being there all evening, feeling more and more disappointed if he doesn't say anything."

"Then don't think about him," Grace said. "There are lots of other people to hang out with. He's not the only person in town.

Give him a couple more days, and leave him an opportunity to talk to you if he wants. But try not to worry about it in the meantime."

Alex's forehead furrowed. "You really still think there's a chance he might like me?"

Grace nodded hard. "Absolutely. I don't see how we'd both have been completely wrong about him."

"All right then," Alex said. "I'll go. But if I don't have a good time, I'm going right home."

"Deal."

❧❧❧❧❧

On Saturday, Grace dressed up—she wore her favorite yellow flowered dress, and she bought a bunch of yellow roses from the grocery store so she could put one in her hair—and went to the fire hall with her parents.

The Fraser's Mill Fire Hall had been built in the 1950s in order to raise funds for the town fire department. It serviced wedding receptions, birthday parties, and anything else that needed a large building or a kitchen. For tonight's old-fashioned evening, the building was filled with tables, and the large parking lot was set up with speakers for dancing after dinner. A few people from the area had brought classic cars and parked them around the edges of the lot to give the place a more old-fashioned feel.

Alex arrived with her parents, her brother Sam, and an unfamiliar young woman—it must be Sam's girlfriend. Grace waved. Alex waved back.

Although dinner had just begun, the whole town seemed to be there already. Most of the round tables were occupied. The speakers in the hall played oldies music in the background of the crowd's chatter.

"Reckon we'll have trouble with the fire marshal if any more people show up," Dad said, chuckling. "They're gonna have to put more tables outside."

Dinner was buffet-style, ten dollars a person, offering hamburgers or grilled chicken, potato salad, green beans, and apple or cherry pie for dessert. Charlie was serving food behind the buffet line, but Grace didn't get a chance to notice whether he talked to Alex yet. She got distracted by Hannah coming in, Doc at her heels. They must have come together.

Overall, dinner and the atmosphere were fun. Dorothy and Walt sat at Grace's family's table and reminisced about what the town had been like thirty years ago, when the Murrays had just moved there. Elaine joined them, and so did Ed Hoffman and his wife Janet.

Janet talked about her youngest son, who had joined the Army. "We're really proud of him, but it's hard having all our kids so far away," she said.

Dad nodded. "I know what you mean. It's been nice having Grace here for a few weeks before she goes back to teaching."

"You know your parents brag about you all the time?" Ed asked, and Grace blushed. "They're always talking about their English teacher daughter out in California. We've got a daughter out there. Maybe our grandkids will be in your class someday. Wouldn't that be a coincidence!"

As dinner finished, people trickled out to the parking lot. Chairs and tables were set up for anybody who didn't want to dance, as well as board games and a couple of cornhole boards. Grace didn't think she would dance. Dad's foot was broken, her brother Thomas wasn't there, and Alex's brother Sam had brought his girlfriend. That counted out all her usual dance partners. Maybe she could find people to play cornhole or Battleship or something.

"Hi, Grace," a voice said behind her. It was Natalie. "Wanna play cornhole with us?"

"Sure!"

Natalie had three sisters, two older and one younger, who were with her. They were all good at cornhole. Grace was not surprised to find she was terrible at it. Ball sports weren't her thing, and apparently bean bags were in the same category. But Natalie and her sisters were friendly and sympathetic to Grace's failed shots. And it was a sunny but not-too-hot evening in late spring, with big band music playing and everyone in town having a good time. It would be hard to ruin a night like this.

Wait a minute. What was Doc doing coming over here? He sauntered toward the girls playing cornhole, hands in his pockets. Great. Now he would witness another of Grace's failures. Couldn't he wait until later and get a group of his own people to play cornhole? Grace turned her attention to Natalie, who was throwing a beanbag.

"Nice shot, Natalie," Doc's voice said. Grace looked up and found him right at her elbow.

He held out his hand, palm up. "Dance with me?"

Grace blinked. What?

"Uh—" Grace started to say.

"I could dance with you," one of Natalie's sisters said from behind Doc.

Doc didn't seem to notice. He waited for Grace's answer, hand still outstretched.

"Um—" Grace said. "Sure."

Taking Grace's hand firmly, Doc led her toward the parking lot. "Do you know the foxtrot?"

"I used to, but it's been a while."

He swung her in among the dancers. "Let's give it a try."

Grace tried to remember dances in her college days. Start with the right foot. Back, back, side-together. Back, back, side-together. Then a turn. It wasn't too bad. Even if Doc was the last guy she would have thought she would ever dance with.

"Wanna try a spin?" Doc asked.

What the heck, why not? He swung her around, and she only tripped slightly getting back into the rhythm.

Doc raised his eyebrows, his mouth quirked in a hint of a smile. "See, you remember."

"I think it would be easier if you took smaller steps," Grace told him.

"Whoops, sorry." Doc moderated his steps. "Better?"

"Much better."

He was good. Of course he was good. Everything Grace had seen him do, he did competently. He was probably a world champion cornhole player too.

Over Doc's shoulder, Hannah stood on the sidelines of the dance floor with her arms folded. She didn't look happy. Maybe she thought Grace was chasing Doc. Well, she wasn't.

"So you don't dance much out in California?" Doc asked.

Grace shook her head. "I haven't danced since college—except at weddings."

"The town's put on three or four dances since I moved here," Doc said. "A few of these old-timers could teach a ballroom dance class all by themselves."

Dorothy and Walt passed by, doing a fancy step. Grace laughed. "I believe it."

Doc spun her around. "Dang, I just remembered—that's your burned hand, isn't it? Let me look at that." He stopped in the middle of the parking lot and scrutinized Grace's hand. "How long has the bandage been off?"

"Since a few days ago. Wednesday, maybe." From dance to doctor checkup in two seconds flat. Doc must like multi-tasking.

"Does it hurt when I touch it?" Doc asked.

"Not anymore. I think it's pretty much healed."

"Good." Doc swung Grace back into the foxtrot. "I wouldn't want to be the one who re-injured it. It could damage my professional reputation." His face was serious, but his eyes twinkled.

They danced. The step felt more familiar now. The song kept going. It must be a long one. Surprisingly, Grace didn't mind.

"We haven't argued about anything today," Doc said. "That's a change."

Grace raised her eyebrows. "The evening's still young."

He spun her again, with assurance, as though he'd done it a hundred times. He must have done a lot of dancing in college.

Another couple bumped into them. Doc grimaced. "Watch where you're going, Kevin," he called.

"Sorry," the couple both called back.

"Let's go where there's more room," Doc said, and led Grace into a smooth traveling step toward the edge of the parking lot.

Grace had forgotten how much dancing—with a partner who knew the step and kept in time—felt like flying. As they whirled around, and Doc forgot to moderate his long steps, Grace felt as though she would lift off into the air any moment.

Doc spun her out and back into a dip, his arm solid behind her back, just as the music came to a stop. His dark hair fell tousled across his forehead. His eyes were blue—light blue and laughing.

He set her upright, grinning down at her. "Good timing?"

"Yeah," Grace said, breathless.

He guided her to the side of the parking lot.

"Thanks," he said, and headed toward the fire hall.

"Thanks."

Well, that had been unexpected. Doc showing up out of nowhere, asking Grace to dance, and then leaving with only an abrupt thank you. What was up with him?

Grace was still staring after Doc's departing back when she felt a tap on her shoulder. She turned around. Wrong shoulder.

"You always fall for it," Alex's voice said from the other side.

Grace turned around. "And you and everybody else always sneak up on me."

Alex was wearing an orange dress with embroidered flowers, and the bright color matched her excited expression. Something must have changed since yesterday, because the bouncy, energetic Alex standing there now was far different from the listless, drooping Alex that had walked into the store yesterday.

"Guess what?" she asked.

"What?"

Alex looked around, dropping her voice. "Charlie asked me out!"

"Really? That's wonderful!"

"I know!" Alex bounced on her toes. "You don't know how happy I am right now."

"I can tell just by looking at you!" Grace said. "So what happened? Tell me about it!"

"Well, I was going through the food line," Alex said, "and when I came to him, he asked if I could meet him outside in five minutes. So I waited five minutes out by the side door, and he came rushing out with his cooking apron still on. He wanted to ask me to go to the movies with him, and said he'd been waiting for a chance to ask me ever since I gave him those cookies, but it kept seeming like a bad time. So I said sure, I'd love to go to the movies with him."

"Yay! Alex, I'm so happy for you!"

"I can hardly believe it." Alex's face glowed. "I thought he'd never ask!"

"Now aren't you glad I convinced you to come?" Grace asked. "Otherwise, he still wouldn't have had a chance to ask you."

"Oh, you can rub it in," Alex said. "Your cookie idea was a big success, and then you practically dragged me here tonight. You can have all the credit."

Grace laughed. "Well, thanks."

"Now I've got a question for you." Alex folded her arms, a mischievous gleam in her eye. "Did I see you dancing with Doc?"

"Oh, good grief!" Grace should have known Alex the matchmaker was keeping an eye on her. "He came out of nowhere and asked me to dance. I couldn't think of a reason to say no."

"Uh-huh." Alex raised an eyebrow.

"Knock it off, Alex—that's the whole story!"

"Well, I think you looked cute dancing."

"Cute? Ha! I don't know why in the world he asked me."

"Maybe because he doesn't think you're as terrible as you think he is?"

"Well, it doesn't matter," Grace said. "I hold to what I told you before. He and I would drive each other absolutely crazy."

"I think that just means you'd have chemistry," Alex said. "I've gotta go—Charlie's almost done in the kitchen, and I said I would meet him." She raced away.

Charlie and Alex would be wonderful together. They were both cheery and friendly and liked to cook and sing in the choir. Their personalities didn't clash. Unlike Grace and Doc, whose personalities clashed horribly.

In the parking lot, Hannah and Doc were dancing together. They were doing a lot of spins and dips. Hannah was better at the foxtrot than Grace was.

Maybe Grace should see where her parents had gone. She headed toward the fire hall. On the way she ran into Dorothy.

"Hi, Grace. Having a good time?" Dorothy was carrying a

big box—it looked like more lawn games. She must have gotten roped into helping. She got roped into everything.

"Yes—everything is really nice. The classic cars are so cool, and I love the oldies music. Can I help you carry that box?"

Smiling, Dorothy handed the box over. "Thanks. I didn't realize it was going to be so heavy. It goes there by the cornhole."

"Dorothy, do you ever get any rest?" Grace asked.

"I'll sit down in a minute. I wasn't working during the dinner—I got to spend time with your parents, remember? They seem chipper tonight."

Grace set down the box in a spot that wasn't in the way of the cornhole players. "They were really looking forward to this. By the way, have you seen them anywhere?"

"I think they're over there somewhere." Dorothy motioned to the far side of the parking lot, near the classic cars, where more chairs were set up. "I'm glad it worked out for the grocery store to supply tonight's food. Your parents need all the business they can get, especially with that dollar store about to open this week."

"Dollar store? Is that the new building down by the gas station?"

"Yes, that's it—it's going to be a dollar store."

"You think that'll hurt my parents' business? It's not a competing grocery store."

Dorothy shook her head. "They'll sell a lot of the same things at lower prices and undercut you," she said. "People will start going there instead. It's happening all over the place. A dollar store comes into a town and the local businesses—especially grocery stores—struggle. Didn't your parents mention it?"

Grace shook her head. "They never said anything about it. I guess they must not be too worried."

"Well, if they're not, they should be," Dorothy said. "I've heard of grocery stores that had to close down within a year of a dollar store coming in. Some places are changing their zoning laws to limit new dollar stores. Maple City prevented one from being built there, just a couple years ago. It's too bad we weren't able to do that here."

"Wow." If true, this wasn't good. "I'd better talk to my parents. We definitely couldn't afford to lose a lot of business to a dollar store or anything else."

Dorothy nodded. "If you want me to help with any advertising, let me know."

"Thanks a lot, Dorothy. You're a good friend."

Dorothy smiled. "Your parents have been good friends ever since they bought the store and moved in here. We're all lucky to have them in Fraser's Mill."

Dorothy went toward the building, and Grace went to find her parents. This dollar store business worried her. She'd have to ask her parents about it.

The Dollar Store

They got home late, and Grace's parents were tired, so she decided not to mention the dollar store to them that evening. She would look it up herself and see what she found.

She ended up staying up much later than she had meant to, until she realized, long past midnight, that she had to sing at Mass in the morning. The information about dollar stores was so worrisome that she hadn't been able to tear herself away.

She'd found one interview with a man who used to own two grocery stores in different towns. A dollar store had moved into one town and put the first grocery store out of business. Now the man was trying hard to keep his second store afloat, but he was worried and just trying to get through the year.

Grace would never have thought a dollar store would be a big competitor for a grocery store. She had thought of dollar stores as places where you could get cheap silverware and plastic dishware for parties. But apparently the goods the stores sold overlapped a decent amount. Moreover, the dollar stores got their goods at rock-bottom prices because they were part of huge chains with central distribution hubs. They could afford to sell things more cheaply than small grocery stores.

The dollar stores didn't sell fresh fruits or vegetables or meat. They just had pre-packaged, non-perishable foods. If a dollar store put a small-area grocery store out of business, that would leave the area without fresh food — a "food desert." People would have to travel to get healthy food. The elderly, the poor, and those without good transportation tended to shop close to home. They couldn't travel to get their groceries, so without a grocery store nearby they would end up eating unhealthy processed food from the dollar store.

Why weren't more people talking about this? Grace was amazed she'd never heard about it before. She found article after article about the rise of dollar stores, how they were moving into small rural areas and stealing all the business, and how the chains were opening new stores at an alarming rate. It was an epidemic.

Did her parents know all this? Were they keeping it from her so they wouldn't worry her? She'd ask them tomorrow. In the meantime, she needed to say her prayers — especially for the wellbeing of Murray's Grocery — and get some sleep. What was that old saying, "Give it to God and go to bed?" Ultimately, the grocery store was in God's hands. Although Grace would still need to do her part helping the store too.

Grace decided to approach her parents about the dollar store issue on Sunday afternoon, after they had finished dinner. She felt bad talking about business things on a Sunday, but if she left this for one more day she would burst. Besides, maybe there were things they could do to help the store that they could start implementing tomorrow.

Grace's parents were sitting on the front porch. Because it was Sunday, they weren't working on Mom's story. Dad read aloud from a magazine article about an archaeological dig. He liked reading things aloud, and his wife liked to listen to them. Grace didn't have the patience to listen to things being read aloud. She liked to read them more quickly herself.

Grace came out on the porch barefoot, guiding the screen door so it wouldn't bang. "Hi," she said.

"Oh, hi," Mom said. "How's your afternoon going?"

"Well, it's pretty good, but there's something I'm worried about, and I wanted to talk to both of you about it. It's about the store."

Dad put down the magazine, taking off his reading glasses. "Sure, Gracie," he said. "Go ahead."

"Well, yesterday I was talking to Dorothy, and she told me that when dollar stores come into a town, the local grocery stores lose a lot of business. I didn't want to stress you out last night, because we were all having a nice time at the dance and then it was late. So I looked it up myself, and it's really scary! I keep finding all these articles about how dollar stores come in and have lower prices for everything, and then the grocery store loses business and eventually has to close. And that dollar store at the edge of town is opening this week!"

"Oh, sweetie, I'm sorry," Mom said. "Your father and I did hear dollar stores can be a challenge to local grocery stores. We've been talking about it, on and off, but we didn't want to worry you when you were just here for a few weeks helping out."

"Oh, Mom, I wish you had told me," Grace said. "I feel terrible about you and Dad sitting around worrying about the store and trying to be cheery for my sake."

Mom shook her head. "We've been so busy lately with your dad's broken foot, we haven't had time to sit around and worry about anything else. Besides, who knows if it'll be a problem at all? The dollar store is all the way down at the end of town. It's not as though it moved in right next door. We've been doing all right competing with the Walmart in Cadillac—lots of people from town go out there for their groceries, but we're still doing fine."

"The stuff I read last night said loss of profits is pretty much inevitable," Grace said. "Even if the dollar store isn't right next door. If it's in the same community, it starts stealing your business."

Dad sighed. "I've seen some of those articles too. But there's nothing we can do about it. That store is going to open up in Fraser's Mill, this week, and everybody's gonna have to live with it there."

"Well, maybe there's something we can do about it," Grace said. "I know it's too late to stop them from coming into town, but there's gotta be something we can do to improve our own business. I'm here for almost another month—I can help!"

This outburst brought a smile to Dad's face. "That's my girl. As stubborn as they come."

"That's right," Grace said. "I'm absolutely determined about this. No dollar store is gonna drive us out of business."

"I'll tell you what," Dad said. "Liz, tell me what you think about this. Why don't we wait and see how things go with the store totals for a week or two after the dollar store opens. I reckon that's enough time for the excitement of the grand opening to wear off. If it turns out the dollar store is hurting business, we can start talking about possibilities then. No need to get all worked up if there isn't a problem."

"That sounds good to me," Mom said. "Things went pretty well this past week. I'd like to keep on doing what we're doing unless we need to change it."

Grace could have expected her parents' plan to be conservative. "All right," she said. "But I'm going to do some research on my own, too, to see what kinds of things store owners can do to improve business."

"You're not going to use up all the time for your National Board prep, are you?" Mom asked.

"No, I won't," Grace said. "Besides, this is more time-sensitive. I have only a few weeks to help you in the store, and there isn't actually a deadline for the National Board stuff until I'm in the school year putting portfolios together for the different components. It'll be all right if I focus on the store for now."

"Well, you're a good daughter," Dad said. "Thank you."

"Of course, Dad."

The dollar store opened on Wednesday, advertised by an enormous banner out front. Grace had to go down to the gas station that morning and passed the big parking lot full of cars. The townspeople must be checking the place out. Of course, those cars could all be out-of-towners, but since Fraser's Mill wasn't on the direct route to any larger cities, it was unlikely so many people would be passing through.

Grace was tempted to go in to see what the store was like, but she wouldn't want to buy anything, so it felt like spying. She looked away from the dollar store and finished pumping gas. She had the morning off, and she was going to Alex's farm to help harvest produce.

At this time of year, most of the farm's produce came from their greenhouses. Greenhouses were great to have in Michigan—you could start planting seeds months before you could grow anything outside. But the Martins also had a strawberry patch that was ripe for picking, and asparagus was in season as well.

Grace found Alex in the first of the greenhouses on her hands and knees, cutting cucumbers off the vine. "Hey, Grace," she said. "Grab some shears and come help. We've got enough cucumbers to feed the whole county."

The farm didn't just sell vegetables to the grocery store. They had a roadside stand, and twice a week they sold goods at the farmer's market in Cadillac. This was an all-day event, and Alex's family took turns doing it. Today wasn't a market day, however, so all four of the Martins—Alex, her parents, and Sam—were home working on the farm.

"Good thing you're wearing jeans," Alex said. "I forgot to tell you to wear old clothes."

Grace laughed. "It hasn't been that long since I helped on the farm," she said. "I bet I still remember how to milk a goat."

"Unfortunately, I already milked the goats." Alex smirked. "I'm supposed to pick strawberries after this. It's pretty hot work."

"That's all right. I brought a hat."

A lot had happened since the girls had last seen each other. Alex told Grace she was seeing a movie with Charlie on Friday night. Good movies in theaters were scarce right now, but a theater in Cadillac was showing *The Princess Bride,* a favorite of both Alex and Charlie.

"What are you going to wear?" Grace asked.

"I don't know yet. Probably jeans and a plaid shirt, with cowboy boots. Do you think that's too casual?"

"No, it'll be great. The cowgirl look is good on you."

Alex laughed. "Good thing, because I wear it all the time," she said. "Well, I'm sure Charlie won't show up in a three-piece suit."

They finished the cucumbers and went out to pick strawberries, a warm, prickly job. Alex hadn't heard about the situation with the dollar store yet, so Grace filled her in.

"How could the town let a dollar store move in when it was going to hurt the town's businesses?" Alex threw up her hands. "Who sold them the land? Do you know who used to own that piece of land by the gas station?"

"Maybe whoever sold it didn't know it was for a dollar store," Grace said. "The articles I read said dollar stores often buy land through other companies so they don't need to disclose what the land is being used for."

Alex shook her head. "Sounds awfully shady to me."

"No kidding," Grace said. "Their business model is great for them and terrible for everybody else. It's only the first day, and that store is crawling with customers. I'll bet we haven't had a customer at the grocery store all morning."

"People are probably just interested in the grand opening." Alex brushed off a strawberry and bit into it. "Maybe it'll die down in the next day or two."

"I sure hope so." Grace sighed. "I wish I knew how to keep them from stealing all our business."

"Have you been inside the store yet?" Alex asked.

Grace shook her head. "I don't want to darken their door. If they learn I'm from the grocery store they'll know I'm competition. It feels like spying."

Alex's eyes gleamed. "I'm not above a little spying. Why don't I check it out after we drop off the produce, and I can tell you all about it?"

"You're incorrigible," Grace said. "But you might as well. I'm dying to know what that place is like inside. Let's hurry up and get the rest of these berries picked."

❧❧❧❧❧

Done with the farm work, the girls drove into town and parked at the gas station. Grace waited in the truck while Alex walked over to the dollar store. There were just as many people at the dollar store as before—people who might become regular customers there.

Less than five minutes later, Alex hurried out of the store. As she approached the truck she slowed down and did an exaggerated stealth walk.

Grace laughed. "You look like the Pink Panther," she said. "So what's it like in there?"

"Busy." Alex hopped in the truck and started the engine. "The store's packed with stuff. They have lots of things you don't sell at the grocery store — like party supplies and craft stuff — but they've got lots of items you do sell. Canned food, pasta, soap, toilet paper, toothbrushes, things like that. It's all awfully cheap. Some of it's more than a dollar, but it's still really low-priced."

"Did you happen to notice what any of the specific prices were?" Grace asked.

Alex shook her head. "Sorry — I didn't think to notice."

"I didn't think of it either until just now," Grace said. "Well, thanks. I like to have some idea of what I'm up against."

"Do you know what you're going to do about it?"

"I have no idea. But I'm gonna do something."

St. John the Baptist Bonfire and Picnic

On June 23rd, the vigil of the Feast of St. John the Baptist, St. Anthony's Church sang Vespers in the evening. The Vespers were followed by a huge bonfire and a picnic on the church grounds.

The evening before, at choir practice, Mary Jane had encouraged all the choir members to come to Vespers. All the chants were simple chant tones in English, so the singing wouldn't be difficult.

Grace got out of work just in time to make it to the church before Vespers began at six.

Mary Jane stood in the front pew leading the singing for the women's side, and Father John, the pastor of St. Anthony's, was leading the men's side. The high and low voices alternated pleasantly. It was easy to follow the music in the booklets Elaine and Mary Jane had put together. Grace sang cheerfully from her seat a few pews from the front. She had planned to sit with Alex, but Alex was late — she probably had a lot of things to do on the farm.

They were about halfway through when Alex slid into Grace's pew, her lace chapel veil slipping off her head. Grace scooted closer so Alex could share her booklet.

Vespers over, everyone headed outside to the church grounds, where everything was set up for a big bonfire in honor of St. John the Baptist. Several Christmas trees, which had been drying out since the previous Christmas, would be the fuel. Around the church lawn were a number of Swedish torches, logs that had been set upright and cut most of the way through with a chainsaw. When lit in the center, they would burn for a long time.

Grace had never been to a St. John the Baptist bonfire before. Father John had brought the custom to the parish when he came two years ago. Besides being an excellent priest, he was an avid outdoorsman, and he liked nothing better than leading the parish in prayers followed by outdoor activities. Right now he was bustling around, starting the bonfire.

Grace eyed the Christmas trees warily. Living in California during the aftermath of the devastating wildfires of 2017 and 2018 had left her cautious about outdoor fires. "Do you think we'd better get a fire extinguisher, just in case?" she asked Alex.

Alex laughed. "The sheriff's got the hose," she said. "And the ground's not that dry. It'll be fine."

Someone had set up a canopy tent with a few tables and chairs under it, and a few of the older parishioners were already sitting there. Everyone else milled around near where the bonfire would be.

"So how was your date with Charlie?" Grace asked Alex. "Also, where is Charlie?"

"He had to work," Alex said. "He said he might be able to stop by later if we're still here. I had a great time on our date. Although maybe going to see *The Princess Bride* wasn't the best idea. Half the people in the theater were quoting all the lines right before they happened. It was getting really obnoxious. Then some guy in the front stood up in his seat and yelled, 'We know you've got the movie memorized. Can't you just shut up?'"

Grace laughed. "Wow."

"They actually did get quiet after that," Alex said. "The rest of the movie was great. Then we got ice cream. Charlie said it was nice to go to a restaurant he wasn't working at once in a while."

"That sounds like a lot of fun," Grace said. "So how was it, going around just you and Charlie?"

"It was really fun," Alex said. "We have a lot of stuff in common. Hey, look!"

Grace turned in time to see Father John light the kindling at the base of the bonfire, which had been soaked with lighter fluid. The old Christmas trees went up at once, sending leaping flames many feet into the air. The people who were closest to the bonfire jumped back. Sheriff Liddell, unruffled, stood by with the hose.

"Wow," Grace said.

"It's really something, isn't it?" Alex bounced on her toes.

Father John said a blessing over the bonfire and sprinkled it with holy water. Mary Jane led a Latin hymn for the feast of St. John the Baptist.

It was time to eat. The parish had provided ingredients for s'mores, and some people had brought their own picnic food.

"I'm so glad you and Charlie had a good time," Grace told Alex. "Although I'm not surprised. You know, I thought right at the beginning that there was something going on between you and Charlie, and you flatly denied it."

"I couldn't say there was something going on when I didn't know if there was, now could I?"

"Touché."

"And by the way," Alex said, her brown eyes sparkling mischievously, "Charlie agrees with me that you and Doc would be really good together."

"Charlie? He barely knows me! Him trying to matchmake is even worse than you trying to matchmake."

"Yeah, but he knows Doc," Alex said. "The two of them are good buddies. They play golf and basketball together."

"If they're such good buddies, Charlie ought to know that Doc and Hannah are already an item," Grace said. "I stand by that. I saw her face when Doc was dancing with me last Saturday. She didn't look happy about it at all. Then I saw her dancing with Doc later, and they looked like they had danced together their entire lives. They were ridiculously good. And Hannah—"

"Hey." Alex's face had an odd expression.

"What?"

"Don't look now," Alex said, "but she's coming up right behind you."

"Oh." Grace stood still. She hoped Hannah hadn't been close enough to hear her talking about her.

"Hi, girls!" Hannah breezed in to join them. "I've got a question for you two about the Fourth of July."

"The Fourth of July?" Alex asked.

"Yeah. I hear it's pretty big in Fraser's Mill. I want to make a video for my channel with some of the Fourth of July celebrations. You two both grew up here. Do you know what the town usually does on the Fourth?"

Grace and Alex looked at each other. "I haven't been at the Fourth of July in a few years," Grace said. "But the big thing is always the parade."

"Most of the town is in it," Alex said. "There are a lot of floats and things—people advertising businesses, people riding horses, kids in costumes just walking down the street, veterans in uniform, trucks—but you've probably seen bigger parades than that in Chicago."

Hannah shook her head. "I haven't been to a lot of parades."

"Oh, it'll be extra fun for you then," Alex said. "The mayor reads the Declaration of Independence to kick off the parade. And during the parade there are usually a bunch of booths with things for sale—jewelry, crafts, candied nuts, stuff like that. Then there's lunch at the fire hall. Hamburgers and hot dogs, but mostly pie."

"A lot of pie," Grace said.

"And there's a big firework display in the park at night," Alex said. "The firefighters set them off."

"Wow," Hannah said. "That's a lot to video. I think I'll rope Doc into helping me out. He's good with a camera."

Grace restrained herself from giving Alex an I-told-you-so

look. She nodded at Hannah instead. "The two of you could combine your footage."

"I don't know," Alex said. "I bet Doc will be really busy that day. Fourth of July is prime time for people to get sunstroke. And people get burned on fireworks and kids fall down and skin their knees."

"Maybe I should post on the town page and ask people to be careful on the Fourth, so Doc won't be too busy." Hannah laughed.

"Speaking of Doc," Alex said, "he's right over there."

Grace turned. Doc was coming their direction.

She hadn't seen him since the dance, which was odd, because before that it had felt like she bumped into him every time she turned around. She still couldn't imagine why he had randomly asked her to foxtrot with him.

He sauntered up to the group of girls, his hands in his pockets as usual. He was wearing khakis and a blue button-down shirt with the sleeves rolled up. Could anybody look more suave? "Ladies."

"Doc!" Hannah exclaimed. "You missed Vespers. Where have you been?"

"I'm one of those degenerates that skips the prayers and comes for the picnic." Doc grinned. "Actually, I was still at work. I was behind on paperwork."

"Nice shirt." Hannah appraised Doc's outfit. "It matches your eyes."

This time Grace did shoot Alex a look. Hannah sure wasn't subtle about her interest in Doc.

"Thanks." Doc turned to Grace. "I don't think I've seen you since the dance. Nice little town get-together, wasn't it?"

"Speaking of town get-togethers," Hannah said, "we were just talking about the Fourth of July. It's a good thing you came along. I've got a favor to ask you."

"What's that?" Doc asked.

"I'm going to make a video for the Fourth of July, but there's a lot for one person to videotape. It would work a lot better if I had somebody else going around getting footage." She smiled. "You wouldn't be too busy to help me out, would you?"

"The clinic's closed that day, so I could run around with a camera." Doc's eyes twinkled. "I'll get you some prime footage. Close-up truck wheels, dogs, candy wrappers on the ground—"

Hannah giggled. "If you do that, I'll label it 'Doc's Footage' and have a comparison video showing the difference between your clips and mine," she said. "Hey, look, they've got stuff for s'mores. Come with me. I'll fill you in on what I'm thinking for the video."

She took Doc by the arm, beginning to tow him away.

"What?" Off balance, Doc looked at Hannah, then back at Grace and Alex. "Okay, I'm coming. See you around, Grace." He fell into step with Hannah, and the two walked over to the s'mores table, Hannah's arm still hooked in his.

Grace turned to Alex. "What did I tell you?"

Alex shook her head. "She likes him. That doesn't mean he likes her. If he did, she wouldn't have to try so hard to get his attention. Besides, he seemed like he wanted to stay and talk to you."

"Suit yourself," Grace said. "I still think they're some kind of item. Wanna see if those marshmallows are gluten free?"

"Sure."

They started for the s'mores table too. Some people were already roasting marshmallows over the Swedish torches. A couple brave souls were roasting them by the enormous bonfire.

All this talk about the Fourth of July had given Grace an idea. "Alex, what kinds of floats are there in the parade?"

"Oh, lots of different kinds," Alex said. "Nothing super fancy. They're usually trailers behind pickup trucks, all decked out in streamers and signs and stuff. Lots of the town businesses use them to advertise." She was reading the marshmallow package. "These are gluten free! And the chocolate is too. I'm going to make a chocolate sandwich with a roasted marshmallow in it."

"You'd better get about a dozen napkins then," Grace said, grabbing some extras. "But, I was thinking, the store ought to have a float in the parade. We could get a trailer from somewhere and make a huge display."

"Hey, that's a great idea," Alex said. "We've got a trailer you could borrow. We could hitch it behind the truck."

"Wow, thanks! That would be great."

"Do you think that will bring in more customers?" Alex asked.

"Well, it can't hurt," Grace said. "There are lots of people in town who don't shop at the store. They go all the way out to Cadillac for their groceries. If we do a good enough job advertising, maybe we can get some of those people to start shopping locally."

"Are you going to hand out flyers?"

Grace skewered a marshmallow on a long stick. "Maybe we could give out flyers for the grownups and candy for the kids. I'll ask my parents too. Maybe they'll have some ideas."

They headed toward the Swedish torches to roast their marshmallows.

"Want to join Doc and Hannah?" Alex asked.

Hannah and Doc were roasting marshmallows by one of the Swedish torches. They were both laughing about something.

"No," Grace said. "Let's find our own spot. We can talk more about the float idea for the parade."

Was it her imagination, or did Doc keep glancing over at her and Alex? Probably her imagination. As for Doc's hesitation when Hannah started dragging him away, he was probably just surprised. Grace wasn't about to let her mind be clouded by Alex's crazy theory.

Road Trip

Grace's parents agreed that having a float in the Fourth of July parade was a wonderful idea. "Maybe you could do a float that looks like a shopping cart," Mom said. "I saw one in a parade once."

"I think it would be too hard to make a shopping cart float," Grace said. "Alex says we can use the trailer from the farm. I was figuring we would hang streamers or something from the edge and put something to signify the things we sell at the store—maybe big cardboard food boxes? I'm not the best at designing things."

"I've helped out with a few floats," Dad said. "When I was a boy we always had a big Fourth of July parade. My Boy Scouts troop would do a float. One time a guy lent us a huge deer head to put on it. I was terrified somebody would ruin it and we'd have to pay for it."

Grace laughed. "I don't think we'd better use any deer heads on this float. What if we had some baskets of food and big signs advertising the grocery store?"

"You want it to be exciting," Dad said. "What you want in a parade float is something eye-catching. Something the town is gonna remember."

"You'll have to go into Cadillac to get supplies," Mom said. "There's no place in town to buy that kind of stuff. If you want to do anything with tissue paper, you'll have to find someplace that sells a lot of it cheaply. And you'll want floral sheeting and fringe and stuff."

"Or," Dad said with a grin, "she could get it at the dollar store."

Grace made a face. "I refuse to darken their door."

He laughed. "All right. Cadillac it is."

***

For the next couple evenings, Grace and her parents worked on the float design and looked up materials and pricing. It wouldn't be any use to advertise with a spectacular float if it cost more than they could afford. Grace's sister Katie gave them some suggestions over the phone. She had always liked crafts and was happy to help.

On the Thursday before the Fourth of July, Grace prepared to take Dad's old van into Cadillac. Normally she would take Mom's car, but Mom needed it tonight.

"I don't feel good about you going all that way by yourself," Mom said, when Grace popped into the store to ask if she needed anything from Cadillac. "What if something happens?"

"Mom, nothing's going to happen," Grace said. "And I have my phone."

"You'd better take your phone charger. And keep your ringer on."

"All right, Mom. You know, I drive all over the place in California all the time, and they have much worse traffic."

"Well, you be careful," Mom said. "As long as you stay safe, and your father doesn't try any dangerous projects while I'm gone at the Ladies' Guild meeting, we should be in good shape."

The evening was clear, with a brisk wind. Grace appreciated the warmth of her jean jacket.

The road to Cadillac passed farms and woods—mostly woods—without much of anything alongside the road. Cars driving past were infrequent. Once Grace got to Highway 115, which went through Mesick to Cadillac, it got busier, but not by much.

Still a few miles from Cadillac, Grace heard a noise.

A scraping sound came from underneath the car. That couldn't be good. Either the car had picked up something from the road—Grace didn't remember running over anything—or a car part was dragging on the ground. Either way, she needed to stop and check.

Grace pulled over, grateful for a wide road shoulder. She put her hazards on and jumped out of the car.

Oh, no. A car part was dragging, all right. Two things, in fact—the exhaust pipe and a boxy metal thing Grace couldn't identify.

Why did all the cars she drove have to break down? And why did this one have to break down in the middle of nowhere? Tears of frustration sprang to Grace's eyes, but she got back in the van and pulled out her phone. First things first. She'd better call Dad.

"Howdy, Gracie!" Dad's voice was jovial. "What's going on?"

"Dad." Grace took a deep breath. "The van just broke down. I was driving along and heard this horrible scraping sound, and I'm stopped by the side of the road. The exhaust pipe and this big silver boxy thing are both dragging on the ground."

"Oh, no," Dad said. "Are you in a safe place?"

"Yes. I'm way off the road and it's in the middle of a straight stretch, so nobody's gonna come around a corner and hit me."

"Good. Do you have your hazards on?"

"Yes."

"That thing dragging on the ground is your muffler. You're gonna have to get the van towed. I'll see if I can get a hold of your mom at that Ladies' Guild meeting, and she can come pick you up."

It was bad enough having one wasted trip almost all the way to Cadillac. Grace didn't like the idea of Mom driving out there too, especially when she was in a meeting. "No, I'll be fine," she said. "I'll call AAA and have them come with a tow truck. Thankfully I've had practice dealing with tow trucks recently."

"You're sure? You might have to wait a long time."

"I'm sure."

"Well, you call me the minute you've gotten off the phone with AAA," Dad said. "It's the worst feeling in the world, having my little girl stuck at the side of the road only a few miles away and I can't drive to pick her up. You sure you don't want me to call your mom?"

"Absolutely sure," Grace said. "Just because I'm having a bad evening doesn't mean Mom has to. I'll call you as soon as I've got the tow truck lined up."

She had to wait on hold with AAA for a while. What a waste of an evening—no supplies for the Fourth of July, a broken-down car, and a long wait for a tow truck. Grace was almost ready to cry when a representative answered the phone.

She gave her approximate location. Her phone GPS said she was seven miles from Cadillac on Highway 115. The van would need to be towed to the garage in Fraser's Mill. The garage was closed for the night, but the attached gas station wasn't, so it wouldn't be a problem having the van towed in. The representative said the tow trucks were busy, so it might be about an hour wait. Maybe a lot of Fourth of July travelers had broken-down cars. Grace called Dad with the update.

"About an hour? That's not too bad, considering you're in the middle of nowhere. You're sure you're safe?"

"Yes—I'm all the way off the road, my hazards are on, and my phone's got plenty of battery," Grace said. "I have the car charger in case it starts running low."

"Do you have any water?"

Grace looked over her shoulder to check the backseat for water bottles. "No, but it's not hot. I won't get thirsty that fast."

"Well, I wish I'd thought to keep the car stocked with water bottles and snacks," Dad said. "If you get cold there's a blanket in the back."

He was the best dad. "Thanks." Grace smiled. "I've got a jacket too. I'll be totally fine."

"All right. Well, I won't feel better until you're safely home."

After Dad hung up, Grace pulled up an e-book on her phone. Good thing she had cell service here. It wouldn't be fun to be stranded seven miles from town without a phone. Whatever people had done in the days before cell phones, Grace had no idea.

Cars went by occasionally. One middle-aged woman in a red sports car stopped and asked Grace if she was okay. Grace assured her she was all right and a tow truck was on its way.

Over half an hour passed since she had ordered the tow truck—going on forty-five minutes. Grace wished the truck would hurry.

In her rear-view mirror a blue car was coming down the road. It slowed down. Probably another person asking if she was okay. Grace rolled down her window, preparing to explain that she already had help on the way.

The car pulled up alongside her. It was an antique car, looking strangely familiar. The passenger window rolled down. "You okay?" a male voice asked.

"Yes, I'm fine," Grace called.

That voice was familiar too. Wait a minute. Grace peered at the car. The guy driving the car was tall with dark hair. It couldn't be—yes, it was.

The car pulled ahead and parked in front of Grace's van, and Doc sauntered toward her, hands in his pockets.

"Doc, what in the world are you doing here?" Grace asked. "I'm all right—I called AAA and they're sending a tow truck. The exhaust pipe and the muffler broke apart."

Doc stooped to look under the van. "You're right," he said.

"The only thing you can do is get it towed. Your tailpipe's gonna need replacing too."

He straightened up. "Your dad told me you were stranded out here."

Why did Dad have to send Doc, of all people?

"You mean you drove all the way out here because I was stranded by the side of the road? I'm perfectly fine—there's already a tow truck coming!"

Doc grinned, folding his arms over his chest. "I thought you could use some company while you waited for the tow. And I can give you a ride into Cadillac."

"You don't have to do that," Grace said. "It's all right. I'm fine. I can ride back in the tow truck."

Doc raised an eyebrow. "Without any of the supplies?"

Did Dad have to tell Doc so much? This felt like payback for the time Grace hadn't let Doc help her with the flat tire. If she accepted his help, she'd be stuck with him all evening. On the other hand, she really needed the supplies.

Grace sighed. "All right, I surrender," she said. "Yes, I could use a ride into Cadillac, after the tow truck comes. Thanks."

"Good," Doc said. "Mind if I get in?"

"Sure." Grace unlocked the doors, and Doc swung into the passenger seat.

His long legs barely fit in the space in front of the seat. Wow, he was tall. He was wearing khakis and an orange sweater of a shade Grace had always assumed looked terrible on everybody. For some reason it wasn't bad on him.

"You can move the seat back," Grace told him. "The lever's underneath."

Doc slid the seat back. "Thanks. Nice van—where did your dad get it?"

"Oh boy, I don't even remember," Grace said. "He's had it a long time. He found an ad in a newspaper. Maybe fifteen years ago? That was when the town still had a paper newspaper. It shut down a few years ago. Everybody just gets their news online now."

"Or they hear it through the town grapevine." Doc chuckled. "That's faster than the Internet."

"Like the news about me being stranded in the middle of nowhere with a broken-down car?"

"I got that from a reliable source." Doc grinned. "I was checking on your dad's foot when you called."

"He didn't need to send you out after me," Grace said. "I would have been all right."

Doc shook his head. "He didn't send me," he said. "I wanted to go."

"Oh." Grace stared at him, her face reddening. "Well— thank you."

Instead of spending a relaxing evening at home, Doc had chosen to sit by the side of the road waiting for a tow truck with her. That was a kind thing to do.

"My pleasure," Doc said. "How long did the tow truck say they'd be?"

"They're supposed to be here any minute," Grace said.

"Then where do you want to go after that? Your wish is my command." Doc's eyes, blue and mischievous, seemed to be laughing even when his face was serious.

"I have to get things to make a float for the Fourth of July parade," Grace said. "Floral sheeting, metallic fringe, and big pieces of cardboard—that sort of stuff. It's to advertise the grocery store."

"Uh-huh. What's it gonna look like?"

Grace dug in her purse for the folded paper on which she and Dad had drawn their idea for the float. "Something like this."

Doc looked at it. "Hmm. That's pretty ambitious."

"Does that mean you think we can't do it?" Of course he would think that. He probably thought she had no talent for anything useful. Maybe she didn't know anything about fixing cars, but she wasn't incompetent in every other aspect of her life.

Doc shook his head. "No, but it'll take a lot of work," he said. "You have to decorate all those boxes, put sheeting and fringe on the trailer, and paint a banner. You're not gonna do all this yourself, are you?"

"I was figuring I could get Alex to help since I'm borrowing her family's trailer."

"You need more help than that. I've got an idea. When are you putting all this together?"

"Saturday."

"Where?"

"Alex's place."

"I'll bring some people to help with it. Charlie will be down, if he can get out of work."

"What? You don't need to do that."

"I want to. It'll be fun."

Then Grace would be even more beholden to Doc. On the

other hand, it would be fun for Alex to have Charlie around, and the project would go quicker with more people.

"All right," Grace said. "As long as the other people don't try to take over the project and change everything, that'll be great."

Doc held out his hand. "It's a deal."

"All right." This time Grace let him shake her hand. His handshake was firm, his hand big and strong around hers. Flushing, Grace pulled her hand back.

The tow truck approached, its lights flashing. Grace hopped out of the van and waved, and Doc went to move his car out of the way. The tow truck driver parked in front of the van and lowered the ramp. As he drove the van up, the muffler and exhaust pipe scraped against the metal ramp with a sound that sent shivers down Grace's spine.

"Your dad is probably gonna have to get that muffler replaced," Doc told Grace, as they watched the tow truck driver fasten the van with chains and straps.

Rats. That was bound to be expensive.

The tow truck made a U-turn—Grace had never seen such a large vehicle do a U-turn before—and headed toward Fraser's Mill.

"Shall we go?" Doc waved a hand toward his car. "She's not a flying carpet, but she'll do."

Doc lowered himself into the driver's seat, his head almost touching the ceiling of the car.

"What kind of car is this?" Grace asked, buckling her seat belt.

"It's a Chevy Chevelle. 1970. I got it at an auction two years ago. Best car I've ever had."

Doc must like cars. Many times over the last few weeks,

Grace had seen him out on the driveway, half underneath the car, tinkering with something. It was a greasy job for someone who spent the rest of his time making sure other people were staying healthy.

Dad would be wondering what was going on — Doc said he hadn't told him he was going out to find Grace — so Grace called home. On the phone, Dad sounded jovial. He said to tell Doc thanks from him.

They got into Cadillac, and to her surprise Grace learned Doc was a good shopper. He had a sense of where to find things in the stores, and he walked fast enough that Grace almost had to run to keep up with him. Grace had always been quick in grocery stores, and it frustrated her when she had to go shopping with someone slower. Her roommate Jen was much slower. Grace could go through a store three times in the time it took Jen to go through it once.

They found poster paint, brushes, and cardstock. They still needed supplies to make the big food packages Grace wanted to put on the float.

"Does it count as taking things over if I suggest that a 55-gallon drum would make a great soup can for your float?" Doc asked as Grace picked out a vinyl shower curtain liner which would become a banner.

"Where on earth would I get a 55-gallon drum?"

"Borrow it from somebody in town," Doc suggested. "A bunch of people have them for rain barrels. I think Ed's got a few down at the garage. You can dress them up like big soup cans."

"That's actually not a bad idea," Grace said. "Then we'll

just have to figure out the other big foods for the float. I wanna do some that look like cereal boxes and some that look like fruits and vegetables and stuff. I was thinking we could get posterboard and draw a front and a back for each thing and then sandwich them together. You can use tissue paper to fill in the space between them. I've seen pictures of it online."

Doc shook his head. "That sounds like a lot of work. Why don't you just use regular cardboard boxes and decorate them to look like food packages?"

Did he have to immediately dismiss the idea she'd researched? "Where would I get all the boxes?" Grace asked, her voice sounding shrill in her own ears. "We hardly have any at the store right now. Everybody else in town who has boxes is probably already using them for the Fourth."

"I mean, you don't have to do it if you don't want to," Doc said. He spread out his hands conciliatingly. "It's your project. You can do whatever you want. But I'm sure we can find some if we ask around."

Grace relented. It wasn't fair to be cross with someone who had given up his evening to help her.

"I'm sorry. I'm just stressed. This whole thing is a much bigger project than I thought it was going to be."

Doc surveyed her, arms folded. "I know what you need," he said. "After we're done shopping, we're gonna get something to eat."

"What? It'll be like nine P.M. by that time," Grace said. "And I already had dinner."

"Well, I didn't," Doc said. "And you've had a tough evening.

The good effects of your dinner have probably worn off. You could use a milkshake or something."

Grace crossed her arms. "Is that your professional diagnosis?"

"Nope. I'm out of the office, and you're not my patient. That's an attempt at persuasion."

He looked down at her, his eyes serious for once.

Her dinner did seem to have worn off. And it would take a while to finish shopping and get food, so she'd be hungrier by then. Besides, she was tired. It would be nice to sit down somewhere and decompress.

"All right then," she said. "After we finish getting the supplies. And I'm paying for whatever I eat."

He raised his hand in a salute. "Yes, ma'am!"

On the Waterfront

The Chevelle's back seat and trunk were brimful with float-making supplies, and it was almost nine, as Grace had anticipated.

"Where do you want to go?" Grace asked. "Pretty much everything is closed now except fast food. It might be better to go back to town and stop at the diner."

Doc shook his head. "There's a place down by the lake that stays open until ten. It's right on the water, and you can sit outside if you want. Wanna try it?"

He was asking her, not telling her, which she appreciated. And it sounded better than fast food. "Sure."

They drove down to the restaurant, a small place Grace had passed many times on her way in and out of town. California had many small waterfront restaurants like that. They nearly all served seafood.

"Is this a seafood restaurant?" she asked. If Doc tried to get her to eat oysters, she'd make a run for it and call Mom to get her.

"Well, I think they have seafood, if that's what you like," Doc said. "But it's an American restaurant. Diner food. I like it because it's on the lake."

She could handle diner food.

They went into the restaurant. The hostess, a cheery girl with dark hair in a ponytail, greeted them. "Indoors or outdoors?"

Doc looked at Grace.

The evening air wasn't too cold. "How about outdoors?" Grace asked.

"Follow me," the hostess said. She led them through a set of glass doors and onto a deck with Christmas lights on the railing and small trees all around. She put them at a table for two.

The sun was nearly setting, painting the sky in glorious colors and turning the rippling water to gold. The air was clean, Grace was finally off her feet, and they were going to eat.

"How do you like it?" Doc asked.

"It's beautiful," Grace said. "I can't believe I've never eaten here before."

"It's worth it just for the view." Doc's smiling eyes reflected the glow of the evening light. "I've only been here once myself."

The waitress brought them menus. Grace looked at hers. She wasn't getting any weird appetizers, thank you very much. No strange food choices. She would make her own decisions. She almost felt like breakfast food. It had been a long day, and she didn't feel like a burger or anything like that right now. She really wanted a waffle. And maybe chicken tenders. But she always felt silly ordering things like that. Probably Doc would get the slow-roasted prime rib, at tremendous expense. Doctors usually had money.

What did she care what Doc thought? She would get what she wanted. He could get the prime rib if he wanted to.

"Looks like they have breakfast all day," Doc said. "You know what, it's been a long day. I'm gonna get chicken tenders and a waffle."

Grace burst out laughing.

"What's so funny?" Doc looked up from his menu.

"That's what I was gonna get," Grace said. "This late at night, I'd rather get breakfast food."

"Great minds," Doc said.

He kept overturning Grace's assumptions about him. The mental image she'd formed of him was significantly different from the man in real life.

He folded up his menu. "Speaking of great minds, I hear you're quite the teacher."

"Who'd you hear that from? My dad?"

Doc grinned. "Maybe," he said. "But just because your dad says it doesn't mean it isn't true."

"Well, thanks," Grace said. "It's a good school, and I've got great kids to work with. And the other teachers are nice too. Although I don't know most of them very well."

Doc's face was thoughtful. "One of the most important things about a job is the people you have around you. I'd take a tough job, with a good community, over an easier job without a good community."

"Is that why you took the job in Fraser's Mill?" Grace asked.

She had been wondering, ever since seeing Hannah's video interview with Doc, why he had chosen to move to the middle of nowhere. He could have made more money and had a better career trajectory elsewhere.

Doc nodded. "I did my residency in New York," he said. "Everything was impersonal. There were so many patients I couldn't possibly keep track of them. The medical staff kept changing too. I wanted to live somewhere where I could have an actual relationship with my patients. Besides, I like the country." He motioned to the lake. "You don't have views like this in the city."

Grace laughed. "I suppose you don't." Her apartment in California looked out toward a gray apartment building and some dusty streets. Her school building looked out over a shopping center. But it wasn't as though California wasn't beautiful—you just had to get out of the city to see the beautiful part.

The waitress came back with two glasses of water. "Are you ready to order?"

"I think so," Grace said.

The waitress produced a pen and pad. "Go ahead."

"I'd like a waffle and some chicken tenders, please."

The waitress wrote on her pad and looked at Doc.

"I'll have the same thing," Doc said. "Thank you."

The waitress took their menus and bustled off, leaving Grace and Doc sitting there at the table. No menus to hide behind. No other people. Nothing to do but talk to each other.

Doc leaned forward, his elbows on the table. "So what do you like about California?"

It was refreshing how genuine his interest seemed. "Um,"

Grace said. "Well, I moved there for the school job. After college I worked in Florida for a while—I had a job at the college where I graduated—and some people came to the campus interviewing for a teacher position in Los Angeles. I did an interview, and they offered me the job. So I moved out to L.A., and I'm rooming with a friend of mine from college."

Doc nodded. "Rooming with friends is good."

"The only thing is, I don't see her that much," Grace said. "She's studying to be a nurse and works all the time, and she's also seeing a guy. So she's not at the apartment very much."

Doc's brow furrowed. "That happened to me in New York. I had a roommate, but he was never there."

"I guess a lot of people are pretty busy these days."

"Must be." Doc raised an eyebrow. "You still haven't told me what you like about California."

"Well," Grace said. "I mostly moved there because of the school, not the state—the prices are outrageous, and the policies are worse. But it's nice that it's warm and sunny most of the time."

"And you've got the beach nearby," Doc said. "Although you've got good beaches in Michigan too. They're not so darn crowded as they are out East."

"I've gotta admit, I haven't even been to the beach a lot in California," Grace said. "I've been a few times in the summers. But usually my schedule is too tight for that."

"I get that," Doc said. "When I started my residency I didn't do anything else for three months except Sunday Mass and grocery shopping. When I wasn't at work, I was studying for in-training exams. I used to work out at the gym reading textbooks on the stationary bike."

Grace laughed. "That sounds like me. Except I can't read books while I run."

Doc's phone dinged. "Excuse me," he said. "I'd better make sure that isn't an emergency."

"No problem," Grace said.

Why had she spent so much time this summer assuming she and Doc wouldn't get along? He was friendly and relaxed, and he seemed to be an understanding person. With his background in medical school, he might even relate to all the busyness of being a teacher and getting ready to be an NBCT.

Doc put his phone back in his pocket. "Sorry about that," he said. "Not an emergency. One of my patients wanted to see if he could get an appointment tomorrow."

"Don't worry," Grace said. "I was just thinking, you and I both have pretty busy jobs. This fall's going to be crazy because I'm getting ready for National Board teacher certification. Have you heard of that?"

"If I did, I've forgotten," Doc said. "What's it like?"

"Well, according to a bunch of teachers online, it's the hardest thing they've ever done," Grace said. "But a lot of them said it was the best thing they've done for their teaching career, too."

She told Doc about the process, with the portfolio of class work and the exam at the end of the year. "The more I read about it, the more intimidated I get," she said. "But I know I should be able to get through it, if I put in the work."

"Sounds like something worth working towards," Doc said. "You'll be great. The best teacher in the West."

Grace smiled. "Thanks," she said. "I'm terrified. But I've wanted this for a long time. Teaching is really important to me. Getting kids to appreciate good literature—opening their minds to great thinkers from the past—is so crucial, especially nowadays when they're getting so much of their influence from the internet. Up to this point, I've tried my best, but I always felt inadequate compared to the other teachers. I think the National Board certification process will really help me fill in the gaps. My dream is to learn enough to be able to help other teachers with their classes too."

"Sounds like a good dream to have," Doc said. "To find your way to make a difference in the world, and then go after it as hard as you can—that's important. That's how I feel about my job."

"Did you always know you wanted to be a doctor?"

"I had a few different ideas when I was growing up. I coulda been a contender." Doc smirked. "But my uncle was a doctor, and he had all these stories about the people he helped. I wanted to do that too. So I did pre-med in college and then went into medical school. After my residency in New York, I came straight out here to take over my uncle's practice."

"Do you think you'll be here permanently?"

Doc smiled. "I like it here," he said. "Everybody ought to have a place that feels like home. Fraser's Mill is it for me."

Wow. Fresh out of his residency, in his early thirties, handsome and well-spoken, Doc could have done well anywhere. But he chose to stay here and care for people like Grace's parents, simply because he liked the little town and its people. That made such a difference to the people who lived in Fraser's Mill. He must be quite the guy. Grace understood a little more why so many of the girls in town seemed to swoon over him.

"Is it weird having your patients be your neighbors?" Grace asked.

"Not as weird as you might think," Doc said. "Medical privacy can be a problem in a small town, because everybody knows everybody else's business, but I like knowing my patients outside of the office. It's like taking care of a big family." He took a drink of water. "What's weird is being a doctor in the city. If you see one of your patients out in public you can't even go over and say hi, because it violates patient privacy."

"I would never have thought of that."

Doc nodded. "Another reason I like living here. You can say hello to your neighbors, and it doesn't have anything to do with the fact that you're their doctor."

The waitress returned with the food, which steamed on hot plates and smelled amazing. Grace launched into her waffle the minute she and Doc had finished saying grace.

"So," Doc said, when the food on both his plate and Grace's had diminished significantly, "how did you get roped into this float-making business? Does the store do a float every year?"

Grace shook her head. "This is the first time," she said. "My dad's done floats before, when he was a boy, so he helped me think of ideas. We're hoping to raise awareness for the store. We could use all the extra customers we can get with the new dollar store in town."

"Ah." Doc raised an eyebrow. "Competition."

Grace nodded. "It's a problem all over the country. Dollar stores come in, and the local stores go out of business. I'm not gonna let it happen here."

She told Doc about the videos she had seen, about the grocery store owners whose stores had been closed down, and about the zoning in Maple City which had prevented a dollar store from moving in there. Doc listened intently.

"I know one thing," he said. "Fraser's Mill can't afford to lose its only grocery store. You oughtta get the town involved to help keep the store going. Nobody realizes the dollar store is going to hurt your business."

"What would I do?" Grace asked.

"Get the word out any way you can," Doc said. "Social media. Flyers. Word of mouth."

"Do you think the people in town will care enough to do something about it?"

"If they understand the situation, a lot of them will," Doc said. "These people are your friends and neighbors. They don't want your parents to go out of business. They don't want to drive into Cadillac for all their groceries, either."

Doc was a big voice in the community. He would be a good person to have on her side.

"Hey, your food's getting cold," Doc said. "You've been talking this whole time and forgetting to eat."

"Oh." Grace looked down at her half-full plate. "I guess I got carried away."

Doc smiled. Grace started in again on her chicken.

It was dark when they left the restaurant and started back toward Fraser's Mill. Doc's driving was swift but not anxiety-inducing.

"What time are you building the float on Saturday?" Doc asked.

"I'll text Alex and ask when a good time is." Grace pulled out her phone.

"You can text me when you find out," Doc said. "You can have my number, as long as you don't use it to sell me car insurance or tropical vacations."

"Gee, I was just gonna ask if you wanted to buy a timeshare in Maui."

They got back to Fraser's Mill so late that a number of the houses were already dark. It was nearly eleven when Doc pulled into his driveway.

"I've gotta put all the supplies we bought in the garage," Grace said.

Doc jumped out of the car. "You open the garage. I'll start bringing them in."

It took a few trips to stow everything away.

"Text me when you hear back from Alex," Doc said as Grace locked the garage. He looked especially tall in the dim light of the driveway.

"Sure," Grace said.

"See you around." Doc headed for his house, his hands in his pockets, whistling a tune.

She hadn't thanked him, and he had driven her all around and helped her all evening. "Wait," Grace said, starting after him.

Doc stopped whistling and turned around. "What?"

"I haven't thanked you. You came all the way out to Cadillac to wait for the tow truck with me, and you took me to all those stores and that restaurant. You didn't have to do any of that. It was very kind of you. Thank you."

"You're welcome." Doc's face, as much as she could see of it in this light, was serious. "What you're doing for your parents is a good thing, Grace. You're a good daughter."

"Thanks. They're good parents."

"And they raised a darn impressive woman. Of course," a teasing note came into his voice, "she can't look at a car without it breaking down."

"Oh yeah? Want me to go over there and look real hard at your car?"

Doc laughed. "You'd better get inside, or your parents will think you're getting mugged out here."

"Mugged? In Fraser's Mill?" Grace started toward the house. "Goodnight, Doc," she called over her shoulder.

He was still standing there, his hands in his pockets. "Goodnight, Grace."

❧❧❧

Grace went up to the porch. Was it really the same evening she had set out to buy supplies for the float? Her parents' kitchen was dark, but the living room light was on. Mom and Dad must be waiting up for her. Grace let herself in the front door.

Sure enough, her parents were still awake, sitting in the living room in their pajamas, reading books on the loveseat.

"Hi, Gracie," Dad said. "How'd it go?"

Grace kicked off her shoes by the door and flopped onto the couch. "It was good, actually," she said. "We got everything we needed for the float—except we've still got to dig up some cardboard boxes from somewhere—and Doc's gonna get together some people to help build the float on Saturday. After we got done with all the shopping we stopped at a restaurant in Cadillac, one of those places right on the water, and we both got chicken and waffles."

"You went to a restaurant with Doc?" Mom asked. "I didn't even know you two were friends."

"We weren't," Grace said. "But I think we are now. It's a long story."

She couldn't explain, even to herself, the shift in her feelings about Doc. Somehow, she'd gone from feeling irritated toward him showing up to really enjoying hanging out with him. Gratitude for him picking her up, appreciation for his help, and surprise at his sympathetic understanding swirled together in her mind.

"Well, the van got to the garage," Dad said. "Ed called me when it got in. The muffler and tailpipe broke off when the guy was backing the van off the tow truck. Nothing he could have done about that. It's gonna need a new muffler, exhaust pipe, and tailpipe. That'll set us back quite a bit."

"Dad, I'm so sorry," Grace said. "I didn't have any idea there was something wrong with the van."

"It's not your fault," her mother cut in. "If your father's going to insist on keeping that old thing, he has to take full responsibility for the way it's falling apart."

Dad chuckled. "Your mother's right. It's not your fault. The same thing would have happened to the next person to drive it."

Mom got up from the loveseat. "Well, we'd all better get some sleep," she said. "I'm opening the store tomorrow. Grace, you don't need to come in early. I need you to close the store, and I'm sorry, but I need you to make dinner too. It's Imelda Martin's birthday, and she's having dinner with a few of the ladies at the diner."

"Sure, Mom, no problem," Grace said. "Dinner will be a little late if I've got to close the store at seven and then start cooking. Dad, you might want to eat a snack."

"I'll eat an apple," Dad said. "Don't worry, I won't starve."

Upstairs, after she brushed her teeth, Grace checked her phone. Alex had replied about the float building: "Ten A.M. on Saturday would be great!" Grace texted the information to Doc.

Lucas had also sent an email.

"Grace, I've got great news!" the email read. "This Sunday is my grandma's birthday, and I'm flying in to see her. We're having a big family reunion. I'll be flying in and out of Traverse City. If you're free this weekend or the Fourth of July, we should meet up. I can drive down to Fraser's Mill, and we can get lunch or something. Saturday or Monday would be great."

Oh, boy. When Grace had envisioned going out with Lucas again, she never thought of him coming to Fraser's Mill. She had always connected him with California. From the sinking feeling in her stomach, one thing was evident: she didn't want him to come.

Lucas's interest in her was flattering. And, no doubt, he was an eligible match on the surface. But something was missing.

Grace had seen the way Alex's eyes lit up when she talked about Charlie. Those two seemed so comfortable together and like they had a lot of fun being around each other. Whatever Alex and Charlie had, Grace didn't have that with Lucas. If anything, Lucas made her feel uncomfortable, like she couldn't be herself.

At the same time, what could she say to dissuade him from coming to Fraser's Mill? She couldn't think of a way to uninvite him that wouldn't hurt his feelings. Plus, he was a part of her regular life back in California and one of the only coworkers she'd spent any time with. Even if she wasn't interested in him romantically, it seemed like the friendly thing to do to meet up with him when he was in the area.

But of all possible weekends, this was the worst. Grace had so much to do. She'd be busy on Saturday building the float. Monday was the Fourth of July. Maybe she had a way to get out of the whole thing. She had too many conflicts. Grace emailed Lucas back, explaining about the float-building on Saturday and the parade on Monday.

He must have checked his email immediately, because she got a reply at once: "What if I come to the parade, and then we get lunch when you're done? It could be fun to see the Fourth of July in a small town."

Rats. There was no real reason why she couldn't have lunch with him. She was out of excuses. But she got the feeling the Fourth of July wouldn't be nearly as fun if she had to spend the afternoon showing Lucas around.

She sent Lucas a reply: "OK, after the parade would work."

The Second Dinner

The grocery store was busy before the Fourth of July. On Friday afternoon a truck came from the store's supplier with extra provisions and picnic supplies for the weekend. The Fourth was always a big boost for the store, since many people came to buy cookout food for their families. The town was hosting lunch at the fire hall, and they got their food through the grocery store as well. They needed tremendous numbers of pies. Grace kept busy unloading things. The food coolers were stocked to full capacity.

Grace was helping an evening customer, looking forward to closing the store and making dinner, when Doc came in the door. He often came in after the clinic closed to get food for dinner and the next day's breakfast and lunch. Why he didn't shop once a week or every few days like most people, Grace didn't know. Maybe, living next door, it was easier to shop every day.

Doc approached the register, his arms full of groceries. "Hi," he said. "Did you hear back about the van?"

He looked either tired or sick. Dark circles sat underneath his eyes, and he leaned on the counter.

"Ed called yesterday," Grace said. "The van's gonna need a new muffler, exhaust pipe, and tailpipe. Are you okay? You look awful."

Doc yawned. "I'm fine," he said. "I was up late, and then I got a call at three A.M. A woman down at the other end of town was having a baby, and as it happened, her midwife was in the middle of delivering somebody else's baby. So they called me."

"Good grief! How'd it go? Are the mom and the baby okay?"

"They're doing great. The baby's a girl. She was born an hour after I got there, and then I had appointments at the clinic starting at eight."

"Wow. How do you feel?"

"Oh, I'm fine. I'll get plenty of sleep tonight."

Grace looked at Doc's food — two cans of minestrone soup, a bag of potato chips, and a jug of milk. After staying up all night, he was eating that?

"I'm going to be nosy here," Grace said. "Is this supposed to be your dinner?"

Doc grinned. "I plead the fifth."

Grace shook her head. "This is disgraceful. What you need is a home-cooked meal. You'd better come over for dinner. My mom's at a birthday party and I'm making dinner for myself and my dad."

He raised an eyebrow. "You don't owe me anything for yesterday."

"That's not what I was thinking." Grace pushed his groceries back across the counter toward him. "You're my next-door neighbor, and you just stayed up all night delivering a baby. I'm not going to let you go back to your house to eat canned soup and potato chips."

He raised his hands in surrender. "Okay, okay! I'll come."

"Good. Do you still want me to ring up this stuff?"

"Sure. It might come in handy," Doc said. "For your information, potato chips aren't nearly as bad for you as a lot of other foods."

"All right then." Grace rang up the items and bagged them.

"What time should I come over?" Doc asked. "I can bring a first-aid kit in case you spill boiling juice on your hand again."

Grace made a face at him. "I'm starting dinner as soon as I close up," she said. "It'll be ready around seven-thirty. You can come whenever you want, and leave the first-aid kit at your house. We're having baked salmon, green beans, and pasta with red sauce. Unless you hate any of those things."

Doc laughed. "Sounds like a feast. I'll be over before seven-thirty."

⚬⚬⚬⚬⚬

At seven, Grace closed up the store and went home.

"Hey, Dad," she called as soon as she got in the door. "Where are you? We're gonna have company for dinner."

"In here," Dad's voice called from the living room.

Grace found him sitting in a chair with a dumbbell in each hand. "Dad, what are you doing?"

"Getting some exercise. Don't worry, I'm not putting any weight on that foot." Dad waved away Grace's concern.

"I invited Doc over for dinner," Grace said. "He was up all night helping a woman have a baby, and he was just in the store buying a can of soup and a bag of potato chips for his dinner. I thought he could use a home-cooked meal."

"Fine with me," Dad said. "He's an interesting guy. Tells good stories. You need any help in the kitchen?"

"No, thanks, I've got it," Grace said. "It's all pretty easy."

She hurried into the kitchen, put a pot of water on the stove for the pasta, and placed the frozen salmon onto a baking sheet with butter and lemon pepper. The green beans could wait while she dealt with everything else.

Someone knocked at the front door. Grace opened it to find Doc standing on the porch in khakis and a light green button-down with the sleeves rolled up. He was holding something flat.

"This is for you," Doc said. "Can I help with anything?"

Grace took the thing he handed her. It was a bar of chocolate with raspberry, a kind they didn't carry in the grocery store.

"Thanks!" Grace scrutinized the package. "You didn't buy this at the dollar store, did you?"

He grinned. "I wouldn't live to tell the tale if I did. I got it at the gas station."

"Well, thanks. I like raspberry chocolate," Grace said. "Come on in. You can snap the ends off the string beans if you want."

He came in, seeming extra tall in the small entryway.

"That you, Doc?" Dad called from the living room.

"Hey, Ben." Doc went into the room.

Grace followed him and stopped short. On his hands and knees, Dad was doing kneeling push-ups.

Doc cleared his throat. "I get the feeling you didn't check with your doctor about starting an exercise regimen while still in a cast."

"I'm not putting any weight on my foot," Dad protested. He did another push-up.

Doc shook his head at him. "All right. You can do that if you're careful. But the minute you put any weight on that foot, you'll have to answer to me." He turned to Grace. "Grace, you're my official spy. Make sure your dad doesn't put weight on his cast."

"Sure," Grace said. "If he does, I'll tell my mom on him."

"I don't need half the family ganging up on me." Dad chuckled. "Don't you two have cooking to do?"

In the kitchen, Grace set Doc to work snapping beans while she set the table. Doc still looked tired, but he said he'd had a cup of coffee and was feeling a lot better.

Dinner was cheery. Doc regaled Grace and her dad with tales of his New York residency and his first impressions of Fraser's Mill. He had had a rocky start because people were used to his uncle and didn't trust him at first, but things had improved.

"Grace, you won't believe this," he said. "You asked if people ever paid me in chickens. Well, last week, somebody did. Two fresh ones he'd just killed and plucked. They were in a cooler in his car. I couldn't believe my eyes."

Grace laughed. "Wow," she said. "What did you do with them?"

"I put them in the freezer. I still have to figure out how to roast chickens."

Near the end of dinner Doc was yawning again, but he didn't move to go home.

"You oughtta get some sleep," Grace said, "or you won't be able to function tomorrow."

He grinned. "Do you always get rid of your dinner guests this way?"

"Nonsense. You need sleep."

"I guess I am gonna get up early to work on that float." Doc rose from his chair. "Thanks, Grace. The food was great. The company wasn't bad either."

He held out his hand to Dad. "Ben. Good to see you."

Dad shook Doc's hand heartily. "Thanks for coming, Doc. Come again sometime. You oughtta try my wife's scalloped potatoes—they melt in your mouth."

Doc left, and Grace began to clear the table.

"Can I help with anything?" Dad asked, pushing back his chair.

"No, no, thank you," Grace said. "I've got it."

"Then I'll just keep you company for a while," Dad said. "That was a good dinner. Your mother couldn't have made better salmon."

Grace smiled. "Thanks, Dad." She stacked up the plates and took them to the sink.

"Doc looked like he enjoyed himself, too," Dad said. "The two of you seem to get along well. Must have been a good trip to Cadillac yesterday."

Was that an offhand comment, or was Dad matchmaking? Grace started filling the left side of the sink with water. "Yes," she said. "It was a surprisingly good time, considering it started out with the car breaking down."

"Uh-huh," Dad said.

Grace turned around. He was grinning.

"Dad," she protested. "There's nothing romantic between me and Doc. We're just starting to be friends."

"Whatever you say, Gracie." Dad chuckled. "I'm not trying to make matches here. I know you're getting ready to go back to California. But I'm glad you and Doc are friends now."

Grace smiled. "Thanks, Dad."

It was comfortable talking about Doc with Dad. Of course he would suspect something going on between her and Doc, after she invited Doc to dinner. But Dad didn't press the issue, like others might.

She could just imagine Alex's reaction when she heard about the last couple days. Alex would crow over her, saying that was proof Grace and Doc were good together. Sure, in a way Alex had been right; they did actually get along when they spent time together. Doc was surprisingly fun to hang out with, and it was a lot nicer to be his friend than it had been to imagine herself his enemy. But Alex could forget her matchmaking entirely, because Grace wasn't planning to get involved with anybody from Fraser's Mill right before leaving Michigan. Grace needed to find a guy in California. Doc liked Hannah, anyway.

So what guys were in California? Lucas. Just thinking of him gave Grace a sinking feeling. She should have known long before that she wasn't interested in Lucas. But she hadn't realized it until he asked to visit her. Before that, sending emails back and forth had been low-pressure enough that she hadn't had to think too seriously about it. She couldn't uninvite him now — that would seem rude. But if he asked her for another date, she'd have to kindly tell him they weren't a good match.

There had to be somebody else. Grace hoped he would show up soon, because time was ticking. She was twenty-seven. She'd spent so much time on school and work the last few years that she hadn't spent a lot of time dating. Sure, school and work were important, but Grace didn't want to be an old maid either. Maybe she'd find some other guy out in California, a guy who was less like Lucas and more like…Doc? No, no, no. There was no way Alex was right.

Cardboard and Paper and Fringe, Oh My!

Grace had the next morning and afternoon off to work on the parade float. Before ten A.M., she was at the Martin farm, sitting on the big flat trailer that would be used for the float and explaining her decoration plans to Alex. She had brought a cooler with drinks and sandwiches for the helpers.

Doc had done his recruiting well. By ten o'clock, eight people were there to help with the float. Doc had invited even more, but a few — such as Hannah — had been busy. Not all of the helpers had experience building things, but Grace had been thinking about the project over the last few days and reading instructions for making floats. It couldn't be too bad if they followed the instructions she had saved on her phone. It was hard to read the screen in the sunlight, though. Somebody ought to make phones that were easier to read in bright glare.

"I thought of doing that tissue paper pomping you see on a lot of big floats," Grace told the helpers. "But it looked like it would take weeks, and we don't have weeks, so we're not doing it."

"Thank goodness," Alex said. "My mom said they did that when she was in college, and it took forever. She never wanted to see another piece of tissue paper when they were done."

Their first step was to build a platform on the trailer itself. It was a low-boy trailer with rails, and Grace wanted to make the platform flush with the top of the rails. She had gotten a number of wood pallets from the grocery store, and Alex's dad had provided some large sheets of plywood on the condition that they be returned after the Fourth of July. Charlie Keller and Sam Martin started right away building the platform, using long screws and a cordless drill.

The main other thing for this float was making the big food boxes for display. Doc had gotten two 55-gallon barrels — borrowed from Ed at the garage — and some helpers would put paper on them and make them look like soup cans. Others were going to decorate large boxes to look like cereal and other boxed foods.

Grace undertook the design and painting of the banner for the float. She had a white vinyl shower curtain, which was going to read: "Murray's Grocery Store: Support your Local Grocers!" She just needed to enlarge the text from the small version she had designed to replicate it on the shower curtain.

"I can help with that," Doc said, when Grace explained about resizing the banner image. "You just need to figure out the proportions. Anybody have a yardstick or a tape measure?"

"I've got a tape measure in the house," Alex said, and ran off.

When Alex returned, Grace measured the dimensions and

spacing of the letters on her small banner mock-up and read them out to Doc. He converted the numbers to scale for the larger banner.

"Why can't you just eyeball it?" Charlie asked, taking a break from his platform-building to see what Grace and Doc were doing. They had spread out the banner in the Martins' pole barn.

"Eyeball it!" Grace exclaimed. "Charlie Keller, have you ever tried to eyeball something this big? Especially on a floppy shower curtain liner? If we don't measure the letters, they'll look horrible."

Doc was on his hands and knees marking the placement of the letters on the vinyl. His doctor's hands were steady.

"This'll be ready to paint in a few minutes," he told Grace.

So much was going on, Grace didn't know what to do next. The guys building the platform were almost done. The floral sheeting needed to go on the platform. The fringe needed to be stapled around the edge of the platform.

Where was the staple gun? Also, where was the paint for the banner? She and Doc had bought poster paint in Cadillac. At last she triumphantly fished the paints from the miscellaneous bags and boxes near the trailer.

When she got back in the barn, Doc was finishing his markings on the vinyl. "Just in time," he said. "Why don't you take one side and I'll take the other?"

"All right," Grace said. "Don't forget to paint the part farthest away from you first, so you don't drag your arm through it afterward."

Doc laughed. "I thought the whole point of making a banner was to smear the paint everywhere."

The letters for the sign were outlined in pencil. It wasn't too difficult painting and staying in the lines. It was more difficult trying to stay out of each other's way. With each of them on one side of the vinyl, starting in the middle, there was barely room to work without bonking heads.

Grace was strangely aware of how close Doc was. If she moved her hand a couple inches, she would touch his tanned, muscular arm. Now why had that popped into her head?

"I feel like I'm doing a school project," Doc said. His head was bent over his painting, but there was a grin in his voice. "Do you make your school kids do stuff like this in class?"

"I leave that for the art teacher," Grace said. "My school kids are too busy reading *Tom Sawyer* and *Anne of Green Gables.*"

"You didn't take a day off during your *Tom Sawyer* lessons to whitewash a fence?"

Grace laughed. "Does anybody whitewash fences anymore?"

"We could bring it back." Doc looked up, a twinkle in his eye. "You could get your parents to put in a line of whitewash at the store."

"For a lot of nonexistent fences? Who's going to build all those fences?"

"Hey, Grace," Alex said, appearing again in the barn doorway. "We've got a problem."

Grace sat back on her heels. "What?"

"The staple gun is out of staples and we don't have any more."

"I'll go to the hardware store," Doc said, straightening up. "What size staples?"

"Thanks, Doc, you're a gem," Alex said. "I don't know what size. I'll ask Charlie."

Doc and Alex hustled off, and Grace went back to her painting. It was going to take a long time to fill in those letters.

Grace heard footsteps. "He likes you," Alex's voice said somewhere above her head.

Grace looked up. Alex's hands were on her hips, a smirk on her face.

"Huh?" Grace said. Oh boy, here it came.

"It's obvious," Alex said. "You think he would spend his whole Saturday afternoon running around doing arts and crafts if he didn't like you?"

"Alex, he's a nice guy," Grace said. "He goes out of his way for people. That doesn't mean he likes me."

"A nice guy?" Alex exclaimed. "You didn't think he was a nice guy before. You couldn't stand him! Now you're both painting banners and joking around. What happened?"

"Well, it's a long story," Grace began.

"Enough stuff has happened to be a long story, and I haven't heard a word about it?" Alex sat down cross-legged on the barn floor. "What's going on here?"

"Well, it all started when the van broke down on Thursday," Grace said. "Hey. If I'm gonna tell you a whole long story, you'd better help paint."

"Fine, give me a brush."

They started painting again, and Grace told Alex about the van breakdown, Doc's sudden appearance, and their evening of shopping and dinner on the water.

"Which wasn't a date," Grace told Alex. "I paid for myself. It was just because it was getting late and we were both hungry."

"Uh-huh." Alex didn't sound convinced.

"Then last night I invited him over for dinner with me and my dad, but it was because he had been up all night helping a lady have a baby, and he was going to have canned soup and potato chips for dinner. You'd have done the same thing."

"Wait. You invited him over? To your house? For dinner?" Alex sat up on her heels. "And you still say you're not interested in him?"

"I was just trying to be nice," Grace said. "He drove me all around and took me to get food on Thursday. I owed him one."

Alex shook her head. "I think you like him."

"Nonsense! Besides, he likes Hannah, remember?"

"He likes you," Alex said. "I'm positive."

"Hey, Grace! Alex!" A shout came from outside. "Need some advice!"

Alex got to her feet. "That's Sam. I bet they're done building the platform."

With teamwork, the rest of the float-building went quickly. Doc returned with staples for the staple gun, and after everyone took a lunch break he and Grace finished painting the banner.

Grace's conversation with Alex had heightened her awareness of Doc's behavior. He was certainly in a good mood, joking and teasing as they painted, his eyes twinkling. But that could just be his normal behavior towards anyone. It didn't necessarily mean what Alex thought it meant.

They let the banner dry while everyone arranged the imitation foods around the sides of the float and fastened them down.

"Well, that's not going anywhere," Sam said, slapping a

55-gallon barrel dressed up as a can of soup. "Grace, you wanna hang the banner from the edge of the float or rig it up above the float somehow?"

Grace considered, her head on one side. "I guess we'd better hang it from the edge of the float. I can't imagine how we would rig it up above."

The banner in place, everyone stood back to look at their float.

"Hooray!" Alex bounced on her toes. "It looks terrific!"

The fringe waved in the breeze, and the big food boxes on the float looked great. The girls who had been putting them together had done a nice job on the food packaging and the fruit and vegetable details. The banner clearly showed the float's sponsor.

"Wow," Grace said. "This is perfect." She turned to her helpers. "Thank you all so, so much. I think this is gonna be really good for the store's business."

"It was fun!" Charlie dusted off his hands. "Do we get to ride on the float?"

"Sure, why not?" Grace said. "We can all throw candy and hand out flyers. Unless we're over the weight limit. Alex, do you think this float can hold nine people?"

"Sure, no problem," Alex said.

"Great. Speaking of which, I'd better get some candy and print up some flyers. I think we're done here, unless you think it's going to rain—maybe we'd better get tarps or something to cover the float just in case."

"It's not going to rain," Sam said. "Look at that sky. Not a cloud."

"Just the same, I'd feel better if we had tarps over it," Grace said.

"I'll take care of it, Grace," Alex said. "You better go print those flyers."

Grace went off, leaving the helpers to cover the float. It was great to have a team of people that had your back.

It was going to be hard, leaving all these Fraser's Mill people behind when she went back to California. She'd gotten to know them so much better over the past few weeks. Maybe from now on she could visit here more frequently, if she could save the money for the plane flights. Her parents would always be glad to have her come. And maybe she could keep in better contact with everybody when she was in California, too. Alex...Dorothy...Doc...especially Doc. Now what was that fluttering feeling in Grace's stomach? No, it couldn't be butterflies.

Independence Day

The glorious Fourth dawned sunny and hot. In Michigan, the Fourth always seemed to be the hottest day of the year. It wasn't as hot as California, but it made up for that by being humid.

Grace had been so excited about the float and the parade and the store flyers that she had almost forgotten about Lucas coming—until she got a text from him. "Excited to see you in the parade this morning!" the text read. "See you soon!"

She should have thought of a way to convince him not to come. Today would be hectic enough, and now that she knew for sure she wasn't interested in Lucas, she felt bad about letting him visit. But it was too late now. She'd have to be kind and friendly—but just friendly—to him when he came.

Well, she didn't have to worry about Lucas until later. It was time to get ready for the parade.

Grace had never been in the parade before, and she hadn't realized how early everyone had to get there and how long they had to wait on a side street for the parade to start. The sheriff and his deputies had blocked off Main Street for the parade and were directing traffic.

Sam was driving the farm truck with the float attached. The girls had decorated the truck with streamers and written "Murray's Grocery" on the windows with soap. The helpers from yesterday were hanging around in the vicinity of the float, joking with each other.

Doc was the only one missing — he was helping Hannah take videos. It was too bad he couldn't be part of their group after he had worked so hard on the float, but maybe he preferred helping Hannah. Like Grace had told Alex, Doc was a helpful guy who went out of his way for people. It didn't mean anything special that he'd helped Grace with the shopping and the float.

Since Grace and her friends were too far away to see the goings-on in the center of town, Grace had asked Mom to text her updates. The parade started at eleven with the mayor reading the Declaration of Independence. Following the reading, the mayor gave a speech.

The parade finally began inching along. The sun beat down. Grace had forgotten to wear a hat. She'd be red as a lobster tomorrow.

But when the parade got into town, it became fun. People crowded at the sides of the road, some in lawn chairs, some standing. Some little kids rode on their parents' shoulders to see better. Other kids were out in the road scrambling for thrown candy.

The Murray's Grocery team was throwing flyers with candy taped onto them, which had been Grace's idea. The candy helped weight the flyers so they could be thrown. Charlie had suggested making the flyers into paper airplanes, but Grace and Alex shouted that idea down.

Somewhere ahead of them, a band played. Fraser's Mill didn't have a regular band, but in the weeks leading up to the Fourth the mayor had gone around recruiting anybody who played a band instrument to participate in the parade.

The delectable smell of hot cinnamon sugar wafted over to the float from a roadside cart selling candied nuts.

Hannah stood in front of the firehouse, holding up her phone, videotaping. Her sundress, with a blue top and a red-and-white striped skirt, looked patriotic. Doc was nowhere in sight.

No, there he was, farther down the street, in front of the bank with his own phone. Good, he could get some video footage of their float. He was wearing a red-and-white striped shirt that matched Hannah's outfit, cargo shorts, and sunglasses.

She'd better stop looking around and focus on throwing flyers and candy. Some little kids stood farther from the road, kept safe by parents who didn't feel comfortable with them in the road. Grace tossed candy farther back for them.

"It looks like the whole town is out," she called to Alex.

Alex laughed and threw a handful of flyers. "On a ninety-degree day, too!"

Mom and Dad were waving from their front porch. They liked to sit in the shade and watch the parade in comfort instead of getting hot and sunburned near the road. The grocery store was closed during the parade, although it would be open later in the day.

The parade went down Main Street as far as the church and the sawmill. Then everyone turned down side streets. They had to find alternate routes to get back, since the rest of the parade was still coming down Main Street.

Sam pulled over on the side of the road and stuck his head out the truck window. "Hey, boss," he called, "where do you wanna go now? Want me to drop you guys off and take the truck back to the farm?"

"If that's convenient for you," Grace called to him. "Otherwise I can take it over there."

"Then you'd have to walk all the way back. I'll take it."

"Thanks, Sam."

Grace scrambled off the float. They'd have to figure out about taking it apart later.

"So, what are you up to now?" Alex asked Grace. "Charlie and I are gonna go down to the hall for lunch."

"Do they have anything gluten-free you can eat?" Charlie asked, hovering behind Alex.

"I'll get a hamburger without a bun," Alex told him. "You coming, Grace?"

"No, I've got to meet somebody," Grace said. Now she had to spend the afternoon showing Lucas around. Hannah and Doc would probably have a fun afternoon videotaping without her.

Alex lowered her voice conspiratorially. "Is it who I think it is?"

If only! Grace shook her head. "Nope. It's Lucas. The guy from California I told you about. He's visiting his grandma in Michigan and wanted to stop by while he was here."

Alex's face fell. "Oh. Well, I hope you have a good time. We'd better get going. Come on, Charlie."

"See you, Grace," Charlie called over his shoulder as the pair walked off.

Now where was Lucas? Grace hadn't seen him during the parade. She must have missed him in the crowd. People were milling around everywhere.

She checked her phone and saw Lucas had texted: "Meet me at the park on Main Street when you're done with the parade?"

"Sure," Grace responded. "I'm heading over there right now."

She found Lucas in the park, sitting on a bench and checking his phone. He looked much the same as he had in California, except he was wearing shorts and a T-shirt with loafers instead of his usual suit.

"Grace!" Lucas jumped up from the park bench. "There you are. Did you see me from the float?"

Grace shook her head. "No, I didn't. Too busy throwing flyers, I guess."

"Let's find a place indoors to sit and catch up," Lucas said. "I forgot how hot and humid it gets in Michigan. Any coffee shops in town?"

Grace laughed. "Not one, not even one of the big coffee chains. Which is just as well, because some of the big chains are terrible companies. The only restaurants in town are the diner and the tavern."

Lucas raised his eyebrows. "This really is a small town."

"There's a lunch at the fire hall for the Fourth of July," Grace said. "Right across the street. They've got hamburgers and hot dogs and potato salad and all kinds of pies."

Lucas squinted across the sunny street and shook his head. "It looks crowded. And the food's never good at those things. Why don't we try the tavern? Maybe they've got some decent beer on tap."

She might have known he wouldn't want to eat at the fire hall. Grace tried to forget the burger, fries, and coconut cream pie that had been in the back of her head all morning. *"The food's never good at those things,"* indeed! Murray's Grocery had provided most of it. But Lucas wouldn't know that.

"Sure, we could go to the tavern," Grace said. "They've got a bunch of good beers." If there was one thing Michigan did well, it was brewing beer. Even Lucas would have to agree about that.

Grace and Lucas passed the fire hall as Doc came up to it, wearing his sunglasses. Grace couldn't tell if he saw them.

She and Lucas went into the dim tavern. Bars and restaurants always had to be so dark, and after coming in from the sun it was especially hard to see. But she'd been there enough times to be familiar with the menu and semi-familiar with the beer list.

"Want to sit at the bar?" Grace asked.

"How about a booth?" Lucas said.

"Fine, then we'll have to wait for the waitress to seat us."

Grace kept thinking of the fun she was missing at the fire hall. Even if Doc was still tied up taking videos for Hannah, he had probably stopped for lunch. And it would have been fun third-wheeling with Alex and Charlie, even if Doc wasn't there.

The waitress led Grace and Lucas to a booth.

"Finally," Lucas said, sliding into his side of the booth. "As a local, what do you recommend from this place? Any good appetizers?"

Whatever happened, she wasn't going to let Lucas pick out food for her. She was surprised he hadn't looked up the restaurants in Fraser's Mill before getting here. Grace slid into the booth, which was sticky. "I actually haven't tried any appetizers from here," she told him. "Honestly, I don't usually get appetizers. You can go ahead and get one if you want, of course."

"Okay, that's fine." Lucas opened his menu. "Where's their beer list? What do they have on tap?"

When the waitress came back, Grace ordered a beer and a hamburger with fries. Lucas ordered a beer and a plate of ribs. He must not be worried about sauce on his clothes.

"How was your grandma's birthday?" Grace asked.

"It was great. Most of my extended family was there," Lucas said. "She turned eighty-five, so they had a party with eighty-five guests."

"Wow, that's a big party! That must have been really nice for your grandma."

Lucas nodded. "She had a great time. There was a big tent set up in the backyard, and my uncle was giving people rides around the lake in the pontoon."

"Nice!"

"So tell me," Lucas said, "what have you been doing with yourself these days? Do you get out of town much?"

"No, not really," Grace said. "But there's been a lot to do around here. Especially getting ready for the Fourth of July."

The waitress came back with their beers.

Lucas's forehead creased as he tasted his.

"That's surprisingly good."

"See, I told you they had good beer," Grace said.

Lucas laughed. "No offense, but I don't usually take women's advice about beer."

Grace wouldn't take Lucas's advice about drinks either — or food, for that matter — but to each his own.

Grace's burger tasted good, and Lucas proclaimed the ribs to be all right. He managed to eat them without getting anything on his shirt. It must be nice not to be klutzy.

"So how's your summer going so far?" Grace asked.

Lucas launched into a description of his travels. He had been up and down California, visiting different places, doing a lot of surfing and frisbee. He had been to a few amusement parks.

"Well, that's enough about my summer," Lucas said at last. "I don't want to make you jealous, when you've been stuck here in a grocery store all summer."

Grace shook her head. "Actually, it's been surprisingly fun here. I wouldn't have traded it for a summer in California."

Lucas raised his eyebrows. "Really! You're enjoying working in the grocery store, then?"

"Well, it's not always easy, but it's good," Grace said. "Right now the main thing is that we have to improve our business. We just got a dollar store in town that's competing with us."

She filled Lucas in about the dollar store. He listened, his forehead creased.

"If you ask me," he said, "this is a good time for your parents to sell the store and retire. They must be close to retirement age anyway." He leaned back in his seat. "My dad retired early last year, and he's loving it. He and my mom can travel any time they want now."

"I'm sure my parents don't want to sell the store," Grace said. "Besides, it's the only grocery store in town. If somebody doesn't fight to keep it in business, Fraser's Mill will turn into a food desert. All we'll have is the dollar store. People will have to drive to Cadillac to buy groceries."

Lucas shrugged. "Somebody else could run the store," he said. "Anyway, if your parents sold the store it wouldn't be your family's problem at that point."

"But it would still be the town's problem," Grace said. "You don't understand, Lucas. This is a big issue, and it's important to combat it. Dollar stores are taking over the country, especially in the rural areas. Somebody's got to stand up to them."

"Sure, of course." Lucas ran a hand through his hair. "And I'm sure some people will. All I'm saying is, it would be better for your parents if they retired now."

Didn't he understand what the store meant to her family? "Well, I don't think they'd agree with you," Grace said. "They've worked hard in this store for thirty years."

"All the more reason they should get to retire." Lucas laughed. He leaned forward. "Just trying to be practical, Grace."

"Sure—thanks."

It was easy for Lucas to make a quick analysis of the situation; he wasn't involved in it himself. He didn't understand family businesses or small towns.

The waitress came by with the bill. Grace tried to pay her portion, but Lucas insisted on paying it himself. "Why don't we go get ice cream?" he suggested. "It's a hot day, and that looked like a quaint little ice cream stand down the street."

Grace hesitated. She didn't want to prolong this hangout or have Lucas spend more money on her. But refusing to go to the ice cream stand seemed unkind. She could pay for her own ice cream. "All right," she said. "We can do that."

At the ice cream stand they had to wait in line in the blazing sun. The line was still long in front of them when Grace's phone rang. It was her parents' cell.

"Sorry, I'll be right back," Grace said. "I've gotta take this."

She stepped away and answered the phone. "Hello?"

"Grace, I've got a problem," Mom's voice said. "I hate to ask this, because I know you have the day off, but could you possibly man the cash register from five to seven? Natalie asked me if she could get off at five to go into Cadillac with her family. We've got a lot of customers and I can't handle the store all evening by myself. I'm just really overwhelmed, and it's been a long day. I'm getting too old for this."

In other circumstances Grace might have been disappointed to get called into work, but this provided her with a legitimate reason to end her hangout with Lucas.

"I can do it," Grace said.

"I can't hear you," Mom said. "The connection's bad."

Fraser's Mill reception could be spotty. Grace walked farther from the ice cream stand. "Is this better?"

"That's better. Now I can hear you. What were you saying?"

"I said I can come in from five to seven," Grace said. "I don't have anything pressing to do in the evening anyway."

"Is that guy from California still here? The one that took you out to dinner that time?"

"Lucas? He's still here," Grace said. "We were in line at the ice cream stand when you called."

She peered back down the street toward the ice cream stand. Lucas was still in line, talking to a girl in a red, white, and blue sundress. Hannah. Why was Hannah talking to Lucas? Did she always swoop down on any new guy who came to town? Wasn't it enough that she hung out with Doc all the time?

"Oh, Grace, I don't want to ruin your hangout," Mom said. "Maybe I can manage by myself, after all."

"Huh? No, Mom, it's all right." Grace looked over at Lucas again. Now was a great opportunity to spill her feelings about the situation. "I think we're about done hanging out," she confessed. "It's—well, it's awkward. He's an okay guy, but he just rubs me the wrong way."

"Is he the one who likes oysters?"

"Yeah. There's no way I could see myself dating him. Nothing I like is good enough for him. I don't know why he even wants to hang out with me. He didn't want to eat lunch at the fire hall because he didn't think the food would be good. He doesn't see the point of trying to save the store, either. He thinks you and Dad should just sell the store and retire."

"Well, I have to say, on days like today, that idea sounds pretty attractive," Mom said. "But I'm sorry the two of you don't get along as well as you'd thought you might. He must like you—he took time out of his family's vacation to visit you. If you're not interested, you'd better tell him."

Grace groaned. "I know, I know. I've gotta figure out how to tell him this isn't going to work out. But I don't know how to bring it up."

"Often the best thing is to be direct. Just be honest with him. It's a lot better than letting him go around thinking you like him."

She was right. "Thanks, Mom," Grace said. "Well, I'd better get back before he gets to the front of the line. I can just see him ordering me an ice cream I don't like."

Mom laughed. "All right," she said. "See you at five."

When Grace got back to the ice cream stand, Hannah was gone and Lucas was near the head of the line.

"Just in time." He winked at Grace. "I was about to have to order for you."

"That was my mom," Grace said. "They need me to help out in the store. I was supposed to have the day off today, but the employee that has tonight's shift has to leave, so I've gotta go to work at five."

"What?" Lucas shook his head. "Can't you find anybody to take your place? It's not right for you to have to come in when you have the day off."

"Well, it's my family's grocery store," Grace said. "I don't want some other person to be stuck working when I can do it."

"When do you get off?"

"Seven."

They approached the ordering window. "It's on me," Lucas said.

"But you paid at the tavern," Grace said. "I was thinking I could get my own ice cream."

"As I said, it's on me."

Protest was useless. Grace ordered the smallest ice cream cone on the menu. Lucas got a flurry.

All the tables around the ice cream stand were full, so Grace and Lucas went to the park for some shade. Now would be the time to tell Lucas things wouldn't work between them. Grace still wasn't sure how to start that conversation.

"I've got an idea," Lucas said. "When you get off work, we can find a restaurant for dinner — there must be some in Cadillac. While we're there, we can see the fireworks over the lake. It's not as exciting as I had hoped for our first big holiday together, but that's okay."

Their first big holiday together?

"Wait a minute," Grace said. "You're talking like you and I are dating."

His brow furrowed. "We are dating."

Grace took a step backward. Oh, no. This was bad. He must be confused.

"No," she said, looking Lucas square in the face. "No — we're not. What would make you think that?"

"What do you mean? We've been going out since May."

"Since May?" Grace's volume rose. "We went out to dinner one time."

No wonder Lucas had been so insistent on coming to Fraser's Mill and paying for Grace's food. A sick knot formed in Grace's stomach.

Lucas frowned. "Right. I took you to dinner at the end of May. We were going to go out again before you left, but you couldn't make it. We emailed back and forth for a month. Then you agreed to let me visit you in Michigan. I understood we were seeing each other exclusively."

"Well, I didn't!" Grace said. Her face was heating up, and it wasn't because of the weather. "Nobody said anything like that. I went out with you once. One date. Well, two, counting today. That doesn't mean we're in a relationship!"

Her ice cream cone was dripping all over her hand. Never hold an ice cream cone during an argument.

"So you don't want to date me?" Lucas's face was turning red.

Grace shook her head. "No. I don't think we're a good match for each other."

"Then what were you doing sending all those emails, letting me come to visit you? Just leading me on?" His mouth twisted.

"Leading you on!" Grace exclaimed. "I wasn't trying to lead you on. We were just starting to get to know each other. I was trying to figure out if we were compatible. But now I've figured out that we aren't."

Her hands, sticky with ice cream, were shaking. How could she have made such a hash of this? She should have said no to that second date the minute he suggested it. Then there wouldn't be all this confusion.

"What are you talking about?" Lucas exclaimed. "We would be great for each other. We're both Catholic, we work at the same school, we both like reading and nerdy things and working out—what's so incompatible?"

Grace shook her head. "Lucas, you're a great guy," she said. "And I know we have a bunch of things in common. But I don't think our personalities work well together. I'm sorry, but I don't."

"Well, I think you're delusional," Lucas scoffed. "If we don't work well together, who else do you think you're gonna find? Prince Charming? You're what, twenty-eight? You don't have a lot of time left to be that picky."

That was the last straw. "I'm twenty-seven," Grace said. "And I'd rather be single forever than be with a guy that tells me I'm too old to be picky. Goodbye."

She turned and walked away. On the way out of the park she threw the melting ice cream cone into the trash can. She hoped he saw it.

Aftermath

Grace had to talk about Lucas to somebody, and she couldn't to Mom in the grocery store with the customers listening. Dad wasn't home—he had a checkers tournament at the fire hall. Where was Alex? Probably hanging out with Charlie somewhere. Grace sat down in a rocking chair on the porch and rocked back and forth, thinking.

Alex came up the street, walking briskly despite the heat. Charlie was nowhere in sight. That was convenient. Grace bounced off the porch and hailed her.

"Alex! The wildest thing just happened, and I'm furious about it. Do you have time to listen to a rant?"

"Whoa, slow down." Alex threw up her hands. "What's going on? Are you okay?"

"I'm okay, but I'm just clean mad!" Grace said. "It's about Lucas. The guy from California."

"The guy you were meeting today?" Alex asked. "What happened?"

"Everything was horrible," Grace said. "I don't want to tell the whole thing standing out here in the sun. Let's go sit on the porch."

Alex sat down in a rocking chair. Grace sank into another one.

She explained about Lucas inviting himself to Fraser's Mill. "As soon as he mentioned coming, I didn't want him to," she said, "but I didn't know what to do. It seemed unfriendly to tell him no. I didn't want to alienate one of the few coworkers I knew back in California. Although now I've managed to alienate him anyway."

"What happened?" Alex asked.

Grace filled her in on her time with Lucas at the tavern and the ice cream stand. "I figured I'd go to work and he'd leave. But he said he wanted to take me out to dinner in Cadillac and see the fireworks there. Then—get this—then he said it wasn't as exciting as he had hoped for our first big holiday together. He thought we'd been dating all summer!"

"What in the world?" Alex's eyes widened. "He thought you were in a relationship? Did he ever ask to be your boyfriend?"

"No, he didn't! Nothing like that. But then today he said he had understood we were seeing each other exclusively."

"Wow!"

"I went out to dinner with him once in California. Only once! I would have been okay with going on a second date, but he asked me again when I was getting ready to leave for Michigan. Then after I left he started emailing me. So we've been sending emails back and forth for a few weeks. But I was just trying to get to know him better as a friend while I figured out my feelings. I did think, at the beginning, that we could be right for each other."

"Uh-huh." Alex leaned forward. "And then he asked to visit? Did he fly out here from California just to see you?"

"No, he was in the area," Grace said. "His grandma lives around here. So he asked if he could meet up with me while he was here. I didn't want to say no, because I thought it would seem unfriendly. But I guess when I agreed to meet up with him he took it as more confirmation that I was interested in him."

"Yeah, I can see that."

"I was so floored when he said we were dating. I didn't know what to say! We never had even one conversation about being in a relationship. I tried to explain that, and he got mad. He said I was leading him on all summer. And then—you won't believe this—he said, 'You're what, twenty-eight? You don't have a lot of time left to be that picky.'"

"Oh my goodness!" Alex exclaimed. "That's one of the rudest things I've ever heard."

"I was so mad! I basically told him I'd rather be single forever than be with a guy like him. Then I walked away."

"Good for you," Alex said. "Where is he now?"

"I think he's gone. Probably left town in a huff." Grace sank against the back of her chair. "Alex, do you think I led him on? I wasn't trying to, but now I'm not sure. Maybe I took too long to make up my mind about him. Do you think I should have replied to all those emails?"

"Oh…I don't know." Alex rocked her chair back and forth. "If somebody I worked with sent me an email I'd probably reply too, whether I was interested in him or not. Emailing somebody doesn't mean you're automatically in a relationship."

Grace groaned. "Who knows what he's been telling people back in California about our so-called 'relationship.' It's gonna be so awkward when I get back."

"Well, it probably won't be awkward for too long. Even if he told a bunch of people you were dating, people forget about that kind of thing pretty quickly."

"I hope so." Grace sighed. "We don't have the same break room at the school. Hopefully we won't have to interact too much."

"Yeah," Alex said. "I bet he doesn't want to be around you any more than you want to be around him."

"You're probably right."

"It's too bad you missed all the fun at the fire hall," Alex said. "Charlie and Doc and I had lunch together. Doc asked where you were. He must have missed you." She smiled meaningly.

"Oh, good grief," Grace said. "Well, I sure wish I'd been at the hall with you guys instead of at the tavern with Lucas. What else is going on this afternoon? I have to work at the store from five to seven, so I'll probably miss most of it, unfortunately."

"There's not much going on right now," Alex said. "Tonight Sam's gonna grill hamburgers and stuff down at the farm. His girlfriend's gonna be there, and Charlie's coming. You and your family should come. We've got lots of food."

"That sounds like fun," Grace said. "I'll ask my parents if they want to come. I can't get there until after seven though."

"That's fine. There should still be plenty of food left."

"Yay! Thanks a lot."

Alex got up from the rocking chair and stretched. "I should probably get back to the farm and see if my mom and Sam want any help with dinner."

After Alex left, Grace went a few minutes early to help in the store. She didn't have anything else to do, anyway.

Lucas had probably left town by now. It seemed unlikely he would hang around after Grace's rejection. Good thing he had come to Michigan to visit his grandmother, because if he had come all the way out just to see Grace, he would probably be a lot more upset right now.

Dad was gung-ho to go to the Martins' farm for dinner, and Mom said she had spent a decent amount of her day cooped up in the store and didn't intend to be cooped up anymore. So when Grace got off work they loaded up in the car—bringing Dad's knee scooter and crutches so he could use either—and drove down to the farm.

The Martin family had invited quite a few people. Sam was grilling in front of the house, and a bonfire burned out back. A few people were playing volleyball. Grace wasn't good at volleyball, so she hung out with Alex and with Sam's girlfriend Nadia from Traverse City. Nadia was friendly and smiley, and Grace could see why Sam liked her.

Doc wasn't there. Alex said she'd invited him, but he must have been too busy to come. That was a bummer. It would have been fun to hang out with him by the bonfire. Well, hopefully Grace would see him back in town later that evening.

When it got dark, everyone piled into cars and went back into town to watch the fireworks display in the park. By this time the mosquitos had come out. Grace slapped at them, wishing she had worn long pants and long sleeves, but she didn't want to go change and miss the rest of the fireworks.

Hannah was there with her phone, getting footage of the fireworks. Doc was nowhere in sight. Maybe he had had to deal with a medical emergency. He usually made a point of attending town events if he could.

Grace had less than two weeks left before she flew back to California. That didn't leave a lot of time to hang out with Doc. It was a shame that he and Grace hadn't really seen each other on the Fourth when they had spent so much time prepping for it. Well, at least they had had the fun of making the float.

❧

Grace was working the morning shift the next day when Sam came in with a crate of vegetables. It was Alex's turn to run the stand at the farmer's market, so Sam filled in for her deliveries.

"Hey, Grace," Sam called across the store. "Are you gonna get people to take apart that float? I need that trailer on Thursday, and it's a lot to take apart by myself."

Grace had forgotten about the float. That was the Martins' farm trailer—of course they would need it back. "Sam, I'm so sorry," she said. "I forgot all about it. I'll figure something out today—maybe I can get people to help this evening."

There was a lot to do in the store too. The Fourth had been busy, and Grace had a lot of cleaning and restocking to finish.

262

It was hard to tell at this point how the dollar store would affect the grocery store's business in the long run. Sales had dipped noticeably the week the dollar store opened. The totals for Fourth of July weekend were lower than last year, but Dad wasn't convinced the dollar store had caused that. Fourth of July sales fluctuated from year to year anyway. In a week or so, they might have a better idea of how things were going. Grace hoped the parade float and flyers would bring in more business. At least people had noticed the float—several people had told her they liked it.

She got off work at five and planned to find people to take apart the float. Alex was out of the question, since she wouldn't be back from the farmer's market until late and would probably be exhausted. Grace decided to try Doc first.

The clinic closed at five. This was about the time Doc usually came over to the store to get dinner, but so far he hadn't appeared. Where on earth could he be? She hadn't seen him much since the float-making. It would be fun to hang out with him again. She could see if he was at the clinic.

The clinic door was unlocked. Grace walked in and found an empty waiting room.

"Doc?" she called.

No answer. Maybe he was upstairs. Maybe he wasn't home and had left his house unlocked. Grace was beginning to feel like a burglar.

"Doc?" she called again.

"Come in," Doc's voice said from behind a door.

Grace opened the door and popped her head in. If he was busy she'd go away and come back later.

Doc was sitting at a desk covered with paperwork and mugs, his laptop in front of him, his lab coat on, his hair tousled. Grace's pulse quickened inexplicably. Well, Alex would have had an explanation. But Alex wasn't here.

Doc's eyebrows went up when he saw Grace. "Are you okay? That's quite a sunburn."

"Oh, I forgot about that," Grace said. "I didn't come about that. I already put aloe on it last night."

"Then how can I help you?" he asked, instead of making a joke like she expected. He was frowning. Maybe he'd had a bad day.

"Well, I was wondering if you'd like to help take apart the float we made for the Fourth," Grace said. "Sam needs that trailer on Thursday, so I thought I'd get a group to take it apart sometime in the next couple days."

She had been expecting Doc to perk up, since he had been so excited about the float before. To her surprise he shook his head. "Sorry, Grace. I don't think I can help this time. I'm really behind on my patient charts."

Was something wrong? "What's going on?" Grace asked. She came closer to the desk.

"Just work," Doc said. "I didn't get anything done over the weekend or the Fourth."

He wasn't looking at her, flipping through papers on his desk. Maybe he had gotten himself buried under a pile of paperwork. Grace knew that feeling well enough from her school grading.

"Is there any way I can help?" she asked. "I'm pretty good at paperwork."

He shook his head. "Confidential patient records," he said

flatly. "Thanks anyway. I hope you find people to take apart the float."

Grace stepped back, a cold sensation hitting her in the pit of her stomach. This didn't seem like Doc. She'd seen him when he was tired and overworked. He'd been cheerful then.

"What's the matter?" she asked. "Is something wrong? I haven't seen you much the last couple days."

He shook his head again. "I've been busy. I'm sure you've been too, showing your friend from California around."

Lucas. Maybe Doc had noticed Hannah talking to Lucas. Maybe he thought Hannah and Lucas had been flirting and was upset about it.

"He's gone back to L.A.," Grace said. "Doc, are you all right?"

He looked up at her, his blue eyes tense. "I'm all right," he said. "I've just gotta get this work done. You'd better find some other people to take apart your float."

"I will. But are you sure you're okay? You don't seem okay," Grace said. "If you've got a problem, I'm a pretty good listener."

She wasn't about to ask outright about Hannah. Doc hadn't opened up to her about his love life, and now didn't seem like a good time to bring it up.

Doc's eyebrows drew together. "Why do you care? We barely know each other. I'm just the guy who comes along to help whenever you're in a jam!"

Grace's mouth fell open. He wasn't upset with Hannah or Lucas—he was upset with her. That was how he felt about her? She was a damsel in distress, and he was sick of rescuing her? In one second, all her opinions of Doc flew out the window.

"Well, I didn't know I was a bother to you!" Grace burst out. "I thought we were becoming friends. I didn't know you were gonna resent helping me."

"I don't resent helping you," Doc exclaimed. "I just think—"

"You certainly sound like you resent it," Grace said. "You offered to help—I never expected or forced you to. I didn't make you drive me around when my car broke down. I didn't make you work on that float all Saturday morning. That was your choice!"

"Yeah, that's right," Doc said. "And this is my choice right now: I'm gonna sit here and work on my paperwork!"

"Fine! I'll go find other people to take apart the float."

"Good!" Doc turned back to his papers.

"Fine!" Grace marched toward the door. "Why don't you just send me a bill for all the times you helped me out, and we'll be square?"

"Grace, wait—" Doc's voice came after her.

She slammed the door behind her.

Back home, she flung herself face-down on her bed and cried. If Doc didn't want to help her, he shouldn't have offered to help. Did he expect her to read his mind? It was mortifying that he thought of her as somebody who was always looking for someone to make her life easier. She was a hard-working, independent woman. She didn't normally run around begging for help. All those things he had helped her with were things that didn't usually happen.

And Alex had thought he liked her! He had just been trying to be kind and helpful, the same way he treated the patients who came to the doctor's office. He wasn't interested in her, he was just a nice guy—one who apparently regretted being nice to her now.

From now on, Grace would leave him alone. He could do all the doctor work he wanted. She wouldn't get in his way.

Maybe this town wasn't as friendly as Grace had thought. She still had to find people to take the float apart, but after that, she was going to focus on the store and getting ready to go back to California where she belonged. Dad's cast came off tomorrow, and her flight to L.A. was on the 16th. That didn't leave much time to help her parents save the store.

Changes

Grace manned the store Friday night while her parents were at the hospital in Cadillac, where Dad was getting his cast off.

It was a good thing he'd be back on his feet, because they needed him in the store. The parade float and the flyers seemed to have done some good. The totals were better this week than the previous week, and they had a few new customers from around town. Right now Grace was busy with a line of five customers at the cash register.

"Did you make these, Grace?" the woman at the checkout asked, holding up a package of oatmeal cookies with dried cherries. Grace recognized her as Sheriff Hank's wife.

Grace smiled. "Yes, I did."

"How do you find the time?" Hank's wife asked. "Aren't you busy getting ready to go back to California?"

Everybody in this town knew everything about everybody. "I've been fitting in some baking in the evenings," Grace said. "And getting ready for California at the same time."

"Wow! You are one busy young lady."

Grace laughed. "I guess so," she said. "I just want to help my parents with the store as much as I can before I go. Did you know we've just started a social media page?" She pulled a slip of paper from a box on the counter. "If you want to know what baked goods and local produce we have, we're posting about it daily on the page now."

"My goodness! Thank you, Grace."

Grace was determined to show the people in town that their store could do things the dollar store and the forty-five-minutes-away Walmart couldn't. The main thing she could think of doing herself was making more homemade baked goods, so she had been spending a lot of her free time baking, being careful not to burn herself. She wouldn't want to have to go to Doc's.

As Grace helped the last customer in line, the bell over the door jingled. It was her parents.

"Howdy, Gracie," Dad exclaimed. "Look at my new boot!"

The cast on Dad's foot had been replaced with a bulky boot brace.

"I'm allowed to bear weight on it." He smiled widely. "No more scooter for me. Won't be long before I don't need the crutches either."

"You better make sure you don't overcompensate and injure the other foot," Mom said. "Remember, the doctor told you not to overdo it."

"Now, don't you start fussing over me. I'll be careful. You don't have to worry about a thing."

Mom shook her head at him. "Impossible man!"

"I can't wait to show Doc," Dad said. "He's not around now, is he?"

Grace shook her head. "I haven't seen him."

She hadn't seen Doc since the argument, even in the grocery store. Maybe he was avoiding her, getting his groceries elsewhere or coming in when she wasn't working.

"We'd better get back to the house," Mom said. "Ben, you need to do your physical therapy. I'm going to put some food together and see if I can get any work done on my novel. And Katie said she's going to call. Grace, are you all right closing the store by yourself?"

"Sure, Mom," Grace said. "Please don't wait on me for dinner—I'm going to see if Alex wants to hang out."

She couldn't face the thought of doing National Board prep tonight. Her mind was too full of other thoughts. Improving the store. Doc avoiding her. Getting ready to start the school year. What she needed was a relaxed hangout with a friend before going back to California.

Alex knew all about Grace's argument with Doc—Grace had filled her in on Wednesday, and Alex too was at a loss to understand Doc's sudden change in behavior—but Grace was determined not to make that the topic of the hangout.

∞∞∞∞∞

Alex replied immediately to Grace's text asking if she'd like to hang out. "Sure, I'd love to," she said. "Wanna go down to the diner and get milkshakes?"

"You're just hoping we'll run into Charlie," Grace teased her.

"Maybe." Alex sent back a winky face. "He's working late tonight."

Alex drove over to Grace's house, and she and Grace walked down to the diner. The evening was warm, but not more humid than usual.

Charlie wasn't behind the counter in the diner. Another guy who worked there was taking orders. If Charlie was there, he was in the back someplace.

"Sorry, Alex," Grace said in an undertone. "Maybe Charlie took a break."

Alex elbowed her instead of responding.

"What?" Grace asked.

Alex motioned with her head. Grace looked. It was Doc and Hannah, sitting in the far booth of the diner. Hannah, facing Grace and Alex, must have seen them, but she didn't show any sign of recognition.

Of course Doc and Hannah would be hanging out here. Well, no matter. Wild horses wouldn't drag her to approach those two, and she doubted either of them was likely to approach her.

"What do you think?" Alex hissed in her ear.

"Ssh!" Grace turned back to the counter.

"I think I'm gonna try something new," she said, louder. "I'm not gonna get a milkshake. I'm gonna try that mixed berry smoothie they keep advertising."

"Charlie says it's not actually that great," Alex said.

"Well, I think I'll try it."

They waited for their drinks at the end of the counter. Alex kept glancing over at Doc and Hannah. Grace kept her head turned the other direction.

"I still think they're probably an item," she told Alex, low.

Alex shook her head. "Maybe they're just hanging out—as friends. I was positive he liked you."

"Well, I think you were mistaken."

Drinks in hand, the two girls walked toward the park. A small river ran through the park, making it a favorite summer hangout spot. They sat on the grass by the riverbank. The evening sun turned the rippling water to gold, and the sound of crickets filled the air.

"There's only one more week until you go back," Alex said. "Are you glad you spent your summer here instead of in California?"

"Well, if I hadn't come out here, I wouldn't have gotten to hang out with you," Grace said. "Besides, I might not have learned about the dollar store taking my parents' business."

"That's true."

"I think the main thing we need to do is show people what a good thing they have with the grocery store right here in town. It's close and convenient and has a lot of great stuff—including all your nice farm produce—and we just need to get the word out."

"Mm-hm." Alex took a drink of her milkshake.

"Hopefully the social media page for the store is helping too," Grace said. "A bunch of people have told me they saw my baked goods advertised, so they must be seeing the page. Of course, I won't be able to bake any more things after I go back to California. I don't know how much time my mom will have to do that."

"Hey, I've got an idea," Alex said. "If your mom doesn't have time to bake cookies and stuff for the store, maybe I could do it and sell them there. I think fresh baked goods really do draw people."

"How would you possibly find time to do that? You're super busy already."

"I have odd free hours here and there," Alex said. "It'll be good for me to have another hobby. And I can make cookies and things for Charlie at the same time. It'll be fun."

All in all, Grace was leaving the store in good hands. She would miss Alex in California, though. She didn't have any close friends back in L.A.

She wasn't sorry to leave Doc behind. For a few days, she had thought they could be close friends too. That was in the past. Doc hadn't made any effort to make up with her, and she certainly wasn't going to go over to the clinic to try to make up with him.

Go West

Saturday, July 16th, rolled around, and with it Grace's flight back to California. As usual, she had to fly early in the morning to get the 2,000-mile trip done in one day.

She finished her packing the night before and said goodbye to Alex, Charlie, and a few other townspeople she ran into. Dorothy stopped over at the Murrays' house to bring Grace some cookies to take on her flight.

It was going to be hard, leaving all these people she had seen all summer. Her parents, Alex, Dorothy, Elaine, Charlie, Sam, and all those other people who made Fraser's Mill what it was — they were a great community.

She still hadn't seen Doc even once since their fight, but she didn't care if she said goodbye to him anyway.

Her parents both went with her to the airport, even though it was forty-five minutes away and it was four o'clock in the morning. Grace breathed in the crisp morning air as they drove through the pines. She'd be back in the heat and the smog of California in the evening.

Grace arrived early for her flight. Mom pulled up at the curb outside the airport after Grace insisted there was no point in her parents waiting inside. "You're running the store today," she told them. "I think you both oughtta go home and take a nap until opening time."

Grace's suitcases took up a lot of the car. Dad helped her lift them down—he promised he wasn't going to hurt his foot—and they all stood there on the sidewalk outside the airport doors.

"Gracie," Dad said, "I want you to know how much it meant to me and your mother that you spent more than half of your summer helping us out. You're a good daughter, and I'm proud of you."

Mom squeezed Grace's arm. "Me too," she said. "We couldn't have managed without you, Grace. It's been difficult for your dad and me to run the store even before he broke his foot—I can't imagine what we would have done by ourselves during that time. Thank you so much for everything. I hope all this doesn't make it difficult for you to get ready for the school year."

Grace hugged them both. "I was happy to help. And it was lots of fun spending time with you and being around town again."

"Good luck with everything," Dad said. "Call us often, you hear?"

"Of course! I'm going to need a full update on everything about the dollar store and how your profits are going. I'm not going to stand idly by and watch them drive you out of business!"

The trip out to California was uneventful, which was a mercy, because Grace was in no mood to deal with delays and rescheduled flights. She wanted to get back and dive into all the things she needed to do. School would start in a few weeks, and she wasn't ready at all.

On the plane, Grace rummaged through her backpack and pulled out a notebook. That list of goals she'd made earlier in the summer was in there. She had been so busy working in the store and hanging out with people in Fraser's Mill that she had almost forgotten all the things she had planned to do this summer.

1. Finish the school year well. Prepare reviews and quizzes carefully for the next two days. That was crossed out, finished.

2. Work on National Board prep at least one hour every evening. She had begun strong with that and then slacked off for most of the summer. Her work for the store had been important, but there were so many times she could have worked on National Board materials and had chosen to do other things instead. Now she'd be way behind. She'd better devote a lot more time to that before the school year started.

3. Be more consistent with daily exercise. Over the last few weeks she'd been even worse with her exercise than usual.

4. Make a Shipt shopping schedule for the summer to make enough money but not get overwhelmed so there's no time left for other things. Well, she'd kept busy at Murray's Grocery, but the pay hadn't been much. After she paid for her new catalytic converter, there would be hardly anything left.

She hadn't done much for her planned goals from the beginning of the summer. But she had helped her parents. They should be better equipped now to compete with the dollar store. So she'd done something worth doing. Now she'd have to buckle down and work on attaining the rest of those goals she'd been ignoring for so many weeks.

Somehow, Grace couldn't get excited about those goals right now. She stuffed the notebook into her backpack and looked out the plane window. All she could see were clouds. Somewhere beyond those clouds, far below, Michigan was getting farther and farther away. Grace sighed and turned from the window.

An Evening at Home

It was late afternoon, in blazing heat, when the Uber pulled up in front of Grace's apartment building. Grace struggled to get the suitcases out of the small car and up to the third floor.

She opened the door and breathed in stale air. Jen wasn't there—she was never around at this time of day—and the blinds were closed, making the apartment dark. Grace opened the blinds and let in the strong sunshine. Her plants on the windowsill were wilted and brown. She had forgotten to ask Jen to water them.

Well, she was back. Life was back to normal.

There was nothing good to eat in the apartment. Grace had used up the perishables before she went to Michigan, and she had forgotten there wouldn't be any when she came back. She wasn't going to use Jen's food. They were careful about not eating the other's food without asking.

She checked the cupboard where she kept non-perishable

food. The cupboard held a can of corn, a can of minestrone, a bar of dark chocolate, and a bag of potato chips. She wouldn't have thought her pantry was so empty. But she didn't want to get an Uber and go to the store. The only store within walking distance was a dollar store.

Soup and potato chips—the same dinner she'd saved Doc from eating, that day he was so tired. That had been a fun evening. But the memory was clouded over by the argument they'd had. Now she was in California, and he was in Michigan, and she didn't need to think about him anymore.

Grace opened the can of soup and poured it into a pan. It was food, and she ought to be grateful she had it. Later she could figure out about going shopping.

After dinner she worked out a plan for what to do over the next few weeks, typing it up on her laptop. She needed to get her apartment back in shape by grocery shopping, unpacking, and cleaning. She needed to get her car back from the garage, whenever the catalytic converter came in. And she also needed to get ready for the new school year.

She made a grocery list and ordered the groceries from Shipt. It was cheaper to pay the delivery fee than it would have been to take an Uber and get her own groceries. Besides, this way there was no chance of running into Lucas at the store.

Grace had the whole long evening to herself. Jen had texted her that she hoped she'd gotten in okay, and that she would be home late—she was hanging out with her boyfriend. Grace couldn't stand to plunk herself down at her computer and work on National Board stuff. The goals she had reviewed on the plane were well and good, but they could wait until tomorrow.

Grace flopped down on the flat-cushioned couch, bonking her head on the armrest. What was there to do? Maybe she should read a book or watch something. It was strange not having anybody to talk to. She had gotten used to having her parents and neighbors around all the time. It would be better when school started and she was around the school kids and teachers all day.

How had Jen dealt with being here by herself the whole time Grace was gone? Maybe she was so busy it didn't matter if there was someone else in the apartment or not.

Grace couldn't get herself to read anything or pick something to watch. Maybe she ought to take a nap. It had been a long day, being up since three A.M. Michigan time, which was midnight California time. In Michigan she would be asleep by now.

❧

Grace opened bleary eyes at the sound of keys in the door. The apartment was dim. She must have fallen asleep. Jen was back, unless that was a burglar with keys.

"Grace?" Jen's voice was loud. "Are you here?" The overhead light snapped on, and Grace sat up, blinking in the bright light.

"Hi, Jen," she said, still blinking. "Sorry, I just woke up from a nap."

"You're back!" Jen hugged her. She was wearing a flowered rayon dress. She must have had a fancy date with Ryan. "It's good to see you," Jen said. "You don't know how empty this apartment felt the whole time you were gone."

"I believe it," Grace said. "I've got an idea. I'll make tea, and we can catch up on our summers."

"Oh, Grace, I'm sorry," Jen said. "Ryan's actually waiting for me outside. I just came in to change clothes, and then we're going to the park for a walk."

"Oh, okay," Grace said. "What time is it?"

"It's like ten o'clock. I won't be out way too late—I have to get up early again."

"Have a good time," Grace told her. "Don't get mugged!"

"Don't worry, we won't," Jen said. She whisked off to her room to change, then rushed out the door to meet Ryan.

Grace wasn't tired anymore after her nap. She might as well do something. She turned on an oldies playlist she had made on her phone after the town dance the other week, dragged her suitcases to her room, and started unpacking.

Her phone dinged. It was a message from Alex. What was Alex doing up at this hour?

"I know it's late, but I learned something today," Alex's message read. "Remember when you had to sell all that chicken that was about to expire, and Charlie bought a lot of it? Charlie told me today that they still have to use up a lot of that frozen chicken, and he doesn't know how Doc talked him into buying so much. That wasn't Charlie's idea—it was Doc's!"

"Huh!" Grace replied. "Wow."

If true, that was a nice thing Doc had done for the store. Although it didn't change what had happened later.

"I still think Doc was interested in you," Alex texted. "He never ran around trying to help the store before you came to town."

"Well, I guess he got tired of helping," Grace replied. "You know how I told you he thought I was taking advantage of his helpfulness. He thought I was some kind of moocher. If there's anything I don't want to be, it's a moocher!"

"I don't know," Alex said. "Doc's seemed pretty gloomy the last few days. I think he misses you."

"Misses me? There's no way he misses me," Grace said. "He started that argument. He could have come and talked to me any time before I left, but he was going out of his way to avoid me. And besides, he and Hannah seem glued at the hip. If they're not dating yet, they'll probably start any day."

"OK, OK, I won't push it," Alex replied. "How was your first evening in California?"

It hadn't been great, but what could you expect for the first night back?

"I ordered groceries and took a nap and now I'm unpacking my stuff," Grace told Alex. "For that matter, shouldn't you be asleep?"

"Yeah, you're right, I should get off," Alex said. "I was baking raspberry bars for the store, but they're done now. I just wanted to tell you about Doc and the chicken."

Grace finished unpacking her suitcases and got ready for bed. She had her pajamas on and was looking for a missing phone charger when Jen came back in, smiling from ear to ear.

"Look!" She held out her hand, something sparkling on it. Grace hurried over to look. It was a diamond ring.

Good for Ryan—Jen had been waiting for him to propose for a while. He must have finally asked her.

"Jen, I'm so happy for you!" Grace pulled her roommate into a hug. "That's wonderful!"

"I'm so happy!" Jen was beaming. "Come on, sit down, and I'll tell you all about it."

Ryan had proposed on the top of a hill that overlooked the brilliant lights of the city. Jen said she had never been so surprised as when Ryan got down on one knee and pulled a ring box out of his pocket.

"We're going to get married in the winter," Jen said. "Around New Year's. We can't set the exact date until we check with the church. I won't finish nursing school until the spring, but we didn't see any point in waiting until then, since I'll be just as busy after I finish school."

"You're probably right," Grace said. "They say people are always waiting around to do things when they're less busy, and most of the time 'less busy' never comes."

Jen nodded. "Right, that's exactly what I was thinking. Of course, that means we have to start planning the wedding right away. Did you know lots of reception venues book a year ahead?"

Grace shook her head. "Wow." Her sister Katie had had her wedding reception at the fireman's hall in Fraser's Mill. You could usually get the hall with a couple months' notice.

"Do you want a cup of tea or anything?" Grace asked. "I'll bet you're way too excited to go to sleep."

"Thanks, but I've got to make some calls," Jen said. "Ryan says my parents knew about the proposal ahead of time, but I want to tell them and my sisters how it went before the news leaks out and they hear it from someone else."

That was bound to take a while. Grace decided to go to bed.

She had said her prayers and gotten in bed when a thought struck her. With Jen getting married, she would have to find another roommate. Who in the world would she room with? She didn't want to room with a total stranger. One of the other female teachers from her school could be good, but she didn't know if any of them were looking for a place to live.

If she didn't find anyone, she would have to move to a smaller apartment, because she could never pay rent on a two-bedroom apartment in L.A. by herself. But she didn't want to live by herself. It was hard enough that Jen was gone most of the time. She couldn't imagine never having anyone around — it would drive her crazy.

Why did some people like living by themselves? What was going on in Thoreau's head when he decided to move to Walden Pond?

Grace pulled out her phone and looked up Thoreau and Walden Pond.

Apparently Thoreau wasn't such a hermit as she had thought. She had always believed he lived out there alone with nature at Walden Pond. The Internet informed her that Thoreau walked into town every day and had friends over frequently. His mom did a lot of his laundry and cooking. Some hermit.

Real hermits did live by themselves, but Grace didn't think she was cut out for that kind of life. She'd better find a roommate. She ought to start figuring that out.

She had too many things to do, and all of them seemed like a lot of work. Grace might as well get some sleep while she could.

Family Meeting

The following Wednesday afternoon, Grace was going through National Board paperwork when she got a text from her mother: "Are you available this afternoon for a video call with us and Katie and Thomas? We need to have a family meeting."

Grace hoped nothing terrible had happened. Probably no one was hurt or sick, because Mom would have just said so. They did have family calls occasionally—like on Easter or birthdays or other holidays—but only for fun.

Grace got another text, this one from Katie. "Do you know what's going on with this family meeting thing?" Katie asked. "Mom just told me she and Dad will explain at the meeting. You don't think something terrible has happened, do you?"

"Mom didn't tell me anything either," Grace told her. "I guess we'll find out at the meeting."

At five P.M. California time, which was eight P.M. Michigan time, all five Murrays got on a video call.

There was a flurry of hellos. Katie was holding baby Rosie, who was even cuter than the last time Grace had seen her. The boys were running around in the background. Thomas, calling from Florida, had a new haircut. Grace's parents looked the same as they had a few days ago. They seemed cheery. Some of the tension in Grace's shoulders relaxed.

"Mom, Dad, what's all this about?" Thomas asked. "You said this was a family meeting?"

"Your mom and I have made an important decision, and we wanted to talk to all of you about it in person," Dad said. "Or as close to in person as we can get."

"It's something we've been thinking about for a while," Mom said. "Especially with the dollar store moving into town."

A sinking feeling hit Grace in the gut. Was this about the store?

Dad cleared his throat. "You all know your mother wants to be a novelist," he said.

Grace and her siblings nodded. They all knew about Mom's book.

"I want to find a way for her to have more time to write. She's tried working in the store during the day and moonlighting as a novelist, but that's hard to do."

"Also, your dad's foot isn't what it used to be before he broke it," Mom said. "He still has to be careful with it, and he won't get that boot off for a while. It's been a struggle getting around."

"Now, Liz, it's a lot better than when I had that cast on," Dad said.

"Still, he's not as young as he used to be," Mom said. "He

can't race around the way he did thirty years ago when we first opened the store."

The suspense was killing Grace. "Mom, Dad," she burst out, "please, tell us what the decision was, and then you can roll back and tell us why you made it!"

"Patience, Gracie," Dad said. "We're getting to it."

Grace sank back into her chair with a sigh.

"The other thing is that the dollar store is real competition," Mom said. "We've realized that if we want to compete with it, we're going to have to put in a lot more work than we're doing now just to make the same amount of money. We would need to advertise more and probably expand the business."

Were they giving up on the store?

"So what are you planning to do?" Grace asked.

"We've been thinking about the best thing to do—for ourselves, our family, and the town," Dad said. "And we had an idea that oughtta be good for everybody. We're gonna sell the store and the house and move to southern Michigan. Your mother will have time to write, and we'll be close to our grandkids."

This had to be a bad dream. They were selling the store? After the thirty years of hard work they had put into it?

"You're moving by us?" Katie squealed. "Arthur, get over here and listen to this! Mom and Dad are planning to move close to us!"

"That sounds like a good idea to me," Thomas said. "It'll be great for Mom to work on her book. And I've thought for a while that running the store was getting to be too much for you."

No, no, no. How could they do it? How could they leave Fraser's Mill?

"Gracie, you're mighty quiet," Dad said. "Are you all right?"

"Oh boy, Dad, I don't know what to say," Grace said. "I mean, I don't want you and Mom to be overworked in the store. And it would be great for you to be closer to the grandkids. But I hate the thought of you selling the store and moving. Especially when we were just trying to beat the dollar store. It's like the dollar store won without even having to try!" Tears sprang to her eyes.

Mom shook her head. "Sweetie, it's not like the dollar store put us out of business," she said. "If something like that had happened, I would feel terrible and angry. But the dollar store is just one of the reasons we decided to do this. It's sad having all our children live so far away. We wanted to see at least some of you more often, and that isn't going to happen in Fraser's Mill. Besides, I really do need more time if I'm going to write that book. I'll never get going as a novelist if I never have the time."

"What's going to happen to the store?" Grace asked. "Do you have somebody who's planning to buy it?"

"Not yet," Dad said. "We're going to start looking for a buyer. Chances are we'll find somebody in the area who wants to buy it. We've done a lot to that place in the last thirty years."

"And the house will be for sale right next door," Mom said. "We were thinking we might sell it as a package—the house and the store—if anybody wanted to buy both. It could be a great deal for somebody."

"Well, I think that's just great," Thomas said. "I've felt bad about living down here in Florida and leaving you guys back in Michigan by yourselves. I'll be glad when you're living close to Katie and Arthur."

There was some scuffling in the background, and Katie called over her shoulder, "Boys! Quiet down! No, Grandma and Grandpa aren't coming over today. You can come say hi in a minute."

Dad chuckled. "Those two aren't half as loud as Grace and Thomas used to be."

Grace could see why her parents would want to be closer to Katie and their grandchildren. But she hated the thought of all the work they had put into the store going to waste, especially after the last month and a half she'd spent working with them. And the house! All three Murray kids had grown up in that house. It was the only home Grace had known before she went to college. She couldn't picture strangers living in that house and running the store, while her parents lived in some small unfamiliar house elsewhere.

The conversation was still going on. Mom was explaining cheerfully about her book. "I'm still halfway through the first draft, but I know I can finish it when I get a little time. I was able to get a bit done when Grace was here. I just haven't had a chance to touch it since then."

Grace had known Mom wanted to write this book, but she hadn't understood how much. She had always figured keeping the store running was their first priority. She hadn't realized how much the store work drained her parents' time and energy.

"Another thing is," Dad said, "we'd have to sell the store at some point anyway. Your mother and I aren't as young as we were, and we don't have anybody to pass the store down to."

"We didn't want to push any of you to take it over, just because it was in the family," Mom said. "We wanted you to grow up and do the things you want to do. We're really proud of each of you for following your dreams and talents."

It all made sense, but Grace still had a sick feeling in the pit of her stomach.

"Aren't you sad about leaving the house?" she asked.

"Of course we're sad to leave the house!" Mom exclaimed. "It's been our home for such a long time. But when all's said and done, a house is just a building. People are what's important. And all the people who are most important to us are pretty far away."

That was true. It must be lonely for Grace's parents with their kids scattered across the United States.

Katie's boys had clambered onto her lap to say hello, and the baby was shrieking in the background.

"Well, I think I'd better get off," Katie said. "The boys are supposed to start getting ready for bed, and Rosie needs a diaper change."

"Of course," Mom said. "Well, we should probably get off too. I'm going to see if I can get anything done on my novel before I go to bed."

"Thank you all for coming," Dad said. "We oughtta do this more often. It almost feels like we're all in the same room."

"But not nearly as good," Mom interjected. "Video calls feel so distant. Besides, most of the time someone's camera isn't working, or their mic isn't on, or there's some kind of other problem. It's so distracting. I can't wait to see at least some of you in person soon. When Grace came for the summer, I remembered how much I'd missed my kids."

"Well, we'd better say goodnight," Dad said. "Love you."

"Love you," Grace said. "Bye."

Decision

Grace flopped down on the uncomfortable couch, hugging a pillow to her chest. Why did she feel so awful about this whole thing?

It didn't even affect her. She normally came to visit her parents at Christmas and another time or two during the year. She could still visit them, and what did it matter if their house was different? Mom would set up the familiar furniture and hang the "Horse and Buggy Days" painting over the couch. She and Dad wouldn't be so stressed, and she would finish her book and maybe get it published. It would be great for them.

Meanwhile, Grace had her life out in California. She had school work and National Board prep, which would kick into high gear once classes started and she could gather material to submit for the different components of the certification. She still needed to find a roommate to replace Jen, so that would keep her busy too.

Busy, but lonely. After a summer in a small town, where everyone knew everyone and there was always something going on, Grace's L.A. apartment seemed boring. The myriads of strangers outside were still strangers. Grace's roommate was going off and getting married. She didn't know anybody else that would work to room with. And she didn't have close friends at the school.

She ought to make some friends. She could find a young adult group or something. There was probably a Catholic group somewhere in the area. There was no reason she couldn't meet new people and make new friends.

But hang it all, she wanted the old people and the old friends.

Alex and Charlie, Sam, Dorothy, Elaine, all the other friendly townspeople. She wouldn't see any of them, with her parents moving out of Fraser's Mill. She wouldn't be there for Christmas or holidays. Now if she ever came back, she would be a visitor, and would have to stay at Alex's. The town would be everybody's home except hers.

Home.

Grace looked up from the couch and saw the wall calendar still sitting on that page and quote she had forgotten to change a long time ago: "There is nothing like staying at home for real comfort."

It was still a stupid Mrs. Elton quote misattributed to Jane Austen. Well, Grace was staying at home, but it wasn't real comfort—her head was angled against the hard arm of the couch—and she was beginning to think it wasn't home either.

She didn't like living alone. She didn't want to live in this apartment without Jen. She didn't even like this apartment. She was only here because she taught school here. And why was she teaching school here, exactly?

She taught because she liked English, and she liked teaching kids, and that was what she had wanted to do all through college. And the L.A. school was a prestigious job. She was on her way to becoming a National Board certified teacher, which was something lots of teachers didn't even do. She was doing something worthwhile to help future generations. She had a big future ahead of her, maybe even becoming a principal. It was the big important thing she'd always wanted.

But that didn't take away the feeling that she had reached a dead end, and that she had lost the only home she'd ever had.

This apartment wasn't home. Her parents' new house wouldn't be home. She hadn't even lived there. Fraser's Mill wouldn't be home, because her family wouldn't be there anymore and the house and store would belong to strangers. She wouldn't have anywhere to call home at all.

Grace's stomach growled. She hauled herself off the couch and went to preheat the oven for a flatbread pizza. Good thing she had bought some easy-to-make foods the other day, because she couldn't stand to cook right now.

At the kitchen window, Grace looked out over the streets and buildings outside. Concrete and traffic. She missed the fresh air of Fraser's Mill and the neighbors who were always coming by the house. She even missed seeing Doc on his driveway, tinkering with his car.

She had to get out of her own head and focus on something else. Maybe catching up on her online notifications would help.

She logged onto her social media. The first post on her news feed was from the Fraser's Mill town page, which she had followed earlier in the summer. The post advertised an upcoming church rummage sale. People could bring items to donate, or volunteer to work at the sale, or just come and shop.

That was sure to be fun. Grace could imagine the people bringing in all kinds of items, from furniture to clothing to books, and the volunteers sorting through it and joking around. Probably her parents would bring some things. Probably all kinds of friendly neighbors and townspeople would be involved.

There was a new video from Hannah about the Fourth of July. She had put together the video footage she and Doc had taken. Grace didn't click on it. She didn't care about seeing Hannah's take on the Fourth of July celebration.

Why was she so down on Hannah, anyway?

Was it because Hannah was rich and got to spend the summer going around making videos? If so, that was petty, and Grace ought to be ashamed of herself. Was it because she was unfriendly? Hannah had never been outright unfriendly to her, just cool. And Grace hadn't gone out of her way to be friendly to Hannah, either.

No, it wasn't any of those things — it was because of Doc. From the beginning, Hannah had made it clear she was interested in Doc. And although Grace had said over and over that she didn't care, and that Hannah and Doc deserved each other, something deep down told her she did care. After her argument with Doc, it had hurt to see Hannah and Doc together at the diner.

In any case, it didn't matter, because she wasn't going to see Hannah and Doc again.

The oven timer dinged, and Grace went to get the pizza out. While it cooled she set the table for one. She was sick of eating sitting on the floor in front of the coffee table. What she wanted right now was a nice dinner with family or friends, but Jen wasn't back, and even if she had been, she and Grace had rarely eaten dinner together.

What kind of life was this? Grace didn't want to eat alone in an apartment and work all the time and be thousands of miles from her family. Sure, she had a good job, and she wasn't going hungry, but there was more to life than that.

"Dear Jesus," she prayed, "please, show me what You want me to do."

She couldn't turn her back on a career she had spent years of time and money to build, could she?

On the other hand, Grace's parents had spent thirty years working on that store, and they were letting it go for something they wanted more. Just because you had put a lot of time and money into something didn't mean you had to stay with it forever.

What if she moved back to Fraser's Mill and took over the grocery store herself?

It was a crazy idea. She didn't have money to buy a house or a store. Besides that, she would have to take on the dollar store by herself. Grace thought she recognized a wild idea when she saw one, and this was too wild for her.

Plus, Grace's supervisor, the principal, would be upset. School started in less than three weeks, and Grace had a contract for this year. She had signed the contract before leaving for the summer, and even if she hadn't renewed the contract, the withdrawal deadline would have been the beginning of July. There were penalties for breaking your teacher contract. Grace had heard of people losing their teaching license for the next year by doing things like that.

Of course, if she did decide to go back to Michigan, what would she do with a teacher's license?

It would be hard on the school, leaving like that and giving them such a short time to get another English teacher before school started.

On the other hand, Grace was about to lose the only home she'd ever had. Should she give up her home because of a teaching contract?

That, in a nutshell, was the question. Where did Grace belong: at this job in California, or at her home and her family's store in Fraser's Mill?

Put like that, the question wasn't hard to answer. When Grace was younger, she had dreamed of life out in the big world, of having an important career. But what good was an important career—and being an NBCT didn't even seem that important anymore—if you weren't happy?

Besides, it wasn't true that you couldn't do anything big and important in Fraser's Mill. Doc took care of the health of all those people. That was important. Dorothy volunteered for the church and the unborn and lent a helping hand wherever it was needed.

That was important. And keeping Murray's Grocery open, supplying the whole town with fresh food, was important too.

She had been wrong to think she would be happier outside of Fraser's Mill. She would be happier—even if she had to do a lot of stressful work and fight the dollar store and scrape for money—in that town with the people she cared about. Fraser's Mill mattered to her. She belonged there.

Grace picked up her phone and dialed her parents' land-line.

"Hello?" Dad's voice said on the other end.

"Dad, hi," Grace said. "This is Grace. I have something I want to talk to you and Mom about."

"I'll get her on the extension."

Grace had barely started explaining her idea when Mom interrupted.

"You can't do this," Mom exclaimed. "You'd be throwing away everything you've worked so hard for! I thought that was what you had always wanted to do."

"Yeah, it was," Grace said. "But it isn't anymore. I don't want to be stuck out here in California with nobody around that I know. And I don't want the store to be bought by strangers or have to close down. Even if you got a good buyer for the store, it still might go under if the people weren't able to compete with the dollar store. And also, I want our family to still have roots in Fraser's Mill. If you and Dad move near Katie and Arthur, and we don't have anybody in town, then whenever we go back we'll just be visitors. I couldn't stand that."

"Are you sure?" Dad asked. "Just a few years ago, you couldn't wait to get out of here. You wanted to go do something important."

"The store is important," Grace said. "And the people in town are important. Being in a big city doesn't make anything more important. I know now that I don't belong here. I belong in Fraser's Mill."

"Are you sure you're not panicking because of our news?" Mom asked. "I was afraid you'd be upset, especially after all the work you put into the store the last few weeks. But your father and I agreed that it was the best thing we could do."

"If we weren't moving, would you want to stay in California?" Dad asked. "Think about it. If we were still going to be here, and you could come home on vacations, would you still move back?"

"Yes. Dad, I've been thinking about it all evening, and I know now that I don't want to be out here anymore. I thought I would, but I don't. I work a ton of hours for what isn't the greatest salary, and I don't have a community around me. It's really lonely."

"If you come back and work in the store, you might get bored," Dad said. "A classroom of fifth graders will at least keep you entertained."

"Well, I want to do it," Grace said. "You know how stubborn I am. If you and Mom don't think it's a good idea for me to come back, that's all right, but I'm going to come back anyway. Even if I have to find somewhere else in town to live and work. I'll save a fortune not paying rent on this apartment anymore."

"Of course you can come here if you really want to," Dad said. "Your mom and I would want to talk about our plans, in that case. Don't know if we'd still move if you came back. But no matter what, you're always welcome to stay at the house and work in the store."

"Thanks, Dad."

"Wait a minute," Mom said. "Haven't you already signed a teaching contract for this fall?"

"That's a bit tougher," Grace said. "I did sign the contract, and it's past the deadline for resignation, so I may have some kind of penalty. I might lose my teacher's license for the next year. But I wouldn't be teaching anyway, so even if I do lose my license it won't matter."

"Hmm." Mom sounded dubious. "You'd better be sure you don't make a decision you'll regret. You can't go back once you've quit, and they probably wouldn't want to re-hire you at that school in any case."

"I know, Mom," Grace said. "I've been thinking about all of that. I don't look forward to talking to the principal. But I know this is what I want to do. It's not a snap decision. It's been sort of creeping up on me for a long time, but I never paid attention to it."

Home Sweet Home

The next morning, Grace called the school principal. Melanie was surprised and unhappy to hear her news. She had been looking forward to Grace returning and working on National Board certification, and now she would have to find a new teacher in less than three weeks. Grace had to hold the phone away from her ear as Melanie's voice rose in volume.

It went better telling Jen she was leaving. Jen would miss Grace, but she was happy Grace was going to do something she cared a lot about.

And now Grace was just waiting on her car, still at the garage waiting for a catalytic converter. It had been two months. Would that thing ever get done?

She couldn't go back to Michigan until the car was done. But she could figure out what she needed to take with her and what she needed to leave. Grace got some empty boxes and started packing.

On Monday morning, the car was done, with a price tag of three thousand dollars. By Monday afternoon, a significantly poorer Grace had all her things in her car and was saying goodbye to Jen.

She had made the trip—about 2,200 miles—once before, when she first moved out to California. It was a long drive to take solo. But she planned to stop as needed for breaks, and she could listen to audiobooks and podcasts and pray rosaries and call people on the phone. It would be good. And what better way to see the United States than a cross-country road trip?

Grace started her car, said a prayer for safe travel, and turned on an upbeat playlist. *Michigan, here I come!*

It was surreal, going back to Fraser's Mill for good. This time Grace wouldn't be just a visitor. She looked forward to being a bonafide Fraser's Mill resident and getting involved in all kinds of town activities—when she wasn't busy saving the store, of course.

By the next morning, after a stay in a little Utah hotel (reputed to be clean and safe, based on online reviews), Grace had run through most of her playlists. Now would be a good time to call her parents, if either of them was home.

Mom picked up. Dad was in the store, she said, and she was cleaning the house. She could put Grace on speakerphone and still do the laundry.

"Thanks, Mom," Grace said. "I just really wanted to talk to somebody — this desert is endless!"

The day was warming up, and the breeze from the open car window blew Grace's hair everywhere as she drove along.

Mom laughed. "Are you still in Utah?"

"Yes, I am. I'm going to see if I can make Denver by night," Grace said. "So how are you guys doing? How's the store? How's Dad doing now that he's getting around more?"

"Oh, he's doing fine," Mom said. "He's been telling everybody who comes into the store that you're coming back to take over. I haven't seen him this excited in a long time."

Grace smiled. She could just see Dad now, standing behind the counter, telling everybody his little Gracie was going to follow in his footsteps as a storekeeper.

"So I guess the whole town knows I'm coming back by now?" Grace asked, grinning.

Mom laughed. "Pretty much! We keep hearing from people who want to recruit you for things. Dorothy wants to get you for her ladies' group at the church. And Alex wants you to join the choir as a permanent member. As though you weren't going to have enough to do already!"

Grace laughed. "Alex texted me about the choir. I guess I'll see how much work I have at the store and then decide about the other things."

It was nice to come back to a place where the people liked her and wanted her to join their activities.

"Doc was really surprised you were coming back," Mom said. "He acted like he couldn't believe his ears."

Grace's pulse quickened. "Really? Huh."

"Yes, really," Mom said. "I was in the store when your father was telling him. He wanted to hear all about your decision to come back."

For someone who hadn't even been talking to her before she left, that was unexpected. Maybe Doc was surprised because Grace had talked so much about her plans to teach.

Well, it didn't matter if he was surprised or not, or why. If she ran into him—which she was bound to do at some point, living next door—she would be polite, but not try to strike up a friendship again. It was better to only be slightly acquainted with a guy she couldn't get along with and whose girlfriend probably didn't like her.

"Speaking of being surprised," Mom was saying, "Katie's fit to be tied about your coming back to work in the store. She thinks you can't be serious about really wanting to come back. You'd better call and talk to her, because she doesn't believe us when we tell her."

Oh, Katie. Always the protective older sister. It was easy to see why Katie would think that, since Grace had been so vocal about her wish to be a teacher and to get away from the backwater of Fraser's Mill. Well, it was good that Katie wanted to look out for her. She'd have to give her a call and explain things. She had been too busy the last few days to call a lot of people.

Grace got to Michigan on Friday morning. After a long stop-and-go period through the I-94 corridor, full of summer construction and congested traffic, she was finally speeding north toward home.

She stopped in Grand Haven for lunch. Should she make a quick stop at the beach? No, she wouldn't. She had done enough stopping and sight-seeing as she went through Colorado, Nebraska, and Iowa. All she wanted now was to get to Fraser's Mill.

As she went through the Ludington area the trees were getting thicker and more piney, and the air was delightfully fresh. She was close now. How had she ever thought she wouldn't want to live in Michigan?

At long last, she could see Fraser's Mill in the distance. It was a bummer that the first thing you saw when you got to town was the dollar store. But that made Grace all the more determined to fight it and win.

The town seemed different this time. Before, Grace had been hit with an overwhelming wave of nostalgia—it was the place where she had grown up, and she had returned to it as someone revisiting her youth. Now it wasn't a place for visits and memories. It was home.

There was the grocery store, with several cars in the gravel lot. Good, customers. Grace pulled into the driveway, hopped out, and ran into the store.

Dad stood behind the counter, a grocer's apron on, looking businesslike as he rang up a customer's groceries. He looked up. "Gracie!"

Grace waited, shifting her weight from one foot to the other.

As soon as Dad finished with the customer, she rushed behind the counter. "Dad!"

Dad caught her in a big bear hug. "Welcome home."

Unraveling Mysteries

After bringing her parents up to speed on her adventures, taking a shower, and crashing on her top bunk for a long nap, Grace helped Dad make dinner—sourdough grilled cheese, tomato soup, and some gingersnaps from the store's baked goods display. Alex had done a good job with the gingersnaps. Grace ought to bake something tomorrow, if she wasn't too busy.

Dinner came later than usual because they had waited for Mom to get done with a shift at the store. The sun was low in the sky as Grace helped clear up after the meal.

"Ben, did you get the mail today?" Mom asked from the kitchen sink.

"No, I didn't think of getting it when I got done in the store," Dad said.

"Oh, I'll get it," Grace said, and went out the front door.

It was a nice summer evening, and the front yard grass felt cool under Grace's bare feet. At the mailbox, she stopped to look through the mail. Ads for pizza places—they didn't even have chain pizza places in Fraser's Mill—two credit card offers, political mail from a candidate Grace didn't plan to support in the midterm election, and a large envelope probably from a place trying to sell insurance. All junk.

"Grace!" A masculine voice caused Grace to look up. Doc strode across his lawn toward her.

She had been dreading this moment, and yet, her heartbeat quickened upon seeing him again.

"Doc!" Grace said. "Hi."

He reached the mailbox and stood there, towering over her as usual. "Your dad told me you were coming back."

Grace nodded. "Yes, I'm back. How are you?"

Polite and distant—that was the way to go. But the expression on Doc's face didn't look polite and distant. His eyes were intense, and the set of his mouth was determined.

"Grace," he said. "I was an idiot. I owe you an apology."

"What?"

"When I yelled at you, the day you asked me to help take apart the float. I was wrong, and I'm sorry."

Grace stared. He had still been thinking about that too?

"Still mad?" Doc asked.

Grace shook her head. "No. I'm sorry I yelled too. I was confused. I didn't know why you were upset with me out of the blue like that."

"The fact is, I was jealous," Doc said. "The guy you were with on the Fourth of July—"

"Lucas?"

Doc nodded solemnly. "I hadn't realized you had a boyfriend."

Grace's eyes widened, understanding dawning. That was why Doc had been mad. He thought Lucas was her boyfriend. Alex was right — Doc must have liked her after all. No wonder he'd been irritated. After picking her up when her car broke down, taking her shopping, and helping with the parade float, Doc must have thought she was taking advantage of his help while her supposed boyfriend wasn't around.

"No, no," Grace said, shaking her head. "Lucas and I weren't dating. He was one of my co-workers from California, and he was in the area visiting his grandmother."

Doc's eyebrows shot up. "I heard he said you were dating."

Oh, no! How had that gotten around to Doc?

Grace groaned. "He got the wrong idea. We weren't dating. We went out once."

A smile crept across Doc's face like the sun coming from behind a cloud. But all he said was, "I see."

This puzzle still wasn't fitting together. "But how did you hear that?" Grace asked. Alex and her parents surely wouldn't have told anyone. "Did you meet Lucas when he was here?"

Doc shook his head. "Hannah met him. He told her the two of you had been dating since May."

She remembered Hannah talking to Lucas by the ice cream stand on the Fourth of July. So that's how that story had gotten out. Hannah hadn't seemed to appreciate Grace hanging out with Doc. Of course she would have jumped at the opportunity to tell Doc Grace had a boyfriend. Grace didn't know that she blamed her.

"I went out with Lucas one time in May," Grace told Doc. "And I replied to some emails he sent. That was it."

"And I believed third-hand information instead of asking you about him myself." Doc grimaced. "I'm an even bigger idiot than I thought I was. Jealous, cranky — and stupid."

Grace shook her head at him. "You don't need to call yourself all those names," she said. "It's all right."

"We're good?" Doc asked.

"We're good." Grace smiled.

"Wonderful." He smiled, drawing closer to Grace. "Then I have a question for you. Will you go out with me?"

The world spun around Grace. She hadn't realized it before, but she'd been waiting a long time for Doc to ask that. There was no question how she felt about him, not anymore. But there was still one thing.

"What about Hannah?" Grace heard herself saying.

"Hannah?" Doc's forehead furrowed.

"I thought you two were dating! You've been going around together all summer."

His face cleared. "No, she's just a friend. She came to town this summer and didn't know a lot of people, so I've been showing her around."

"Really?" That was it? The whole thing between Hannah and Doc was one-sided, all this time?

He nodded. "Really."

Wow. Alex had been right about everything. Seeing Doc and Hannah together so often, Grace had completely misjudged the situation.

"So how about it?" Doc's eyes twinkled. "Will you go out with me?"

Grace found herself smiling hugely. "Sure — when?"

"How about tomorrow?"

"That would be wonderful. But not too early — I'm gonna close the store tomorrow at seven."

"I'll pick you up at eight," Doc said. "We could eat at the diner. Unless you don't want to be seen with me in public."

Grace laughed. "The diner would be great."

"Then I'll see you tomorrow." Doc's face crinkled into a smile. "Careful you don't fall down the stairs answering the door."

An Evening at the Diner

It was almost eight o'clock on Saturday night. Doc should be there any minute to pick Grace up for their date. What in the world should she wear?

Jeans and a T-shirt seemed too casual. Her teaching clothes, mostly blouses and pencil skirts, didn't seem to fit in Fraser's Mill. Her favorite yellow flowered dress was in the wash. She had worn it all day Sunday to make herself feel more cheerful and then neglected to do her laundry before leaving California. Her only other summer dress was the red dress that had seemed too Valentiney to wear on a date with Lucas.

The red dress was perfect.

"Grace?" Mom's voice called up the stairs. "Doc's been waiting on the porch for five minutes."

Of course he would be early when she was running late. Grace hurried into the red dress. No time to do anything to her hair. She'd have to leave it down. She tied her Converse, grabbed her purse, and raced downstairs.

Doc was standing on the porch, arms crossed, looking out across the street. Grace opened the door, and Doc turned.

"I wondered what you looked like with your hair down," Doc said.

"Absolutely wild." Grace laughed. "My hair never behaves."

Doc grinned. "Well, I like it that way," he said. "Wanna go in the car, or would you rather walk?"

Grace had had enough of cars lately. "Let's walk."

They started down the street together. Grace had walked down Main Street countless times this summer, but this time felt different from all the others. This was her street, and she was here to stay.

And Doc walked alongside her, moderating his long stride to suit her shorter one. Without warning, he reached out and took her hand.

Grace looked up. Doc had a questioning look on his face, as if to ask, "Is this okay?"

It was more than okay. His large hand was warm around hers, solid, trustworthy. Grace smiled at him, and he smiled back, clasping her hand more firmly.

Her mind went back to the time Doc bandaged her hand, his touch gentle but capable. She should've realized, back then, the subtle spark of attraction she had towards him.

The diner was nearly empty so late in the evening. Charlie wasn't there—maybe he was out somewhere with Alex. Grace and Doc sat down at the end of the bar. Grace had had her fill of sitting in booths with Lucas, and the bar felt more cool and grown-up.

They talked about anything and everything. Doc wanted to hear about Grace's time in California and her decision to come back to Fraser's Mill.

"There's something I want to ask you," Grace asked, when she was almost done with her burger. "When did you realize you liked me?"

Doc raised an eyebrow. "You really wanna know?"

"Mm-hmm. Alex told me you liked me a few weeks ago, and I didn't believe her."

Doc chuckled. "Alex was right," he said. "I knew I liked you when you yelled at me because you thought I was stealing your mom's car. I said to myself, 'Now, that's the kind of woman you've been looking for.'"

Grace groaned. "I might have known. I'm not really sure when I started liking you. I didn't realize it when it happened. I kept telling Alex you and I would be terrible together."

Doc's eyes twinkled. "Probably in denial."

"I thought I didn't want anything to do with you. You kept coming around right when I was in the middle of a disaster."

"I specialize in disasters. Isn't that what doctors are for?" Doc wiped his mouth on his napkin. "Speaking of disasters, what's your plan for saving the grocery store? Need any help?"

"I'm not trying to get you involved in a whole lot of work. It's my job to try to keep the store afloat. You've got your whole medical practice to run."

He nodded. "I know. But I want to help."

"Well, then, you can tell me more about that idea you had for a town meeting," Grace said. "I've been thinking about it, and I think you were right. We need to get the community invested in the idea of saving the store."

Doc leaned his elbows on the bar. "Maybe you can get the town council to schedule a special meeting about the grocery store. You could go to one of the council meetings and speak up during the time for public comment, but it might be better to talk to one of the council members privately and get them to suggest it to the others."

"What would the meeting be like?"

"It would be like a regular town council meeting, but with only one item on the agenda. You and your parents could prepare a presentation about how the dollar store is affecting the grocery store. Then you'd have an opportunity to hear what the townspeople think about the whole thing. They might have suggestions to help your business, too."

"Do you think the town will think the store's just trying to mooch off of them to get higher profits?"

"Some people might. But if the store closes, they're the ones who will have to drive all the way into Cadillac for fruit and vegetables and meat," Doc said. "Keeping the store open will help the whole community."

He was right. "Well, then, let's do it," Grace said. "Who's on the town council, anyway?"

"Walt Daniels is," Doc said. "Aren't he and Dorothy friends with your parents?"

"Yeah, they are," Grace said. "I'll talk to Dorothy about

it. She's good at talking people into stuff. She'll talk Walt into bringing it up at the town meeting, and she'll get the council members to listen, even if she has to march in there and give a speech herself."

"I believe it." Doc chuckled. "You think you could use some help with your presentation? I could say a few things from a doctor's perspective."

"Thanks, Doc. That would be great."

It was late, and the man working behind the counter had finished wiping down every possible surface except where Grace and Doc were sitting. When the man got out a broom and started sweeping around them, Doc got up from his bar stool with a sheepish expression.

"Sorry, you've probably been waiting to close for a while," he told the man. "How much do I owe you?" He turned to Grace. "Mind if I pick up the tab?"

"You're sure?"

Doc grinned. "Absolutely."

Grace smiled. "Then thank you."

They walked back in the dark, fireflies lighting up all around them, the smell of pine in the air. Grace drew a deep breath. "It's good to be home."

They stopped in front of Grace's house, where her parents had left the porch light on for her.

"Thank you, Doc," Grace said. "I had a wonderful evening. And thanks for all the advice."

His face crinkled in a smile. "Do you want to go out with me again?"

"Absolutely."

"Tomorrow night? At the tavern? We're gonna run out of restaurants pretty quickly."

Grace laughed. "Then we can switch over to picnics," she said. "I hear there's a grocery store around here that has everything you could possibly want for a picnic."

Doc crossed his arms. "Well now, what a coincidence," he said. "We may just have to make use of that, Miss Murray."

"Sounds good to me, Dr. Johnson."

"You can call me Jim," he said.

Grace had heard him called Doc so many times she had almost forgotten it wasn't his first name. "All right, I will," she said. "Do you mind being called Doc?"

He shook his head. "I'm used to it. My friends started calling me that in pre-med, and it stuck. It's better than 'the young doc.'"

Grace laughed and held out her hand. "Well, Jim, it's nice to meet you. I'm Grace Murray."

Doc shook her hand heartily, his mouth amused. "Glad to meet you, Grace."

"So, tomorrow evening at the tavern? How about six P.M.?"

"Six is great," Doc said. "Are you singing in the choir tomorrow?"

"I'd better not—I don't know the motets. I don't think Mary Jane would appreciate it."

"You could sit up in the loft with me," Doc said.

"Aren't you next to the soprano section?"

"You don't want to be a soprano for a day?"

She made a face at him. "And hit all those Fs and Gs? No thanks."

"All right, I'll see you after Mass," he said. "I should let you get some sleep."

Grace nodded. "Thank you," she said. "For everything."

Doc pulled her into a hug, and she rested her head against his shoulder. He smelled clean, like soap and the piney Michigan air.

"Goodnight, Grace," he said. "I'm glad you came back."

"Me too," Grace said. "Goodnight, Jim."

Settling In

Still tired from her travels, Grace got up late the next morning and straggled into the church when Father and the altar boys were already in the vestibule, ready to come down the aisle. The choir sang nicely — they could probably use another alto, though. Mary Jane would be happy to have Grace back in the choir.

Grace had a lot of prayer intentions during Mass. Foremost in her mind was the store. She was excited about taking over Murray's Grocery, but did she have what it took to succeed?

As she prayed, Grace came upon a note she'd stuck into her missal a long time ago. It was a quote from Jeremiah: "For surely I know the plans I have for you, says the Lord, plans for your welfare and not for harm, to give you a future with hope."

She had found that verse comforting when she was a recent college graduate, ready to move across the country and start a new scary job. Now, as she prepared to save Murray's Grocery from going out of business — although she felt peace about that, it was possibly the scariest thing she'd ever planned to do — the verse consoled her again. She didn't have to do this alone. The Lord was faithful, and He had Grace's well-being in mind even when things were difficult. She just had to do her best and trust in Him.

Grace had just stepped into the church vestibule after Mass when Alex pounced on her.

"You're back!" Alex's chapel veil was sliding off, and she was juggling an unwieldy armful of choir books and a missal. "I thought you wouldn't be back for another couple days at least."

"I forgot to text, and then I thought I would surprise you," Grace said. "But I got to the church too late to catch you before Mass. It's so great to be back!"

"Are you here for good now, or do you have to go back to California for anything?" Alex asked. Her armload of books was beginning to slide away. Grace caught the top two and held them for her.

"I'm here for good!" Grace said. "I'm done with my apartment lease, and I've brought or given away all my things. I'm an official Fraser's Mill resident now."

"Wonderful!" Alex's dark eyes snapped with excitement. "I want to hear all about everything! Let's go somewhere else though. I can't hear myself think with all these adorable toddlers shrieking."

They went outside, where it wasn't so loud. Little groups of parishioners stood around talking, while most of the kids ran and played by a large shade tree on the parish grounds.

"I can't tell you how glad I am that you've come back," Alex said. "I was wishing you would stay, but I didn't want to try to change your mind when you liked teaching so much. And then after the blow-up with Doc I figured you really wouldn't want to stay. Speaking of Doc—have you seen him? Did you ever figure out why he got mad at you? He's been moping around and acting really gloomy ever since you left."

"What have I been doing?" Doc's voice came from behind them. Grace whirled around.

He stood there, hands in his pockets, grinning. "Do I hear myself being accused of something?"

"Doc!" Alex flushed. "I didn't know you were there."

Grace raised her eyebrows at Doc. "You're sneaking up on me again."

"Whoops," Doc said. "At least you weren't holding anything breakable." He folded his arms across his chest. "I just talked to Walt. He's going to suggest a special meeting about the grocery store during the council meeting tomorrow."

"Wonderful!" Grace said. "Thanks, Jim."

"*Jim*?" Alex looked from Grace to Doc and back again. "You two had better explain what's going on. I listened to a lot of ranting about that big argument you had. Now you're suddenly calling him 'Jim'? Nobody tells me anything!"

Doc pursed his lips. "It's too late now, Grace. You'll have to tell her all your darkest secrets, or she'll never be satisfied."

"Oh, go away," Alex told him. "I know I'm not going to get any information out of *you*."

Doc grinned. "Have fun cross-examining Grace. See you around." He strolled off, whistling.

Alex threw up her hands. "Grace Elizabeth Murray, what in the world is going on?"

"Alex Santiago Martin, I've been trying to tell you, but we keep getting interrupted. Walk home with me, and I'll tell the whole thing."

Grace told Alex the whole story about talking to Doc by the mailbox, the confusion with Hannah and Lucas, and her realization that she had liked Doc the whole time.

Alex pumped a fist in the air. "I told you so! I knew he liked you. And I had a feeling you liked him, too, but didn't want to admit it to yourself."

Grace filled her in on the date at the diner and Doc's suggestion about having a town meeting. Alex was interested in that idea. "I'll see if my dad would want to talk at the meeting," she said. "I mean, if you'd like him to."

"That would be amazing," Grace said. "We need all the help we can get if we're going to get the community to support the store. Thank you."

Grace opened the store on Monday. She had gotten enough rest, and it was pleasant to walk over in the cool morning, her footsteps crunching over the gravel parking lot.

She stopped in the doorway, looking over the tidy store. Her apron hung by the cash register, ready to go. The displays of fresh produce and baked goods looked bright and cheery with the sunlight streaming through the front windows.

Murray's Grocery might just be a little country store. But to Grace, it was a legacy.

If they succeeded in having a town meeting about the store, how would she present her case to the townspeople? How could she get the people to see the store with her eyes? She'd better start preparing what to say.

As a schoolteacher, Grace had had a lot of practice researching things to present to a group. Those skills could be handy now. Some of the lesser-known facts she had learned about dollar stores this summer would probably be useful.

Grace was at the cash register, still mulling things over, when the bell jingled and Hannah Fraser walked in. As usual, her outfit was on point, a lightweight blue-and-white sweater with short sleeves tucked into a high-waisted pair of white shorts. Her hair shone smooth and glossy.

What was Hannah doing here at eight A.M.? The early customers tended to be the town's old-timers.

Grace didn't have more time to wonder, because Hannah approached the register.

"I heard you and Doc were dating," Hannah said. "Congratulations! I'm happy for you guys."

Her tone was cool and her face unreadable, but if she really had liked Doc, it must have taken an effort for her to say that.

"Thanks, Hannah," Grace said, and smiled.

Hannah looked down, fishing in her purse. "You probably heard I told Doc you had a boyfriend." She raised her head, facing Grace straight-on. "I want you to know—I just didn't want him to be hurt, you know?"

"I know," Grace said. "It's all right. Really."

"That's good." Hannah went back to looking in her purse. She pulled out a grocery list. "Does this store carry avocados?"

"Actually, we do," Grace said.

Hannah smiled. "Great. Now I don't have to drive into Cadillac."

Town Meeting

Led by Walt Daniels, the town council agreed to hold a special meeting to discuss the grocery store and its role in the community. The meeting was set for Wednesday night, and so many people were planning to go to it that Mary Jane moved choir practice to Thursday.

Grace had butterflies as she and her parents, dressed in their best, walked up to the town hall. A lot of people were already milling around. It was great that so many people were interested in the grocery store, but the crowd gave Grace nervous jitters. It was one thing to talk to her parents and friends about the grocery store, or to give a lecture to a bunch of fifth- and sixth-graders. It was another thing to tell the whole town that they ought to buy more things from your grocery store.

But Grace would be the store's new owner when her parents retired. She had given up her teaching career for this. Now was not the time to chicken out. If she was going to own a store, she needed to be able to talk about it.

Grace had never been in the town hall before. It was bigger inside than she had envisioned. Dad led the way to the front row of chairs, facing the tables where the council members would sit. "Come on," he said, beckoning his wife and daughter to follow him. "If we're gonna talk, we might as well sit in the front."

Grace sat down, feeling exposed in the front row. Doc appeared at her shoulder, claiming the chair next to her. "Have you ever been to a town meeting?" he asked.

Grace shook her head. "Do they use parliamentary procedures? Like making motions and seconding them?"

"Yeah, but we don't need to worry about that. We just get up and talk when it's our turn."

More people filtered in. It was time to start. The town supervisor called the meeting to order, and everyone stood and recited the Pledge of Allegiance.

Since this was a special meeting, there was only one agenda item: the dollar store's effect on the local grocery store. Before the agenda, however, it was time for public comment. At this time anyone in town could speak, either about the agenda or about anything else.

Dorothy came up to the podium. "My name is Dorothy Daniels," she said. "I've got something to say."

Dorothy used up the three minutes allotted to her. She explained that the dollar store was taking business away from the grocery store and that the townspeople needed to support the grocery store and help it stay open.

"If she talks much longer, we won't need to say anything," Doc said in Grace's ear.

Grace couldn't help smiling. Dorothy was a dear.

Grace wondered if any of the dollar store employees were at the meeting. Maybe, if they lived in Fraser's Mill. They might be interested in the town's thoughts on the dollar store too.

After Dorothy sat down, Matt Pierce, the owner of the hardware store, got up.

"What I want to know," he said, "is whether the town is gonna give the grocery store a bunch of money to stay open. That store's a privately-owned business. It's not up to the town to support privately-owned businesses. I never got a handout from the town to support my hardware store."

He sat down. A murmur went through the audience.

That wasn't good. If the town thought the Murrays were trying to enrich themselves at the town's expense, they wouldn't want to help Murray's Grocery. Grace and her parents hadn't come to ask for money; they had come to raise community awareness. There would be time to explain that later, but for the moment, Matt's speech made things look bad.

Finally public comment was over. "And now," the town supervisor said, "we'll hear from Grace Murray, current employee and future owner of Murray's Grocery."

Grace had come prepared. She had a stack of notes full of statistics about dollar stores and the towns they had wrecked. At the podium, she read testimonies from store owners whose stores had had to close after a dollar store came in. She urged the people of Fraser's Mill to be loyal to their own grocery store, because if that store had to close, they would have to drive forty-five minutes to the next closest one.

Dad came up next. He talked about all the things the store brought to the community, and how the store's prices depended on the prices of its suppliers. Murray's Grocery couldn't sell their items at dollar store prices—they wouldn't even cover expenses if they did.

Mom went to the podium next. At first she had insisted she didn't want to talk in front of the whole town, but after some convincing from her husband and Grace, she'd changed her mind. She told the people about the plans Grace had come up with for having a larger variety of baked goods at the store and rotating special items in and out. The dollar store didn't have anything like that.

That was Doc's cue to speak, and he addressed the town on the subject of health. He talked about food deserts, places where there was no fresh food within a certain radius, and how those food deserts were contributing to the obesity problem in America. As a doctor, he advised that the town do all they could to keep the grocery store open.

"Besides," he added, "even if you don't care about eating healthy, it still makes sense to keep the store in business. Do you really want to drive forty-five minutes to get meat for dinner? Do you wanna drive through ice storms to get food in the middle of winter?"

A voice from the back called out. "Preach it, man! I don't even drive in the snow!" Doc flashed a grin in the man's direction. The supervisor rapped for order.

"When a community doesn't have a grocery store, that whole community suffers," Doc continued. "As a community, we all need to come together and support the store. Don't drive into Cadillac for your groceries if you can get them here. Don't switch over to buying your canned goods at the dollar store. We didn't ask for the dollar store to come here. It's not doing our town any good. I know the prices there are lower for certain items. But it's not worth the price you'll pay if the dollar store drives the grocery out of business."

Amid scattered clapping, the supervisor rapped for order again.

Alex's dad came up next to speak in support of the store. He talked about the way his farm worked with Murray's Grocery. "If you compare a commercial cold-storage strawberry to a strawberry we just picked from the farm this morning, you'll find a big difference," he said. "Murray's Grocery is bringing all that produce right to you."

With the end of Mr. Martin's speech, the official business of the meeting was over, and it was time for more public comment.

A middle-aged woman Grace recognized as a bank teller came to the podium.

"I have something to say," she said. "I get why we need to keep the grocery store open, because if it closes we won't have one at all. But if the town's gonna help keep the store open, the store ought to take some suggestions about how to improve things. If I go into Cadillac, I can get pre-made salads and sandwiches, prepped veggie kits for dinners, and all kinds of deli items. If I go to Murray's Grocery, I have to make dinner from scratch.

This isn't the 1950s. I don't have time to spend hours making dinner every day. If the store had more grab-and-go options for fresh, healthy food, that would be a big improvement."

"I second that," a man's voice said from the back.

Doc leaned over and whispered in Grace's ear. "That would keep me from eating canned soup and potato chips for dinner."

"That's fair," Grace whispered back.

Grace saw Mom nodding. Dad's brow was furrowed. He was probably wondering how that would work with the store's supplier. The Murrays couldn't make deli items for the store themselves, under Michigan's Cottage Food Law, without a commercial kitchen. Maybe they could get a commercial kitchen. Grace guessed that would be expensive.

Hannah was at the podium. "I'm just here for the summer," she said, "but I agree about having more pre-made salads and sandwiches. All the big stores do it. Also, the store could have more variety in their products. If you want coconut water you have to drive all the way into Cadillac for it. If Murray's Grocery is going to be a real grocery store—not a mini-mart—they ought to expand their stock."

Expand? That was another thing for Grace to discuss with her parents. She ought to be taking notes. She pulled out her phone to type a note with the substance of Hannah's comment.

A mom came up after that. "My family was excited when the dollar store moved in," she said, "because you can get all kinds of craft supplies there, and my kids love doing crafts. Is there any chance the grocery store would be able to get in a line of craft supplies?"

Another man said he wasn't convinced this whole thing wasn't just the Murrays trying to line their pockets. "It's clear the Murrays can't keep the store open themselves," he said. "They oughtta sell it to the town, and we can turn it into a nonprofit. I've heard of places that had food co-ops that did really well."

Turning around, Grace saw a few heads nodding. Oh, dear. Food co-ops were all very well, but she didn't want to sell the store to the town, and it wasn't fair to say her family couldn't keep the store open themselves. No business could stay open if it didn't have customers buying its products. It wasn't as though the Murrays were asking the people to give them money for nothing. They weren't looking for the community's charity, just their business.

She started to rise from her seat to reply to the man, but Doc put a hand on her arm. "Wait."

A woman at the podium seconded what the man had said. She thought a nonprofit co-op was a great idea. That way the people of the town had more control over what was sold at the store.

Grace had a sinking feeling in the pit of her stomach. If a lot of people wanted a co-op, it wouldn't be good. They cared about keeping a grocery store in town, but not about supporting her family's business.

Ed from the garage came up to the podium.

"I had to close the garage to come to this meeting," he said. "And it was worth it, just so I could come up and say this. You people talking about making the store into a nonprofit, taking it away from the Murrays—what's wrong with you? They're not trying to take money from the town to line their pockets. I've known them for thirty years. They're just trying to make their living like the rest of us."

A cheer arose somewhere in the back.

"That's their family business," Ed went on, "and when Ben and Liz retire, their daughter Grace is gonna take it over. The Murrays care just as much about this town as you do. Grace cared enough to come back all the way from California, where she was a darn good teacher, to work in the store. Don't you say one more thing about co-ops. This is America, and people have the right to work their own family business and advertise for it without other people trying to take it away from them."

More cheering. Good old Ed, saving the day. Grace beamed at him as he came down from the podium.

One of the trustees, an elderly man Grace recognized from St. Anthony's, got up. "Thank you all for your input," he said. "I'm glad you're all involved in your community and want to have a say on what goes on around town."

The town treasurer, Charlie's uncle, cleared his throat. "I recommend that the grocery store put in a suggestion box so the townspeople can give ideas for improvement. I'm sure the Murrays will be open to suggestions and will implement anything that's feasible."

The meeting adjourned. People surrounded Grace's parents asking questions and making suggestions. Grace stood listening for a few minutes, but too many people were talking at once.

Doc grinned at her. "Come on, let's go. I've got a box in my office we can turn into a suggestion box for the store."

In Doc's office, Grace sank down into one of the waiting room chairs.

Doc sat in a chair opposite her. "Careful what you touch—this waiting room's full of germs."

Grace had enough things to worry about besides germs. "Jim, do you think the meeting went all right? It really worried me when people started talking about a co-op."

"I thought the meeting was really good. You and your parents made a strong argument for the store, and a bunch of other people did too."

"Like you. Thank you."

Doc nodded. "Anytime," he said. "Anyway, I don't think the co-op idea is likely to get much traction. Your family's too well-liked in this town—the townspeople won't try to force you out like that."

He spoke confidently, and Grace couldn't help but feel better. "I'm glad to hear that from you," she said. "I wasn't expecting the co-op suggestion at all, so I got really scared when that second lady said she liked the idea too."

"I think the main takeaway you need to focus on is improving the store to bring in more business," Doc said. "Getting more healthy pre-prepped foods. Expanding your stock in areas where the dollar store can't compete. Those are valid ideas to make Murray's Grocery even more indispensable than it is now."

Grace nodded. "You're right," she said. "It's pretty scary, though—the dollar store probably has a whole team of people figuring out how to attract all the small-town business. I feel like we're up against Goliath."

"Yeah, but you've got something the dollar store doesn't," Doc said, his eyes serious. "You've got the home team advantage. This is your home, and you care about it. You've also got your parents, me, and Alex, and most of the town behind you. You're not going to let them beat you."

Grace smiled. "No way. Not if I can do anything to prevent it."

"That's the spirit!" Doc said. "Come on, let's find that box to put suggestions in."

The Great Thaw

The suggestion box proved helpful, and the Murrays began working on some of the town's ideas right away. Dad ordered some pre-made salads and sandwiches to carry in the store. Grace and Mom spent a whole evening making cookies and raspberry bars. (Doc had offered to bake with them, but he got called away to help a kid who had gotten hurt falling out of a tree.)

Grace opened the store on Monday. Before things got too busy, she wanted to look at the new suggestions people had put in the box over the last few days. She had brought a notebook and pen with her so she could brainstorm ideas.

The suggestion box was a shoebox, covered in wrapping paper, with a slot in the top. Grace opened it and found half a dozen folded papers. She unfolded the first one.

"Suggestion," it read in large letters. "The store ought to have apple crisp more often. But don't burn your hand making it!"

It was easy to guess who had written that. Grace shoved Doc's note into her pocket and went on to the next one.

She was brainstorming a way to serve fresh coffee in the store without taking too much time or costing too much money when Elaine Keller approached the counter.

"I hate to be the bearer of bad news, but I think there's something wrong with your freezer," she said. "Everything's much warmer than it should be. Look at this ice cream."

She held out a carton to Grace. The carton was warm and soft, and Grace could tell even before she opened it that the ice cream inside was melted.

"Oh, no. Is it all like this?"

"I'm afraid so," Elaine said.

Grace set the carton on the counter with a thump and hurried over to the rest of the ice cream, kept in one of the store's three-door freezers.

She opened the door. It was suspiciously warm inside. Oh, no. All that food! It must have been thawing for a long time. They probably wouldn't be able to salvage anything. It would cost hundreds of dollars to replace all the product.

Were all three of the freezers like that? Grace whisked to the next freezer. A blast of cold air greeted her. It must be just the one.

Maybe it wasn't actually broken. Maybe it had come unplugged or blown a fuse. Grace called her parents.

"Well, howdy, Gracie," Dad said on the other end of the line. "What's going on?"

"Dad, the ice cream freezer isn't working! Everything inside is completely melted!"

"Oh, no. I'll be right down."

After investigating the broken freezer, the two working freezers, and the circuit breaker box, Dad eliminated the possibility of a power supply problem. There must be something wrong with the freezer itself.

Dad called an appliance repairman he knew in Cadillac. The man said he was booked solid all day, but he'd drop in as a favor after his last house call.

In the meantime, they had to deal with all the food that had defrosted. Besides the ice cream, the freezer held frozen fruit.

"I know we can't sell it," Grace said, surveying the food in the freezer, "but could we eat any of it ourselves?"

Bags of strawberries, blueberries, peaches, and raspberries were all defrosted. Dad surveyed them, stroking his chin.

"Guess it depends how long it's been," he said. "I wish I knew when the freezer stopped working. Why don't you ask your mother?"

Mom was dubious when confronted with several bags of mushy defrosted fruit. "Rats. I don't know," she said. "I heard if it still has ice crystals in it, it's okay to refreeze. But I'm not seeing any ice crystals in this stuff. Who knows how long it was sitting there?"

"Well, it's still cold," Grace said. "It's like somebody defrosted it in the fridge."

"Hmm," Mom said. "I'll see if it tastes all right, and if it does, I'll bake it into something. I'm certainly not going to serve it plain."

The ice cream was a total loss. The store stocked a lot of ice cream in the summer, and losing it all at once was a blow. A large percentage of it was local ice cream from a nearby dairy farm. Grace had to go back and forth to the dumpster throwing it out, and by the time she had finished, angry tears stood in her eyes. Why did this have to happen? Hundreds of dollars gone, just because the freezer decided to quit.

And it had to happen just as Grace was trying to improve the store. What would the townspeople think when they came in and couldn't get ice cream or frozen fruit? Grace hoped the freezer could be fixed quickly so the Murrays could restock.

The repairman dealt a blow when he came. "Sorry, Ben," he told Dad. "Fixing that thing wouldn't be worth it. It's so old something else would probably break right away. If you take my advice you'll find a used one on Craigslist or eBay."

Dad sighed. "I was afraid of that. That freezer was over twenty years old. We got the others around the same time. I hope they're not gonna give out on us too."

The repairman shook his head. "It's too bad," he said. "Look at it this way: it lasted a long time before it broke. They did a good job making those old freezers. The modern ones break when you look at them."

Over dinner, Grace and her parents discussed their options.

"We can't get a brand new freezer," Dad said. "Too expensive. Even a used one is probably too much. We don't have a lot of extra cash after all those doctor bills, and we can't get anything for the old freezer."

"Won't the scrap metal people take the freezer?" Grace asked.

Dad shook his head. "Unfortunately not. We've got to get the refrigerant taken out—Bill's gonna come over again and do that—and then we've gotta pay to get it hauled down to the landfill."

There had to be a way to get a freezer without breaking the bank, and Grace was determined to find it. After dinner, she went on her computer and looked up freezers. A new one cost well over ten thousand dollars. Dad was right, there was no way they could afford that.

However, some freezers on eBay were less than half the price. Of course, they'd have to make sure the seller was legitimate, but it seemed like a better option.

Grace found Dad and showed him the freezers on eBay.

"We'll have to hold off on it for a while, even for a used one," he said. "I don't wanna take out a loan to buy one. Then you've gotta pay interest forever. We can limp along with two freezers—pack things a little tighter, use the freezer chests in the back room to store extra stuff, and restock as things get bought out. It's not good, but it could be worse. We oughtta be grateful we've got two freezers that still work."

Grace was still looking at freezers on eBay when someone knocked on the door. She peered out the window and saw Doc on the front porch. She'd called him to tell about the freezer earlier, but he had been out at the Cadillac hospital with a patient he'd driven there.

Grace opened the door. "Jim! Come in!"

He came in, tall in the entryway. "Sorry I couldn't get here sooner. What's going on with the freezer situation?"

"It's awful," Grace said. "Just when things were going well, this had to happen. It's going to be so expensive to get another one, I've been looking all over the Internet to see if I can find a deal on one somewhere."

Doc pursed his lips. "You look like you could use a break. Wanna go for a walk and tell me about it?"

"That sounds heavenly. I've been stewing over eBay and Craigslist for hours — I could use some fresh air."

They started up Main Street, away from the businesses and into the residential part of town. The sun had set, and dusk was falling.

"Thanks for coming over," Grace said. "You must be exhausted after such a long day. And hungry, too."

Doc shook his head. "Oh, I'm not tired," he said. "And I ate at the hospital in Cadillac. It's cheaper than going to a restaurant."

"And probably better than eating canned soup at home," Grace said.

Doc grinned. "I'm just 'the guy who eats canned soup' to you, aren't I?" he said. "Tell me about the freezer. Do you have any leads on a replacement?"

"Dad said we can't get one for a while," Grace said. "Too much money, on top of all the medical bills and everything. I guess we just won't be able to stock as much freezer food. Right now we don't have any ice cream at all, because it all melted before we discovered the freezer was broken. The supplier isn't coming until Wednesday. I'm gonna make a run into Cadillac tomorrow morning to get a few things to tide us over. I'll have to bring coolers to bring the stuff back."

"There ought to be some way you can get another freezer," Doc said. "You can't limp along with two of them for long, especially when some people are saying you can't run your store and it ought to be turned into a co-op."

"That's what I'm worried about—people will probably pounce on this and say it proves we aren't capable of running the store," Grace said. "Well, what else can we do? We don't have the money to buy a freezer."

"Have you thought of taking out a loan?"

"My dad doesn't want to have to pay interest on a loan. That would just put us farther in the hole."

They walked along in silence.

Doc stopped in his tracks. "I've got it!"

"What?"

"An idea. Why doesn't the store host a fundraiser?"

"A fundraiser? Jim, we just finished telling the town we weren't asking people to give us money!"

"There isn't any shame in asking for money if you need it," Doc said. "But this isn't asking people to give you money. You'll be selling them something. You can do a fundraising dinner. The store provides the ingredients, we get some people to cook, and the town comes and eats. How does that sound?"

"That sounds like a good idea," Grace said, "but how would we pull it off? We'd have to find someplace to cook all the food and serve everybody, and my dad still has to be careful of his ankle. It sounds like way too big a project."

"Your friends would help out," Doc said. "I would. And I know Alex and Charlie and probably some of the church ladies would want to help too. Maybe we could use the fire hall for the dinner."

"Well," Grace said, "I feel bad putting you all to a lot of work like that. Most of you already help me with so much!"

Doc shook his head. "I can't speak for the others, but I think it would be fun."

"Well, if you really, actually, want to do it," Grace said, "I won't say no."

Doc grinned down at her. "I'll start rounding up the troops. When do you think we ought to have the fundraiser? The sooner, the better, I'd say."

"I guess we'd better talk to my parents about that," Grace said, "and we should see when the fire hall is available. But, Jim, do you think the people in town will actually come to a store fundraiser? Maybe they'll think this is just a sign that the store is circling the drain already—we have to fundraise in order to keep going!"

"Anybody can have equipment that breaks down on them," Doc said. "It's the way you handle an incident like that that shows what kind of a storekeeper you are. You're going to show the town that you take action when things go wrong. That's a good look for the store."

Grace smiled. "I hope you're right. Thanks, Jim. I feel better."

He grinned. "Just wait until you see my cooking skills in action at the fundraiser."

"Oh, you mean opening cans of soup?" Grace asked.

"Of course," Doc said.

The Freezer

Grace's parents loved the fundraiser idea, and Doc started recruiting volunteers to help cook, serve the food, and spread the word. Spreading the word was important so they could serve the maximum number of people and make the most money for the freezer. The food could be eaten there or taken as a carry-out. Privately, Grace didn't understand why anyone would want take-out spaghetti—it was so rubbery left over.

When inquiring about the fire hall, they met with a piece of unexpected charity Grace couldn't refuse: the firefighters insisted on renting them the hall at half-price.

"The sooner you've got your ice cream freezer back, the happier I'll be," the fire chief told Grace. "Good luck with your fundraiser!"

There was no lack of volunteers for the dinner. Alex and Charlie, Dorothy and Walt, Elaine, Ed and Janet, Natalie and her sisters, and a few friends of Doc's all said they would help.

The day of the dinner arrived. In the afternoon, Grace went over to the hall with a van full of supplies. A number of cars sat in the parking lot already—those must be the volunteers.

Grace grabbed a large box full of dry pasta packages, both regular and gluten free, from the van and went into the hall. The place was set up with round tables. Natalie and her sisters were putting tablecloths on them.

She found Doc, Alex, and Charlie in the kitchen, looking at the available pots and pans.

"Grace!" Doc hurried over and took the pasta box from her. "Now we can get cooking. Is there more stuff in the car? Charlie, come help bring stuff in."

He set the box on the counter and hurried off.

Grace followed after Doc and Charlie to bring in more boxes, Alex at her heels. Grace had brought enough pasta for several hundred people. She didn't know how many would come to the dinner, but after all the advertising, she had prepared for a crowd. The van was jammed with supplies. The volunteers were going to make homemade spaghetti sauce with sausage and peppers according to Dorothy's family recipe, which was famous in Fraser's Mill. Besides the pasta and sauce, Grace had brought bread and butter, supplies for Italian salad, and chocolate chip cookies for dessert. She and Mom had made the cookies themselves.

A few more volunteers were coming in. Time to start cooking.

"Listen up," Doc announced, over the noise. He rolled up his sleeves. "Grace is gonna tell you guys what to do, and you're gonna do it. She's your chef for the evening. I'm the sous chef—

hey, Charlie, toss me an apron — and the rest of you are the kitchen crew. Everybody wash your hands and get ready to cook."

He caught the red apron Charlie tossed him and tied it on. It was too short for him.

"Well, chef," he said, coming over to Grace, "you're in charge — what do you want us to do?"

She wanted to be businesslike, but she couldn't help smiling. "I feel like a chef at a Michelin 3-star restaurant. Thank you, Jim."

His eyes twinkled down at her. "Here's to making Michelin 3-star restaurant profits!"

The next few hours were chaos. Some people cooked pasta and sauce, others put together salad, others plated food and sent it out to the line of waiting people. Doc in his red apron was here, there, and everywhere, carrying heavy pots, telling people what to do, and making sure nobody got burned draining the pasta. Grace didn't think she had ever seen anything so attractive before in her whole life.

The kitchen was hot — it was a sweltering day, and the air conditioning didn't do much for the crowded space with so many stove burners going. People kept taking breaks to splash cold water on their faces and necks before returning to work.

Grace took a moment to breathe and peek into the hall. It was crowded.

"I think our advertising worked," Doc's voice said behind Grace.

She jumped.

Doc chuckled. "Sorry."

She turned around. "Are you ever gonna stop creeping up on me?"

He grinned. "I could start wearing squeaky shoes so you'd hear me coming up. Or a bell around my neck, like in the story about the mice who wanted to put a bell on the cat."

Grace laughed. "So I'm a mouse and you're a cat?"

He raised an eyebrow. "If the shoe fits…"

Something crashed to the floor on the other side of the kitchen, and Grace jumped again.

"Hey, Doc!" Charlie called. "Little help?"

It had been an open can of crushed tomatoes, the large size. Tomatoes and juice flowed in a huge puddle over the kitchen floor.

"Oh, no!" Grace exclaimed. "What a mess!"

Doc put a hand on her arm. "It's okay," he said. "At least there isn't broken glass like last time."

It was going to be okay. Grace took a deep breath and addressed the kitchen volunteers. "Hey, guys," she said. "You keep going, and I'll get some things to clean up the mess."

At this point things were winding down. The steady line of customers had thinned out to a trickle. Alex and a few others were able to keep the food supply going while Grace, Doc, and Charlie cleaned up the spilled tomatoes.

When no more customers came through, the volunteers got to eat. They picked out a long table in the corner of the hall and crowded around it, fitting in more chairs than were supposed to fit. Grace was at one corner of the table with Alex squeezed in on one side of her and Doc on the other.

Natalie, who had been in the hallway selling tickets to the people coming in, came in with the cashbox. "Here's all the money we took in," she said. "I haven't counted it. A bunch of people kept paying with larger bills and saying to keep the change."

"I'll count it tonight," Grace said. "The bank's closed, so we'll have to put it in a safe somewhere."

"I've got a safe," Doc said, "unless you'd rather not keep it there. I could be a thief who's been playing the long game with you all summer."

She wrinkled her nose at him. "I know where you live."

Everyone helped clean up, and Charlie fired up the dishwasher. It was old-fashioned, but so was the one in the diner, and he was used to it. He kept the dish drying crew supplied with steaming plates that were nearly dry already and almost too hot to touch.

"Do enough dishes, and you won't have any nerves in your hands," he said.

It was all over. Grace thanked the volunteers nearly a dozen times each, and she, Doc, Charlie, and Alex put the empty boxes and other things she had brought with her in Dad's van.

The dusky outdoors felt pleasantly cool after the steamy kitchen. Grace hadn't realized how much her feet hurt. She leaned back against the side of the van, not caring how dirty the back of her shirt was getting, and sighed. "Ah, that's better."

"Want me to come over and help count the money?" Doc asked.

"Hey, what about me?" Alex asked, coming around the van. "I want to help count."

"Fine, we'll have a counting party at my house," Grace said. "Charlie can come too, if he wants. Just don't invite any burglars."

They sat around the Murrays' kitchen table with Grace's parents, pen and paper ready to keep track of the totals as they counted.

"Wow, this looks like a lot," Mom said, surveying the full cashbox.

Dad cleared his throat. "Don't get too excited, Liz—we've gotta subtract the money for the hall rental and the cost of the groceries. Do we know how many meals we sold?"

Grace didn't know. Unless Natalie had counted the people, there was no record of how many meals they sold.

"We could count the money and divide by the cost of the meals to figure out how many meals we sold," Alex suggested.

Grace shook her head. "No, that won't give us the right number. Natalie said some people paid with larger bills and said to keep the change."

"That's probably only a few dollars here or there," Dad said. "It won't affect the total much."

"Look at this!" Doc pulled a bill out of the cash box, Ben Franklin's face prominent on it.

"Somebody broke a hundred?" Grace asked. "You sure that thing isn't counterfeit?"

Doc put his head on one side. "In this town? Wanna test it?"

"No, you're right. I doubt any of those people would do that. Besides, the counterfeit pen's all the way down in the store."

Doc rummaged in the cash box. Natalie hadn't sorted the money, and all the denominations of bills were mixed together.

"That's not the only hundred," Doc said. "I've seen at least four or five more so far."

"Really?" Dad scooted his chair closer.

"Come on, let's count it," Alex said, bouncing in her chair. "I want to see how we did!"

"I'll make some tea," Mom said. "Unless you'd rather have coffee."

"You don't want to keep these poor young people up all night, Liz," Dad said. "Better stick with the tea."

Mom bustled around with the tea kettle and stacks of teacups, and the others counted the money.

A while in they were still only halfway through the cash box, and they kept finding more hundred-dollar bills. "I'll tell you what," Dad said. "There's no way you made all this money just selling dinner tickets."

"You mean people were just donating money?" Grace asked.

Doc held up another Benjamin Franklin. "I told you the people around here cared about the store. I wouldn't be surprised if there was enough money here to pay for the freezer."

"I wouldn't go so far as to say that," Dad said. "I'd be surprised if we made over a couple thousand. We'll still need to raise money some other way."

"Guys, you're making me lose count," Charlie said. "I've gotta start over again on this stack. Let's talk when we're done."

"Sorry, Charlie," Grace said. "Come on, let's finish up."

The money was counted. Grace held her breath as Alex subtracted the hall rental and the food costs from the total.

Alex looked up, her face bright. "After you take away the hall rental and the food costs," she said, "you made a total of $3,564!"

"Hooray!" Grace jumped up from the table. "That's wonderful! That's most of the money we need for the freezer!"

"Wahoo!" Charlie pumped his fists in the air.

Dad cleared his throat. "Wow," he said. "This is a lot more than I thought you were going to make. There must have been multiple people just donating money."

"You're right," Doc said. "There's no way we sold anywhere near that number of dinners."

"And we don't know who any of the people are," Mom said. "We don't know who to thank."

"They're our friends and neighbors here in Fraser's Mill," Grace said. "Maybe there's a way we can thank them all together."

"So what are you going to do about the freezer?" Charlie asked. "How much money is it gonna be?"

"The best listing I found so far was $4,500 if you pick it up yourself," Grace said.

"Raising that last thousand might not be too hard," Dad said.

"Wait a minute." Grace pulled out her phone. "Let me look at something."

She pulled up her bank account balance. That account had been drained pretty low when she moved back to Fraser's Mill—she had to pay extra rent money because her lease wasn't up, and the gas and hotels for the trip had set her back even farther—but there was still some money there: $1,056. Her paycheck was a week away.

"I'll give the last thousand," Grace said.

Everyone looked at her.

"Are you sure?" Mom asked. "I'm not going to ask how much money is in your account, but can you afford that?"

Grace nodded. "I want to do it," she said. "After all, I'm

the one who's going to take over the store. All our friends and neighbors have contributed. I'm going to give something too."

"I seem to remember you saying you had barely enough money to get back to Michigan," Dad said, his forehead creased.

"Dad, I get my paycheck in a week," Grace said. "And I have barely any expenses right now. I'll be fine."

Doc nudged her. "I know a guy who wouldn't mind saving you some grocery money by taking you out to dinner."

Grace grinned. "I'll bet you do." She turned to her parents. "It's settled. I'm going to give the rest of the money for the freezer."

"You're a good girl, Gracie," Dad said. "Thank you."

"Yay!" Alex clapped her hands. "Let's go get the freezer."

Everyone laughed. "Not tonight!" Grace said. "Let's all get some sleep, and we can figure that out later."

⸨

The next day, after a lot of research, the Murrays settled on a freezer for the store. It was on eBay, and after Dad had talked to the seller, he was satisfied. The hard part would be getting the freezer on a truck and bringing it to the store. The Martins' trailer was too small to haul a 3-door freezer. Grace posted on the town social media page about it.

She got a reply almost right away from someone she hadn't expected: Hannah Fraser. Hannah said the sawmill had a truck they could use. She called her dad to get permission to lend it to the Murrays.

A triumphant group went out to Cadillac, where the used freezer was. They had brought a lot of people, which was good, because it took seven men to get the freezer onto the truck. Grace had the envelope with the money for the freezer. She had never held so much cash in her hand before. She felt like a real businesswoman, doing big—and scary—transactions, as she handed it to the seller.

Back at Murray's Grocery, they could hardly get into the store because so many people were standing around to watch the freezer installation. Grace slipped in ahead of the freezer and parked herself by the baked goods display, where she'd be out of the way.

"Hey, I gave money toward that freezer," Ed Hoffman said, when one of the guys suggested everybody ought to clear the area. "I wanna see that it gets put in in one piece."

When the freezer was in place, Dad plugged it in. The lights went on, and a cheer arose.

"All right, Ben," a man's voice called from the doorway. It was Sheriff Hank Liddell. "You better go fill that thing up now. It's been two weeks since I had a decent bowl of ice cream!"

"Hank!" The sheriff's wife, standing near Grace, protested with a smile.

"I'll make an ice cream run today," Grace said. "Don't worry, Sheriff, you won't have to wait much longer."

The sheriff smiled. "I'll depend on that," he said, and tipped his hat to Grace. "We can always count on the Murrays to keep this town fed. It wouldn't be the same place without you."

Grace couldn't have smiled more broadly. "Thanks, Sheriff!"

Meet Me At The Fair

With the new freezer in, Grace and her parents could focus on implementing more of the town's suggestions for improving the store. They had a lot of dinnertime planning sessions to talk about new products and displays, as well as ways to save money without cutting back on the quality of the products they sold. Doc was often part of these dinner discussions. He said it was relaxing after a long day in the doctor's office. He did seem relaxed, cracking jokes and contributing good ideas. He made such a natural part of the family gathering, Grace could hardly believe there had been a time when she thought she wouldn't get along with him.

August had come, and with it the county fair. The fair had always been one of Grace's favorite events of the year. It didn't matter to her that she didn't have any animals to show. Her family usually had a booth there, and it was always a good time.

This time, based on the success of her baked goods at the

store, Grace had talked her parents into having a booth centered on homemade treats for the hungry fair-goers. Mom was dubious.

"Isn't there enough sweet stuff at the fair already? Will people want to buy pies and cookies and fudge when they can get elephant ears and cotton candy?"

"I'm sure they will," Grace said. "I know I'd buy them. And Alex said she would make more of her gluten-free raspberry bars for us to sell."

"All right, all right," her mother said. "Mind you, we're only doing a booth on Monday, Tuesday, and Wednesday. It takes too much manpower away from the store to run a booth all week."

Grace and Natalie were in charge of running the booth all day on Monday. They packed up the food in boxes the night before, ready to be taken in the van. Besides baked goods, the booth would sell produce from the Martin farm, jars of pickles and jams, honey sticks in many flavors, fudge, and chocolates.

Before sunrise on Monday, Grace got ready for the fair. It was going to be a sunny day, probably a scorcher. She'd need a hat if she didn't want to get sunburned again. There was a cowboy hat on the top shelf of the coat closet downstairs — it had been hers when she was a teenager. After a hurried breakfast and cup of coffee, on Grace's way out the door, she grabbed the hat and jammed it on.

Natalie was waiting outside, tapping her foot with excitement, her arms folded as she shivered in the snappy morning air. Maybe Grace should have brought a jacket. But it was bound to warm up soon.

Dad followed her out to give instructions. Neither of the

girls had run the fair booth without one of Grace's parents. He wanted to make sure that the paperwork had been filled out, that none of the food would be kept in the sun, and that there was enough change in the cash box.

The drive was dark and foggy, but the sun was up by the time the girls got to the fairgrounds. They had two hours to set up before the fair opened. As they walked across the grounds carrying the first of two portable gazebos, the place already bustled with people—food vendors setting up, little kids leading livestock, people bringing food and handiwork to enter in contests, and police on horseback making sure everything was going all right. The midway was quiet and still at this hour, but Grace could see the top of the Ferris wheel through the trees.

They finished setting up just as the fair opened. Their booth was near the entrance alongside many other vendors. There were stands selling jewelry, lots of candy, people supporting political candidates, a group with pro-life flyers and bumper stickers, and a booth selling American flags.

People began to wander through, a few at first and more as the morning went on. Business was slower than at Murray's Grocery, but Grace still thought it was a good thing they were there. The supply of pies and other foods went down slowly but steadily. Grace gave out lollipops attached to flyers with the store's information. The free candy brought a lot of kids to the booth. Of course, most of the flyers from the lollipops ended up in the trash or on the ground, but the important thing was that people heard about Murray's Grocery.

Grace's phone buzzed in her pocket. It was a text from Doc.

"See you at the fair tonight! I'm coming out as soon as the clinic closes."

Natalie had been exploring. She returned now, her freckles darker than usual in a face that was beginning to sunburn. "Hey, Grace," she said. "Some of my friends are gonna be here in the afternoon, maybe around two. Could you man the booth while I go around with them? I can take it over for you when they leave."

"Sure, no problem," Grace said. "You look a little sunburned, Nat—you might wanna get a hat."

"There's somebody selling baseball caps," Natalie said. "I guess I'll get one."

She dashed off. Just then a customer came up and wanted to know what kinds of fudge they had. Grace hurried to find her list of fudge flavors.

A number of people from Fraser's Mill came by the booth in the afternoon, including Father John, who bought two jars of pickles and a large peach pie and told Grace she had the best booth at the fair. "Your parents are mighty proud of all the hard work you're doing to keep the store going," he said. "That's a big thing to do. Murray's Grocery is important to all of us."

"Thank you, Father," Grace said. "I couldn't do any of it without all the people who keep helping me out."

It was great, feeling like a part of the community.

Natalie's friends—three girls Grace recognized from Fraser's Mill—showed up in the afternoon and whisked Natalie away to the midway. Grace manned the booth in the gazebo's shade, not envying the chance to rush around in the heat.

At length Natalie showed up again with a large bag of cotton candy. She plunked herself down on a chair with a sigh.

"Don't go on that zipper ride," she told Grace. "The one that flips around and goes upside down. I tried it. Worst thing ever. I thought I was gonna throw up the whole time."

"Yikes," Grace said. "You went on that? I couldn't. I just know I'd throw up. Did you have fun, though?"

"Lots of fun." Natalie folded her arms on the table and rested her chin on her arms. "I'm wiped out. I can man the booth by myself if you wanna see the fair now."

Doc wasn't there yet—it was only five-thirty, and it would take him a while to drive over after closing up the clinic. Grace decided to go down to the grandstand, where draft horse pulls were happening.

The blazing sun made Grace glad for her cowboy hat. She strolled toward the grandstand, taking in everything—the kids running around, the mingled smell of frying food and dust and livestock and pine trees, the noise of people shrieking on the rides. There were lots of American flags and lots of people wearing cowboy hats and boots. Rural Michigan was out in full force.

The grandstand was mostly empty. Draft horse pulls weren't as popular as some of the other events, like the demolition derby set to take place on Tuesday. Grace found a seat midway up the bleachers in the middle of the grandstand and watched Clydesdales pull weighted sleds. It was amazing how much muscle those animals had.

"On your left," a male voice said behind her.

Grace turned. "Jim!"

He sat down next to her, stretching his long legs out in front of him.

"When did you get here?" Grace asked.

"A few minutes ago. I found your booth. Natalie said you went to the draft horse pulls."

"Yeah, they're just finishing up."

"What do you want to do? Have you been around the whole fair yet?"

Grace shook her head. "I wanted to wait for you."

"Wonderful," Doc said. "You can show me around. I haven't been to a fair since I was eleven or twelve. Do you come every year?"

"Not since I moved to California, but I used to come every year. The fair's changed some, but not much."

Doc stood up. "Lead the way, Miss Murray. Have you eaten?"

"Not since lunch. I do know where I want to eat. You don't have to eat there if you don't want to."

Doc raised an eyebrow. "The food truck with the deep-fried butter?"

Grace laughed. "Deep-fried butter? Is that a thing?"

"Right by the carousel. I saw it as I came through."

"Good grief. Well, I'm not getting that. I always get food from the fair kitchen. Although I do like having all those food trucks around. It's part of the atmosphere. And I always get an elephant ear before I go home."

Doc laughed. "I wouldn't have pegged you as an elephant ear eater."

"It's part of the experience. Come on—it's this way."

At the fair kitchen, they got hot dogs, French fries, and pie.

Grace's pie was coconut cream and Doc's was apple. They found a picnic table near the livestock judging arena. Other than the hot sun and a few wasps, which came along to see what Grace and Doc were eating, it was a wonderful dinner.

"Mmm." Doc groaned, finishing the last bite of his pie. "That was good. Hey, do you bake pies? Or are you a cookies-and-apple-crisp-only kind of girl?"

Grace put her head on one side. "What possible reason could you have for asking that?"

He grinned. "I'm a Hollywood reporter, here to interview the famous Miss Grace Murray for a documentary we're doing on rural grocery stores."

Grace laughed. "Next they'll make documentaries about grass growing. I do bake pies, Mr. Reporter. Not very often, because it takes a long time and always makes a huge mess, but I do bake them. My favorite's peach pie, made with fresh peaches."

"Peach pie." Doc pretended to write on an invisible notepad. "Thank you, Miss Murray. The American public will be thrilled with your interview. Now that's over, how about joining me on the midway?"

"Why thank you, Mr. Reporter, I think I will."

They threw away the trash from their meal and headed toward the midway. It was the busiest part of the evening, and the rides were going nonstop — most of them had long lines of people waiting. Grace and Doc stopped at a ticket booth and bought a sheet of tickets for rides and games.

Doc stopped in front of one of the games, a basketball free throw. Large stuffed animal prizes hung all over the booth.

"That thing's bound to be rigged," Grace told Doc. "There's probably something weird about the basketball or the hoops."

He appraised the basketball hoop. "We can test that," he said. "I've always wanted to win a prize at a fair. Don't you want an enormous plush duck?"

Grace laughed. "Go ahead. Don't say I didn't warn you."

It was two tickets a throw. The man in charge of the game gave Doc a basketball. Doc examined it on all sides, hefting it. "This looks all right. The hoops are pretty high."

"I wouldn't have a chance," Grace said. "I don't play basketball."

"I play with the guys every once in a while." Doc took careful aim and shot. The ball bounced off the rim of the hoop.

"Rigged," Grace said. "I'll bet even if you get it in the hoop there's a sheet of plastic or something inside that makes it bounce off anyway."

Doc shook his head at her. "You're not very trusting, are you?" He gave the man two more tickets. "Let's try this again."

The basketball bounced off the rim again.

"Third time's the charm," Doc said.

He balanced the ball in his hands, a determined look on his face, and let out a long breath. He shot. The ball swished through the hoop.

Grace clapped her hands. "Nice shot!"

Doc was grinning. He turned to the man. "I'll take that duck, please."

"I thought you were kidding!" Grace exclaimed.

"Nope." Doc shook his head. The man handed him the plush duck, and he held it out toward Grace. "It's all yours."

"I can't possibly carry that around for the rest of the fair. It's gigantic!"

"Then we'll put it at your booth," Doc said. "Come on."

With the duck left under Natalie's supervision at the booth, they returned to the midway. "Now what?" Doc asked.

"Well, not the Scrambler or anything fast," Grace said. "I don't want to lose my dinner. Why don't we go on the Ferris wheel?"

The view from the Ferris wheel was magnificent. They could see far over pine woods, out to a deep-blue lake. The wind ruffled their hair and tugged at Grace's cowboy hat. Grace held onto her hat and took a deep breath.

"Hard to beat that view, isn't it?"

Grace looked at Doc and found him watching her, his blue eyes serious.

She nodded. "It's gorgeous."

Doc smiled. "Better than the view from your apartment in L.A.?"

"Much better."

After the Ferris wheel they stopped at one of the food trucks and ordered an elephant ear with cherries on it. "I used to get one and bring it home in the car," Grace said. "But I always managed to get the cherries all over everything. Mom made a rule that I could only get one if I ate it at the fair."

Doc looked askance at the enormous elephant ear, covered in sticky cherries and balanced on a tiny paper plate. "We'd better get a lot of napkins."

Grace laughed and pulled out a large stack from a napkin dispenser. "This enough napkins for you?"

Music came from a small stage set up not far away, where a bluegrass band was playing. "Why don't we sit over there?" Doc suggested.

They found a picnic table and sat down with the elephant ear. It was as messy as Doc had predicted and Grace had remembered. No amount of napkins was sufficient to deal with the stickiness.

"I feel like a caveman. But isn't it good though?" Grace tried to wipe her hands on yet another napkin.

Doc grinned through a bite of elephant ear. "I'll concede. It's good."

The sky turned golden as the sun sank, and they still hadn't seen the animals. They stopped at a handwashing station to get un-sticky, then made their way to the barns.

Grace didn't know much about livestock except what Alex had told her about the animals on the Martin farm. She couldn't tell the difference between a blue ribbon winner and an animal that didn't even place in the same category, but she loved looking at all of them. In some of the barns kids were mucking out stalls or leading their animals out to be sprayed down at a watering area in order to stay cool. A small girl with an enormous white bow in her hair came by leading a reluctant pig. Sheep nosed at the bars of their pens, interested in the passersby.

"What's your favorite animal?" Grace asked Doc. They had left the sheep and were walking through the wide area between two rows of barns. The setting sun painted streaks of vivid coral across the sky.

"Well," Doc said, "I've gotta say horses. They're intelligent and work well with humans. And they're magnificent animals. When I was little, I wanted to be a cowboy."

Grace laughed. "Well, I wanted to be a cowgirl. Especially when Alex's dad let me ride on their horse. He was a very old horse, and he just plodded along, but I thought it was the most exciting thing in the world."

Doc grinned. "That explains the hat."

"Oh, yeah." Grace adjusted her hat. "I haven't worn it in ages. I didn't want to get sunburned, and I hate sunscreen."

"Uh-huh." Doc's expression was thoughtful.

"Is everything okay?" Grace asked.

"Absolutely." Doc reached up and brushed back a stray curl that had fallen across Grace's face. His hand lingered on her cheek. "Did I tell you how happy I am that you decided to come back?"

Grace smiled. "I think you might have said it on our first date. I can't remember."

Doc shook his head. "Then I'd better tell you again." His eyes were steady. "Grace Murray. I was impressed the first time I met you, but I'm even more impressed now that I know you. You're a smart, hard-working, self-sacrificing, generous woman. I'd go anywhere and do anything if it meant we could be together."

"Even if we fight?" Grace asked. Her heart was going a hundred miles an hour. Good thing he was a doctor and knew CPR.

Doc smiled. "Who says we fight?"

He leaned down and kissed her, slowly but with assurance. Her eyes fluttered closed as she leaned into him and the world came to a standstill.

He pulled back to look at her, and a smile tugged at the corner of his mouth. "I should warn you, I'm gonna talk you into marrying me someday."

Grace raised her eyebrows. "I'm a pretty stubborn person. It might take a lot of talking."

Doc chuckled. "Then it's a good thing I live right next door." He leaned down and kissed her again. "Come on, we oughtta see the rest of the fair before it's time to pack up for the night."

She smiled at him. "Why don't we go see the horses?"

Hand in hand, they walked off into the setting sun.

If you enjoyed this story, please leave a review on Amazon and Goodreads!

Coming Soon…
Hannah Fraser's Autumn
Releasing Fall 2025

Acknowledgements

It's taken three years to write and publish this book, and throughout the process, I've received help and encouragement from so many wonderful people.

A huge thank you to my dad, who first modeled the idea of "being a writer" for me, and my mom, who told me such great bedtime stories that I just had to start coming up with my own. To my siblings—Cili, for being my alpha reader and my forever target audience, and Michael and Peter, for encouraging me throughout the lengthy process.

Thank you to my editor, Amber, for helping this story through so many large- and small-scale issues and for always being so upbeat and cheerful. You're the best!

Thanks to Alt19 Designs for the incredible book cover—it's even prettier than I could have imagined.

A big thank you to Suzie Andres, for her kind publishing advice; to Dom and Paul, for filling me in on catalytic converter theft; to the men who voted on the make and model of Doc's muscle car; to my beta readers, ARC readers, and cover reveal team; and to Rachel Parker and the clean book community on Instagram.

And another big thank you to Grandma, Uncle Rich, and all the cousins, relatives, and friends who have been so kind and enthusiastic about this project. Many thanks, in particular, to the good people of St. Mary's, whose warm little community is my own real-life Fraser's Mill.

Above all, thanks be to God for all His blessings. To Him be all glory, now and forever!

About the Author

Ursi Engebretsen has always loved a good love story with a happy ending. So she decided to write her own—cozy clean romances with sparks flying, strong family themes, and picturesque settings, with the light and joy of the Gospel shining through. Although her characters have their struggles and problems, she wants her readers to walk away happy and uplifted at the end of every book.

Ursi grew up in Michigan and received her BA in liberal arts from Thomas Aquinas College in California. She's a Catholic Christian, a writer, a musician, a voracious reader, and a country girl at heart. Her day job is directing music and playing the pipe organ at her church. She likes bubble tea, a good sunrise, and using too many exclamation points. (She's working on that last one.)

https://ursiengebretsen.com
https://www.instagram.com/ursiengebretsenauthor